FEB -- 2024

A
Different
Kind *of*
Gone

Also by Catherine Ryan Hyde

Just a Regular Boy

So Long, Chester Wheeler

Dreaming of Flight

Boy Underground

Seven Perfect Things

My Name is Anton

Brave Girl, Quiet Girl

Stay

Have You Seen Luis Velez?

Just After Midnight

Heaven Adjacent

The Wake Up

Allie and Bea

Say Goodbye for Now

Leaving Blythe River

Ask Him Why

Worthy

The Language of Hoofbeats

Pay It Forward: Young Readers Edition

Take Me with You

Paw It Forward

365 Days of Gratitude: Photos from a Beautiful World

Where We Belong

Subway Dancer and Other Stories

Walk Me Home

Always Chloe and Other Stories

The Long, Steep Path: Everyday Inspiration from the Author of Pay It Forward

How to Be a Writer in the E-Age: A Self-Help Guide

When You Were Older
Don't Let Me Go
Jumpstart the World
Second Hand Heart
When I Found You
Diary of a Witness
The Day I Killed James
Chasing Windmills
The Year of My Miraculous Reappearance
Love in the Present Tense
Becoming Chloe
Walter's Purple Heart
Electric God/The Hardest Part of Love
Pay It Forward
Earthquake Weather and Other Stories
Funerals for Horses

A
Different
Kind *of*
Gone

A Novel

Catherine
Ryan Hyde

LAKE UNION
PUBLISHING

Text copyright © 2023 by Catherine Ryan Hyde, Trustee, or Successor Trustee, of the Catherine Ryan Hyde Revocable Trust created under that certain declaration dated September 27, 1999.

Published by Lake Union Publishing, Seattle

www.apub.com

Amazon, the Amazon logo, and Lake Union Publishing are trademarks of Amazon.com, Inc., or its affiliates.

ISBN-13: 9781662504389 (hardcover)
ISBN-13: 9781662504402 (paperback)
ISBN-13: 9781662504396 (digital)

Cover design by Shasti O'Leary Soudant
Cover image: © Mint Images / Alamy; © Creative Travel Projects / Shutterstock

Printed in the United States of America

First edition

A
Different
Kind *of*
Gone

PART ONE

Chapter One

Just Another Night in Sloot

On the day Jill Moss was reported missing, Norma showed up at the pub at 8:00 p.m. Nothing remarkable about that. She showed up at 8:00 p.m. every night she was scheduled to work. Nothing remarkable about any part of that day, really. Norma had no idea anything significant was about to happen, because nobody ever does. It was one of those many aspects of her life that only revealed themselves in the figurative rearview mirror.

Betty was on shift with her that night, and was already behind the bar dealing with a large male tourist. They were the only people in the place. She shot Norma an exasperated glance, and Norma hung up her jacket and moved in as backup.

The guy was young, but then again everybody seemed that way to Norma. He wore a beard that he apparently never saw fit to trim. He was on his cell phone with somebody.

"I'm in a little town called Sploot," he said, shouting. Maybe the connection was bad. Maybe he was just a shouter.

"Sloot," Norma corrected.

"What? Wait. You're both talking to me at once. I don't know Sploot what. It's either Sploot, Arizona, or Sploot, Utah. I don't know which."

He covered the phone and looked first to Betty and then to Norma.

"We don't know, either," Betty said.

"Nobody really does," Norma added.

He uncovered the phone and held it to his ear again.

"And the locals are messing with me," he said into the phone.

"We're not messing with you," Norma said. "It's just not a question with an easy answer."

But she had no idea if her words were getting through. He seemed to be paying more attention to the person on the other end of the cell connection.

"Right," he said. "Right, I will. Bye."

He slipped the phone into his pocket and drilled his gaze into Norma's eyes. Why her eyes and not Betty's she didn't know. Especially since Norma had joined the conversation so recently.

"What do you mean it's not a question with an easy answer?"

"We're smack dab on the state line. The pub where we're standing is in Utah. When I drive home at the end of my shift, I'll be in Arizona. And it's only a four-minute drive. And it's Sloot, not Sploot. A sploot is what you call it when your dog lies on his belly with his back legs straight out."

"Wait, what?" the big man said.

It dawned on Norma for the first time that he was probably mildly drunk.

"Never mind," she said. "Just . . . no 'P.' Sloot, with no 'P.'"

"Don't say 'no pee,'" he said, suddenly shifting from foot to foot. "I've been driving for hours and drinking beers all the way. I gotta use your bathroom."

Betty pointed to a sign in the corner behind him and he turned to go. Then he stopped and looked over his shoulder with a crooked little smile on his face.

"I wanted it to be Utah, so I could call it Sloot Ute."

Norma looked up into his ridiculous face.

"We never heard that one before," she said.

For a few seconds, he took the statement at face value.

"See, I can be funny," he said, his face bright. "And I made that one up all . . ."

The sentence drifted off as he looked at Betty's face. Norma glanced over to see her coworker give the guy a slight eye roll and an almost imperceptible shake of the head.

"Oh," he said. "Got it."

Then he disappeared into the men's room.

"He's cut off?" she asked Betty.

"Oh yeah. He's cut off."

Norma got busy drying a fresh batch of beer steins that Betty had washed and left to drain.

"God save us all from spring break," she muttered over her shoulder. "I can't stand guys like him."

"Oh, you can't stand people in general, Norma. Why not admit it?"

Norma's hands stopped, and she turned to look her coworker directly in the face.

Betty was a tall, brassy woman with a ton of bleached blond hair and false eyelashes. She wore makeup—lots and lots of makeup—and flirted with the male patrons if they were worth the time. Which made her about as different from Norma as any two women in their late fifties could possibly be. Still, Norma liked Betty. At least to the extent that she liked anybody.

"Admit it? Are you kidding me? I've done everything but tattoo it on my forehead. I'm arranging to get it carved on my gravestone. And stop saying that like it's a bad thing. It just shows I have good judgment."

"There must be some people you think are decent."

Norma sighed.

"Yeah. I suppose. A few of them are okay." She turned back to the beer steins and took to drying them again. Mostly under her breath she muttered, "But even the best of them are no dogs and horses."

"What was that?"

"Oh, nothing."

Betty opened her mouth to answer, but the bearded man was back.

"I'll have a beer," he said.

"No you won't," Norma said. "You're cut off."

"How can I be cut off? I just got here. I haven't even ordered anything yet."

"You told me you've been drinking and driving. State law says if I have reason to believe a patron has been, or will be, violating the open-container law, then it's not legal to serve that person."

For a moment he just teetered there.

Then he said, "How can you tell me what the state law says when you don't even know what state we're in?"

"Arizona and Utah both have that same law."

Norma braced slightly for whatever would come next. As a general rule, people were not their best selves when you cut off their alcohol supply. Especially when they had a fair bit in them already. For what seemed like a long time, nothing happened at all. Probably it was only seconds. The kind of seconds you could count on one hand.

Then he turned and stomped to the door, hitting it hard with the heel of his hand and disappearing into the dark parking lot.

They waited a moment or two without talking. Just to be sure that was that.

"Here's hoping he doesn't get an assault rifle out of his car and come back."

"Amen," Betty said. "Is there really a state law that says that?"

"I have no idea," Norma said. "But it sounded good."

—

The place was buzzing when Norma got the text.

The pub had filled nearly to overflowing with a group of maybe twenty-five climbers on their way back from Canyonlands. They were all exhausted and filthy, and their exhaustion seemed to help the alcohol go to their heads all that much faster. They were too loud, like one solid roar of sound. They were in the process of finding something excessively amusing, and had been for quite some time.

Norma didn't know what was so funny. Then again, she figured it was best not to know. The chances she'd find it as funny as they did were slim.

One young man stepped briskly up to the bar, still laughing.

"Three more pitchers," he called, shouting to be heard over the din.

Norma planted her elbows on the bar, leaned her chin in her hands, and stared directly into his face.

He backed up a step. Norma had that effect on people.

"And who's driving?"

"Paul and Suzy," he said, "and they don't drink."

"Okay then," Norma said.

She set about pouring the pitchers.

The young man seemed to want to break the tension by small-talking with her. Norma hated small talk. Especially when you had to nearly shout to be heard.

"That was so funny," he said.

"What was so funny?"

"This new guy, Greg. He didn't know how to set a cam right. But he didn't want to tell us so. He was embarrassed. He led on this pitch and it held him because he weighs like a hundred. But he nearly killed the guy behind him. Fortunately the guy behind him knew to test it before he put his weight on it. And it just came flying off the face of the rock wall. Good thing he had a nice solid foothold."

Norma finished pouring the three pitchers and set them on a tray on the bar. In her peripheral vision she saw Betty watching her to see if she was about to lose it all over this guy.

"You've got a strange sense of humor," she told the young man. "All of you. Because I've seen a young man lying broken and dead at the bottom of a wall because he didn't know how to place a cam. And guess what? It wasn't funny at all."

"Sorry," the guy said. His voice was lower now, his head bowed.

He grabbed the tray of pitchers and hurried off.

"I'd say you showed great restraint," Betty said. "Especially seeing as it was only a few weeks ago."

"I got a new theory," Norma said, her voice feeling strained from the shouting. "I figure nobody ever changes anybody else's mind about anything. Why get invested? Tell an idiot they're an idiot and they don't straighten up and fly right. They just keep being an idiot. I figure I'll just live my life and stay out of their way."

And it was right at that moment, right at the end of that last sentence, that Norma got the text. She knew it was Ian because she had her phone set to produce a different notification tone when it was him. And it brought that little jolt into her stomach, that sickening lurch, because it meant someone was missing. Someone was in trouble. The person in trouble was never anyone Norma knew, so she wasn't sure why it hit her that way every time. But it always did.

She pulled her phone out of her apron pocket and read the group text he had sent.

"First light. Rocky Ridge Campground. If you get to bed late like Norma, just get there as soon as you can."

But Norma knew she would be there as early as anybody else on the team.

"Search and rescue?" Betty asked, moving closer.

"How'd you know that?"

"It's a different tone."

"I'll be damned."

"You didn't know it was a different tone?"

"Yeah, of course. *I* knew it. It's my phone. I'm the one who sets the tone. I just didn't know *you* knew it."

Betty moved even closer, her shoulder bumping against Norma's, as if to read the text. But Norma was already sliding the phone back into her pocket.

"Who went missing this time?"

"He never does say. Not in the text. Just tells you where and when to show up. Then when you get there he'll brief you in person on who you're looking for."

"Well, let's just hope it's not another lone climber."

"I'll say. Or another hiker who doesn't understand the value of water."

Because, in her time with the volunteer search and rescue team, Norma had actually found two dead bodies. And, bizarrely, after going several years with only good luck, she had found them both in the last six months.

"You should go home and sleep," Betty said. "I can close up here."

"You sure? It's busy."

"Won't be in a minute. I'm about to cut these fools off."

"Well, maybe I'll take you up on that," Norma said.

Though she suspected she would go home and fail to sleep. That was what usually happened the night before an early search call.

———

Her two hound dogs, Gracie and Lonny, didn't even get up when she came in. They whipped their tails, but held their positions on the rug in front of the fireplace. Even though there was no fire. Force of habit, maybe.

Gracie stretched out long behind her brother's back. She pushed her rear legs out behind her and wiggled forward on her belly, her rear paw pads straight up in the air. Then she turned her head to the side and set her chin on Lonny's back.

"Now that's a sploot," Norma said.

The dogs whipped their tails again at the sound of her voice.

She changed into pajamas, brushed her teeth, set the alarm, and put herself to bed.

—

She never did sleep much. As predicted.

She lay there, wide awake, periodically glancing at the time readout on the alarm clock. Figuring how much sleep she'd get if she could doze off right about then.

The earlier the alarm was set to go off, the less likely she was to sleep. She knew from experience that keeping track of that dwindling sleep window only made matters worse, but somehow she couldn't seem to kick the habit.

Somewhere around 3:15 she might have dozed for an hour or so. But that was it for the night.

And it was too bad, because the next couple of days would push Norma harder than she was used to being pushed. And she was used to some pretty hard days.

Chapter Two

Whatever We Find

The last half mile of dirt road to the campground was in washboard condition, so Norma took it slow and kept an eye on her horse in the trailer behind.

She had a camera in the trailer, with a little monitor on her dashboard, so she could see what he was doing back there. But lately she'd begun wondering why she had it, because Fred was never doing much. He was a champion at staying on his feet in bumpy conditions, and all he was ever up to was pulling little tufts of hay out of his hay bag with expressive lips and daintily bared teeth.

Meanwhile the hound dogs shifted from window to window in the back seat of the extra-cab truck, whimpering with excitement.

She pulled up a few feet from where Ian stood, jumped down from the truck's cab, and let the dogs out. Then she opened the back of the trailer and left it open.

She stepped up to Ian.

He was a small, sturdily built man of about forty, with a no-nonsense attitude. Norma wasn't a fan of nonsense, so they got along fine.

The dogs circled him happily, whipping his legs with their tails.

"Ma'am," someone shouted immediately. "Ma'am, ma'am."

It was a young man with long hair. Someone Norma had not met before.

"*What?*" she said, her voice and patience straining.

"Your horse is not tied up."

"I know he's not tied up."

She looked back to Ian, ready for her instructions. But the young man would not let it die.

"Ma'am, he's about to walk right out of that open trailer."

"Well, I should hope he does," Norma said. "We've got riding to do."

She stood facing Ian, listening to the measured sounds of Fred's hooves banging on the trailer floor as he unloaded himself. She glanced over her shoulder to see the young man reach for the horse's reins.

As was always the case, she had Fred completely tacked up, with a bitless bridle and the long split reins wrapped loosely around the saddle horn so he couldn't step on them.

Norma opened her mouth to tell the kid not to touch her horse.

Ian beat her to it.

"Don't touch the horse," he said. "You don't ever touch somebody else's horse."

His voice was firm. Firm enough that the young man threw both hands in the air as if he were being robbed or surrendering to the police.

"What if he's running off?"

"If the owner says, 'Hey, grab my horse,' then you do. If they don't, you don't. Besides. That horse look like he's running off to you?"

Fred ambled up behind Norma and stood behind her right shoulder. Then he stretched his neck out so his nose got closer and closer to Ian.

"You better have brought him a carrot," Norma said.

"Of course I brought him a carrot."

He produced one from his shirt pocket and broke it into three pieces, offering it to the big buckskin one chunk at a time.

"Good morning, Saint Fred," he said.

The horse chewed contentedly, and noisily, near Norma's ear.

"You could've slept a little," Ian said, turning his attention to Norma.

"I *wish* I could've. But not so much. What've we got today?"

But the young man wasn't done interrupting their routine.

"That horse is huge!" he said. "What is he, like eighteen hands?"

Norma tried not to laugh. Some people could judge the size of a horse just by eyeballing him. Others not so much. This guy fell into the latter category.

"Sixteen three," she said, and tried to turn her attention back to Ian.

"Some kind of warmblood or something?"

"He's a quarter."

"Oh no, he can't be. A quarter horse is usually around fifteen hands."

"Usually so," Norma said, and tried again to ignore him.

"Maybe an appendix quarter horse? They tend to go taller."

"No. A quarter. A regular registered American Quarter Horse. Just bigger than most. Now if you'll excuse me."

"Nobody would want him for running cattle, that's for sure. The reason they breed 'em so compact is so they can get down and look the steer right in the eye."

"I don't run cattle."

"Not sure a horse that big is the best thing for a lady rider," he said.

That was when Norma really began to feel the ire building up around her ears. She opened her mouth to blast him, but he was still blabbing.

"Why, you don't even have a bit on him," the kid said. "You don't even have him in one of those hackamores that stop 'em with nose pressure or by cutting off their wind. What if he decided to take off on you?"

"Fred's not going anywhere," she said.

She shot Ian a furious glance.

Ian walked around behind the young man, grabbed him by the back of the shirt, and began walking backward, pulling the kid along with him. Pulling him away from Norma.

"Hey!" the kid squawked. "Hey! What're you doing?"

"Saving your life," Ian said. "Now get your supplies and get out on the trail and let me get my best rider out on the trail. Starting now."

The young man turned and walked off, and Ian came back to where she and Fred stood waiting.

"Sorry about that," he said. "My sister's kid. From LA. He's been here a week, and he wants you to know how much he's learned about horses in that time."

"Impressive," Norma said, making it clear by her tone of voice that she was not impressed. "Now . . . what've we got?"

Ian held out his phone to show her a picture of a girl. Or maybe "young woman" would be a better description. It was hard for Norma to judge. She had long, straight blond hair and blue eyes. A perky nose. But her smile seemed unsure.

"Jill Moss," Ian said. "Age nineteen. Reported missing last night from this campground by her boyfriend, Jake. The two were on their way to Capitol Reef for spring break, but it was mostly his idea. She's not much of an outdoor person, from what he says. Not really a hiker. No experience in route finding. They had a compass, and a GPS unit, but she didn't take either one."

"Okay," Norma said. "We're good to go, then. Just do me a favor and give me a leg up. I'm not as young as I used to be."

"Wait, though. Before you go."

There was something in his voice. Some note of caution that Norma recognized. There was something different about this case. Something wrong about it. It set up a little fort of defense in her gut.

"Okay, what?"

"Before the boyfriend reported her missing last night, the ranger got a different kind of report altogether. There was a family two campsites over who put in a report. They said they saw this same young woman take off down the dirt road toward the exit, looking upset. Looking like she'd been crying. Boyfriend comes tearing after her, catches up. Physically catches her. Grabs hold of her by the arm. She tries to pull her arm away, he twists it behind her back and forces her back to their campsite. Forces her into the tent."

"Well, now we know why she wanted to get away from him."

"There's more."

Norma was not surprised. Somehow she had sensed there would be more.

"Yesterday, when she was still in cell-phone range, she sent her very worried parents a text. It said, 'Leaving Jake for good. Wish me luck. If you don't hear from me in 24 hours, call the cops.'"

They stood a moment while Norma took that in. She had one hand on the horse's neck.

"I just want you to be prepared," Ian said. "Hopefully she just ran off to get away from him. But brace yourself, you know? Every search and rescue volunteer likes to find a living individual. Nobody likes to find a body."

"I've found bodies. You know that."

"Yeah. You have. You've found people who died from a big fall, or from dehydration. I expect if you ever found somebody who was murdered by the person supposed to love her the most, that might feel different."

"You think he killed her."

"I sure hope not. I want you to brace for the possibility, though."

He walked around the horse, lacing his two hands together. Norma put her left knee in those hands, and he swung her up into the saddle.

The dogs immediately began baying, excited to go.

"Thanks for the warning," she said. "But we can handle whatever we find."

—

They moved along a ridge, in the direction of the high forest, with a good view of the campground below them. With a good view of miles and miles of valley. Norma could see two four-wheel-drive Jeeps searching the flatter areas below. She could see a couple of hikers she was pretty sure were part of the team.

Not everybody went out on horseback, to put it mildly. On a good day there were maybe three mounted team members. The hikers and the riders could both go lots of places the Jeeps could not. But the riders could cover more ground in a day.

She rode leaning her forearms on the pommel of the saddle—especially on the steep uphill stretches—with the reins hanging loose.

She looked around behind her to be sure she was out of earshot of those in the campground.

Then, when she was sure it was just her, the horse, and the dogs, Norma started to sing.

She had made a point of never telling the search and rescue folks that she sang all the way through that wilderness. She wasn't sure if they would make fun of her for it or not. But it made sense. It was easier on the throat than shouting a person's name all day long, and it kept a horse and rider from that awkward situation of rounding a curve and surprising a bear. The higher she climbed, the closer she got to the forest, the more likely she was to meet one. Some riders had bells on their belts or saddles to let bears know they were coming. Norma preferred to sing.

Other people probably sang on the trail from time to time, she figured, but she was afraid people would make fun of her for *what* she sang. She liked the old classics. Those familiar tunes that get stuck in your head for weeks. "Take Me Out to the Ball Game." "Camptown Races." "Beautiful Dreamer." The more old-fashioned the song, the more she liked it. It reminded her of her mother, singing in the kitchen while ironing or making a meat loaf. And if Norma was in earshot of a lost individual, she knew from experience they would hear her, and follow her voice. It drew them to her.

The sky was a steely color of morning. Not really blue yet, because the sun was not quite up over the ridge. The red-rock scenery Norma loved so much looked washed out and pale in that early light.

Soon the sun came up and turned the red rocks red, and heated up Norma, her horse, and her dogs. She didn't carry water, except for a couple of bottles in her saddlebag for a dehydrated hiker or an emergency, because it wasn't fair of her—or her and the dogs—to drink when the horse couldn't. When she was thirsty, so was Fred.

She looped back around to the campground, belting out "Bill Bailey, Won't You Please Come Home." Noting, as she did, that any man who had ever run off on Norma could just keep running as far as she was concerned.

Ian was there when she rode back in, briefing a late search and rescue volunteer.

"Just came back for some water," she said. "I didn't find Jill."

———

It was almost one thirty in the afternoon when the boy hound, Lonny, stopped dead in the middle of the trail. Fred had to stop quite suddenly to keep from trampling him, and it threw Norma forward over his withers. It stopped her cold in the middle of a line from a song.

"She's only a bird in a gild—"

Lonny threw his head back and let loose with a wild sound—something between a bay and a howl. Then Gracie started up barking like a coyote.

A second later they took off up the face of a steep hill together.

Norma sat in the saddle and watched them go. They stopped at a pile of car-sized fallen boulders. It was possible that those boulders had fallen in such a way that there was a gap under some of them. A kind of impromptu cave. That was common in these parts.

Then the dogs just stood there, looking in. They sniffed and sniffed and sniffed. And wagged and wagged and wagged.

Gracie turned her head and looked back down the hill at Norma, as if questioning why she hadn't come along yet.

As she sat watching, Norma realized something that she would never have admitted to anyone. She was afraid. Afraid to go up there. Afraid to know.

She thought of Ian's warning from a few hours earlier.

Brace yourself.

But how does one go about doing that, really? Sure, you make your gut feel like steel. But then you see what there is to see, and does that steely gut really defend you? Does all that bracing really change anything?

What if she found the body of a young girl who had been strangled? What kind of memories would that bring back to life?

Norma dismounted, dropping onto her boot soles on the hard-packed dirt trail.

It didn't look like a slope the horse should try to navigate, so she took the reins over his head and ground-tied him—dropped the reins on the ground in front of him, which he had been trained to understand meant "stay put."

She began to scramble up the hill.

The dogs resumed baying up a storm, and in the midst of all that noise, Norma thought she heard a different sound. But she wasn't sure. If she was right, it was something like air leaking out of a punctured tire.

Or like a person saying "Shhhhhh."

Huffing and puffing from the exertion, Norma joined her dogs, and pulled them off by the collars. They obeyed her. They backed up and sat.

There did indeed appear to be a small cave formed by the pile of boulders. Norma crouched down and looked in.

A young woman looked back at her, blinking too much. Norma couldn't see a great deal of detail, because it was dark in there, and her eyes were adjusted to the bright sun of a spring day. She did seem to have long hair, the girl.

This was probably the girl she was looking for. And that was a huge relief, because her boyfriend had not killed her. Not only was she alive, but she looked none the worse for her experience. And that meant Norma could breathe now. Really, fully breathe.

"Jill Moss?" Norma asked.

"Yeah," the girl said. "But you can't tell anybody. Please."

Norma's brain began to run in circles. Fortunately, at that moment, she had no idea how many years that condition would persist. She knew only that she had no idea what to make of this initial exchange. How can a lost person be found by search and rescue and then demand that their rescue be kept secret? It made no sense.

Norma moved just inside the darkness of the cave and sat cross-legged, allowing her eyes to adjust. She was maybe a yardstick away from the young woman's side.

"Make it make sense," she said.

"I'm running away from my boyfriend."

"Okay. That makes sense enough. I guess. But now you're found. Now you can go someplace where he won't hurt you."

"There *is* no place where he won't hurt me. That place doesn't exist. If he knows I'm out there, if he knows where I am, he'll kill me. Literally, physically kill me. Dead."

"You sure about this? How do you know he'd really kill you dead?"

"I can't tell you. I mean, I'd rather not say. But I know. I just know and you have to believe me. He would."

"Then you get a restraining order against him. And we get you police protection."

"For how long? Are the police going to guard me every minute of every day, everywhere I go, for years? Because he has a long memory."

"No," Norma said. "I don't suppose they will."

"Then you can't tell anybody you found me."

They sat in silence for a moment. Norma watched Fred standing down the hill in the sun. He had moved his head just enough to nibble on some scrubby weeds at the edge of the trail. But he had to stretch his neck out. Because he couldn't move his feet. Because Norma had ground-tied him, and he took Norma's instructions seriously.

She looked over at the girl. Now that Norma's eyes had adjusted to the dim light in the cave, she could see that Jill had been crying. A lot, from the look of it.

"What's the plan here?" Norma asked. "You got food?"

"No."

"Water?"

"No."

"What was your plan when you left that campground yesterday?"

"My plan," Jill said, "was to make it to the highway and hitchhike out of here. Without getting lost. But it didn't quite work out that way."

"I'll say it didn't. You're farther from the highway than you were when you started."

They sat in silence for an uncomfortable length of time.

Then Jill said, "You don't believe me."

"About what? That your plan was not to get lost? Because, in my experience, nobody ever has 'lost' as part of their plan."

"That Jake would kill me."

"Oh. That."

Another brief silence fell as Norma chewed that over. She knew the answer. She just wasn't sure she had access to the right words, or to a way to convey it. She watched the hound dogs, lying stretched out on their sides in the sun.

"The world is full of people who don't know what they don't know," Norma said.

The girl stared at her, blinking a lot.

"Meaning . . . ?"

"Meaning everybody thinks they know everything, and half the time it's stuff they can't possibly know. I don't know you. And I don't know Jake. As far as whether he's capable of killing you or not, the only possible answer is that I don't know."

"You're saying you don't believe me."

"I didn't say that. I said I don't know."

"People decide what they *think* about certain things. That's not so wrong."

"No, that's not so wrong. Provided you know the difference between thinking and knowing."

"Do you *think* I'm right to be afraid of him?"

"Yeah," Norma said. "Probably so."

That seemed to surprise the girl.

"Because . . ."

"Because there are a lot of men who hurt women. Especially the women they're supposed to love. Not most men, but enough that probably every day somebody dies at the hands of someone who promised to love her. And if a woman tries to tell us she's in danger, and we just pass that off as a woman being emotional, or see her as an unreliable narrator, then that makes the way awful damn easy for those men. Besides. I know he twisted your arm behind your back and forced you into your tent."

Norma saw the girl's eyes go wide in the dim light.

"How did you know that?"

"Somebody reported it to the ranger."

"Who?"

"Now how would I know that? Somebody else at the campground. Some other campers."

"That's pretty humiliating."

"Which is the last thing you should be worrying about right now."

"It's the way he was raised," Jill said. "He wants to be a good person, and he is, most of the time, but then his anger gets the best of him and sometimes he—"

"Stop it," Norma said. "Don't even. Just stop it right now."

"I was just trying to say—"

"That he's a prince of a guy but you can't let on where you are or he'll kill you dead."

"I was just going to say that sometimes he just becomes this whole different person."

"No he doesn't," Norma said.

Norma looked over to see the girl staring back at her with her mouth open.

"I thought you were the one who only says what you know, not what you think."

"Right. And this I know. He's one person, right?"

"Well, yeah."

"Is he one person, or do you have two boyfriends named Jake?"

"One, but—"

"Then this 'whole different person' is part of him. It's also him. You may not see it all the time, but it's still him. People only say otherwise when they want to make excuses for somebody. Look, I know you love the guy. Most of us have had some kind of experience loving somebody we shouldn't have, so I'm not judging. But at least admit that, if there's no safe place for you in the world if he knows where you are, his aim to be a good person has failed miserably."

She waited, but the girl never answered. Which was better than arguing, Norma figured.

"Hey," Jill said after a time. "Have *you* got any food or water?"

"Yeah, I got a few things in my saddlebag," Norma said.

She shimmied out of that cramped space and picked her way down the hill, the dogs wagging along. When she reached the trail, Fred raised his head, curved his long neck, and looked into her face.

"Sorry," she said. "We seem to have ourselves a situation here. Let me just move you over where you've got something to eat."

She picked up his reins and led him a few steps into the scrubby weeds. Then she dropped the reins again. Fred lowered his head and sighed contentedly as he grazed. Norma took two bottles of water and two energy bars out of his saddlebags.

Then she committed herself to the part she dreaded most: scrambling back up that steep incline.

"Here," she said to the girl when she got there. Her voice sounded breathy with the exertion.

"Thanks," the girl said.

Jill opened one of the bottles of water and downed it all in one go, without setting it down or taking a break to breathe.

"What's the plan here?" Norma asked, feeling her patience stretching thin.

"Good question."

"You can't just live under these boulders for the rest of your life."

"True," Jill said, tearing the wrapper off an energy bar. "It would be nice, though."

"Let's get real for a minute here."

"Okay," the girl said. She took a huge bite of the energy bar—nearly half of it—and then tried to talk around it. "I definitely need help getting to the highway."

"Some problems I see," Norma said. "First of all, like I said before, you're farther from the highway than you were when you started out. More than twenty miles if I'm figuring right. And I usually am. And there are a whole bunch of people out looking for you. One of them is bound to notice us before we get there."

"Maybe we could go at night when they stop looking."

"It's a long trip, like I keep telling you. You walked so far in exactly the wrong direction that you're only a couple miles from my house."

"Then maybe you could take me to your house."

"You're putting me in a bad position here, my young friend."

Norma was just at the edge of losing her temper, and it came through in her voice. When the girl answered, she sounded hurt and scared.

"How am I doing that?"

"Because I'm a volunteer with search and rescue. We're loosely associated with the sheriff's department. It's my job to find people and bring them back, not take them to my house and hide them."

"I figured your job was to save people's lives," Jill said.

"It is."

"Well, this would be saving my life."

Norma sat with her face in her hands for a time. Then she dropped her hands, sniffled, and sighed deeply.

"And how do you suppose I'm going to feel if anybody finds out I lied regarding your whereabouts?"

"How are you going to feel if you don't and he kills me?" Her voice sounded more sure now. Just at the edge of hard.

"That's not very fair," Norma said.

"I'm sorry. I've gotta do what I've gotta do here. I'm trying to survive."

"And what about your parents? You don't think they're going crazy with worry?"

"Maybe you could call them. Here. Give me your phone. I'll put their number in."

Norma gave the girl her phone. Not because she was convinced she wanted to be any part of this mess, but because talking to the girl's parents might offer some welcome perspective.

She needed time. She needed to go off on her own and really think about all this.

"Tell you what," Norma said. "I've got some trail mix down in the saddlebag to go with those two energy bars. Eat it all before dark, because we're close enough to the high forests that we get black bears here. I'll go back and try not to say whether I found you or I didn't. I'll call your parents and I'll come back in the dark tonight and let you know what I've decided we're going to do. That sound fair to you?"

"Sure. Just please don't decide to let on where I am."

"Don't push me anymore. I've got thinking to do."

Norma stepped out into the blinding daylight. She picked her way down to the horse again, mad at the prospect of scrambling up that hill a third time.

"Almost done," she told Fred as she pulled the trail mix out of his saddlebag.

"Hey," she hissed up the hill.

She didn't think the girl would hear at so much distance. But a minute later Jill stuck her head out into the light.

Norma sailed the bag of trail mix as far as she could. It landed about four feet below the fallen boulders. Jill scrambled out and grabbed it, then ran for cover again.

Then Norma took out her GPS unit and created a waypoint for the spot where she stood. She picked up Fred's reins and they walked together back down the trail, the dogs weaving and wagging around her legs. They walked that way until she found a boulder she liked well enough for mounting.

They rode back to the campground, Norma's brain running in aggravated circles.

When she got back and saw Ian again, he didn't ask "Did you find her?"

Somehow she had been expecting him to ask straight out, putting her in the untenable position of having to lie. Then again, she realized after the fact, why would he ask? If a search-team member rides back empty-handed, that's the answer.

Usually.

"Good job anyway, Norma," he said. "You tried. We'll go out again tomorrow."

That was when Norma realized she would have to ride these hills for days, looking for a missing girl who wasn't missing at all.

The whole thing was creating a sour feeling in her stomach. Norma was unusually picky and particular about the way her life was supposed to go. And this was not the way it was supposed to go at all.

Chapter Three

Against Her Better Judgment

Norma drove home, unloaded Fred—or rather stood back and waited while he unloaded himself—stripped off his tack, and fed him his evening meal of hay and oats.

"Thank you for being a horse and not a human," she said as he dug in and started eating.

Then she fed the dogs.

"Thank you for being dogs and not people," she told them as she set their bowls down.

They did not look up to acknowledge her words, because food was important to them.

She didn't feed herself, because her stomach was off. She hadn't eaten all day, and she knew the lack of nourishment was only adding to the unsettled feeling. But she purposely chose hunger anyway. She wanted to be upset. She didn't want anybody or anything talking her out of it yet.

Instead she did something she almost never did. She poured herself a drink.

It was bourbon, and she poured it from a bottle Betty had given her for her birthday the year she started working at the pub. Which made the bottle more than seven years old. It was the only bottle in the house, the only bottle that ever *had* been in her house since she'd received it, and she was still in the top one-third of it. That was how much Norma drank.

She got very poor cellular reception at home, so she picked up the receiver of her landline and punched in the number the girl had given her, reading it off her cell phone. The contact the girl had entered was labeled "Owen and Teresa Moss." The area code was recognizably Southern California.

Norma changed the name on the contact to "O and T." Then she hit the call button.

A woman picked up.

"Hello?" the woman said, but it sounded like an unusually hesitant question.

Her voice was breathy. Desperate. Like a woman who was waiting to hear whether her daughter was alive or dead. Because she was.

It almost made Norma wish she'd called them first and then fed the horse and the dogs after. Almost. Then again, the horse had worked hard that day, and the dogs were the ones who had found this woman's daughter. They would always come first.

"Your daughter is okay," Norma said.

She heard a great rush of air. Like a sigh, but more forceful. It went on for a while. When it was over, nothing was said for a time. Norma got the sense that the woman had to get ahold of herself before she could speak.

"Oh thank God," she said, her voice a breathy whisper. "Owen," she said. "Owen. It's okay. She's okay." Then, bringing her attention back to Norma, she said, "And you are . . . ?"

"I'm with the volunteer search and rescue in Sloot. Little nothing town on the Arizona-Utah border. It's only a couple of miles from the campground where your daughter was staying when she was reported missing."

She quite purposely did not tell Teresa Moss her name.

The woman began to speak, but Norma decisively cut her off.

"Listen," she said. "Just listen to me for a minute. Because we have a situation on our hands here. Nobody knows I found your daughter today. I did *not* bring her back to the campground. I did *not* ride back to the campground and announce that I'd found her. And that's messing with me. That's a problem. It's something I did against my better judgment. I only did it because your daughter begged me. Begged me not to tell. She thinks Jake'll kill her if he has any idea where she is. I tried to talk her into police protection. You know. A restraining order. The usual stuff. But she figures this guy's got a long memory, and I'm not going to be the one to tell her a restraining order is guaranteed to save her life. Lots of women are dead now because the guy they had a restraining order against showed up at their house. You can call the police to come enforce it, but some women die before the police get there. Some die before they can pick up the phone to call."

Norma stopped talking and took another sip of her bourbon. At first, Teresa Moss said nothing in reply.

Norma looked out the window. In the fading twilight she could see Fred standing in his corral. She could see the comforting action of his jawline moving in silhouette as he chewed his hay. She watched a few strands fall, and the horse drop his head to get them.

When it was obvious Norma was done talking for the time being, Teresa spoke.

"What are you going to do?"

"I haven't figured that out yet," Norma said. "I'm having a tough time with that. It's really messing with me. But maybe I said that before." A brief silence fell. Then Norma asked a question she figured was the key to the whole troublesome situation. "You think Jake would really kill her?"

"I know Jake would hurt her." Teresa's voice sounded stronger now. More sure of itself. "I think he already has. Probably on more than one occasion. And I think my daughter knows him best. If she says he's capable of it, I figure she's right."

"This is a question no mom will like," Norma said, "so I apologize in advance. But I gotta ask. Is your daughter prone to any kind of exaggeration? Does she fall into hyperbole every now and again? I just need to know if I've got a reliable narrator on my hands here. Please don't take offense."

"I understand. But no. A solid no. She tries to downplay Jake's behavior. She defends him. She makes his anger sound like no big deal. This is alarming, then, that she's saying straight out he'd kill her."

A silence. Norma did not feel inclined to fill it, so she didn't.

"I didn't catch your name," Teresa said.

"I didn't throw it. And I'm not going to. Because what your daughter's asking me to do might be illegal. At the very least it's a breach of my ethics as a volunteer search and rescue team member."

"What's she asking you to do?"

"She wants me to get her to the highway in the dark of night and then never tell anybody I found her. Which is pretty much asking me to lie. If nobody asks me straight out if I found her it might not be a technical lie, but it's still the sin of omission. But even if I do it, I'm not gonna leave her out on the highway all by herself. Girl that young and that pretty hitchhiking alone in the dark? Why, she might end up getting into more trouble than she would with her boyfriend. No, if I do it, I'll bring her all the way to you."

"We'd be so grateful to you for that. You'd be saving our daughter from that . . . animal."

"He's not an animal," Norma said.

"How can you say that?"

"Because he's not. Were his parents both four-legged beings of some kind? Or were they humans? Then he's human. People love to do that. Revoke other people's humanity. Before we give people the death penalty, we do that. Get up in court and say he's not even human. He's a monster or an animal. Because if we admit he's a human then it's a lot harder to say 'Yeah, go ahead and kill him now.' In your case I can understand how it might be comforting to want to think there's no such thing as a human being who would do something as terrible as murder your daughter. But human beings do terrible things all the time, and we just have to deal with that. Clearly Jake has anger-management issues, and he's not fit to be around. Maybe he's abused your daughter already. Maybe he really would kill her for leaving him. Does that make him somebody who should be locked up so nobody gets hurt? Probably. Does it make him a terrible human being? Definitely. Does it make him nonhuman? Sorry. No."

Norma waited for a reaction to all that. First she heard only silence. Then Teresa Moss took the conversation in an entirely different direction.

"My husband and I will pay you a reward to bring her here. A substantial reward."

"Oh no you will not," Norma said. "That's the last thing I need, to be caught profiting off lying to the sheriff's department. And by the way, if anybody ever sees this call on either of our phone records, I need you to say I only called to wish you the best and promise you we were doing everything in our power to find your daughter. That's a trifle out of the ordinary and it might even have them questioning my judgment, but it's not breaking any laws as far as I know."

"So . . . ," Teresa began. Norma got the idea that she almost couldn't bring herself to go there. Wherever "there" was. Actually, Norma had a pretty good idea. ". . . does that mean you're going to do it?"

"I still don't know," Norma said. "It's a conundrum."

"My husband and I would be forever grateful to you if you would. We can keep her safe from here. We can hide her. Or whatever we need to do. You might very well be saving our only child's life."

Norma took another long swallow of bourbon. She figured Teresa could hear the gulping sound on the other end of the line.

"I don't think you've thought this all the way through," Norma said. "If we never tell anybody she's been found, the search will go on for weeks. Months. In some respects, almost indefinitely. The sheriff will have to keep the case open. The resources that'll go into it are considerable. Time and money, both. Resources that could be used for other public good. Law enforcement will be in touch with you. All the time. Asking you if you've heard from her. You'll say no. That's a crime, to lie to them. Filing a false police report. You sure you're ready to bring all this down on yourself? And before you answer, let me tell you the really scary part. The really scary part is that I'm not sure *I'm* even thinking it all the way through. I'm trying. But I just keep getting a nagging sense there could be more unintended consequences, stuff we really never saw coming. I'll ask again. Are. You. *Sure?*"

"I would risk a hundred times more than that to keep my daughter alive. A few minutes ago I thought that boy might've killed her and hidden her body."

"We all considered the possibility."

"Do you know how hard that was for Owen and me? Have you got any children?"

"Yeah," Norma said. "Two boys. Grown men now. But I prefer not to talk about that."

"Oh. I'm sorry. Well, anyway . . . then you know the lengths I would go to. To keep her in the category of the living. To never get that phone call we thought we were getting just now."

Norma sighed deeply and took another slug of her drink. Out the window, Fred had finished his dinner and ambled into his run-in shed for the night. Or so he thought. She might be about to spring a surprise on him.

"If I do this," Norma said into the phone, "you will leave me out of this forever." Her voice was solid and hard. Even more so than usual. "If it comes out that she's alive, and found, you will go to your grave swearing she just turned up on your doorstep all on her own."

"We will. We promise. We give you our word as parents. Please bring Jill to us."

"It's against my better judgment."

"But you'll do it?"

"I'm afraid it's beginning to look that way," Norma said.

———

Norma sat for several minutes after the call ended, feeling the alcohol going to her head.

Then she decided all her misgivings were of no use to her now, and it was time to put them away. Put them to bed once and for all. When you're deciding, they serve a very important purpose. Once you've decided, they're of no use to you. Even if what you've decided is a mistake.

And there was a very real chance that what Norma had decided was a mistake.

She picked up the phone again and called Betty at home.

"Hey," Norma said.

"You okay? You don't sound so good."

"Oh, I'm kind of a mess. I've been riding all day on no sleep. My stomach is upset. And I've got to do it all over again at dawn. You think there's any chance you could handle tonight on your own?"

"I prob'ly could," Betty said. "Seeing as it's Monday and all."

"Oh, is it Monday? I'd totally lost track of the days."

"Get some sleep, girl."

"I absolutely will," she said, and ended the call.

Of course, she already knew she absolutely wouldn't.

"You stay here," she told the hounds.

They gave her desperate looks of confusion and concern. They seemed to know it was something more than just going to work. How dogs knew so much, Norma could never fathom.

Still, she couldn't afford to have them barking at shadows all along the trail.

She slipped into her boots again on the front porch. Let herself into the tack room, where she hung Fred's bridle over one shoulder and slung the heavy saddle by its horn over her back.

She walked the few steps to his corral.

His head came out of the shed immediately, and he blinked at her in the moonlight.

"I realize this is out of the ordinary," she said to the horse. "But, anyway. Here goes."

———

As she was riding out, she realized that she had gained very little by withholding her name. After all, she was the only woman with the volunteer search and rescue in Sloot.

Chapter Four

Why

The sky was clear that night, and the moon was bright, which was both a blessing and a potential curse. It made it relatively easy for Norma and Saint Fred to see where they were riding. It also made it easier for someone to see *them*, if anyone was out and about.

But the way back to where she had left Jill was a sparsely traveled use-trail even by day. After dark they had it blessedly to themselves.

Norma's night vision was not the best, so she rode with one arm outstretched in front of her face, palm out, to be sure she could identify any overhanging branches before they smacked her in the face. With the other hand she held her LED-illuminated GPS unit, its arrow turning slightly as the trail turned, always pointing to the spot where she had left the girl. It left Norma riding more or less with no hands. She could have told the horse a great deal with her legs if any guidance had been needed, but, as always, Fred seemed to know what he was doing.

The moon cast ghostly shadows of rock formations down in the valley, and what few stars the moon could not wash out looked more brilliant than Norma could ever remember seeing them.

She leaned back slightly as the trail led downhill, to make balance easier for the horse.

Then the ground leveled off and, without realizing it, she dropped off to sleep.

She woke because she was drifting forward over the horse's withers, and slightly to the left. Also he had stopped, which might have added to her overbalancing forward. She figured that was why he had stopped—because the weight of the rider felt insecure. But when she opened her eyes and looked down at her GPS unit, she saw they had arrived. And she had no idea whether Fred had stopped because he knew they'd arrived—or if such a thing was possible, even for Fred—or whether her falling asleep and almost coming off in that exact spot was an odd coincidence.

She looked up the hill and saw only a vague shape of the fallen boulders, and the moon shadows they cast.

Norma whistled a birdcall. A song sparrow, though she didn't figure Jill would know that. They didn't sing at night, but she didn't trust the girl to know that, either.

She stopped. Waited.

Nothing.

She whistled the song-sparrow call again.

Still nothing.

It irritated Norma, who had no intention of getting down off her horse and scrambling up that hill in the dark.

She made a distinctly human sound, about as loudly as that soft sound could be made.

"Psst!"

At that, she saw motion above. Then she heard the sounds of the girl scrambling and sliding down the hill.

"It's you," Jill said when she arrived.

"Yeah. Me. Didn't you hear me whistling birdcalls?"

"Yeah."

"And . . . ?"

"I thought it was a bird."

"Songbirds don't sing at night."

"Oh. Sorry."

"Whatever. Here's what I want you to do." Norma kicked her foot out of her left stirrup as she spoke. "I've got my foot out of the stirrup on your side. I want you to put your foot in there. You'll have to really reach up. He's a big horse."

"I'll say," Jill said, sounding a little intimidated.

"Then I want you to grab hold of my arm and swing up behind me. You won't end up in the saddle. There's barely room in the saddle for me these days. I want you to land as lightly as possible just behind the cantle."

"What's a cantle?"

"This thing," Norma said, indicating the hard raised leather ridge at the back of the seat. "There's some flat skirt of the saddle behind it and you'll be partly on that and partly on his butt."

"Is that fair to him?"

"What do you weigh, like one ten?"

"One hundred even."

"Sorry I asked. He's a big horse. He'll manage."

She sat her horse in silence for a full minute or so, waiting for the girl to follow directions. Nothing seemed to happen.

"We need to get out of here," Norma said. "Why aren't you getting up?"

"And after I get up there . . . then what? Where are you taking me?"

"Oh. That's the hang-up, is it? I'm taking you to my house. When we get there, I'll make you some food. And then somehow I'm going to get you to your parents' house in Southern California."

"You talked to them?"

"I did. I said I would, so I did."

Norma saw the girl fumbling for the stirrup in the dark, her right leg very high.

"You don't know horses much," Norma said, "do you?"

"No, why?"

"You put your *left* foot in the stirrup."

"You couldn't have told me that?"

"I thought it went without saying. If you put your right foot in there and swing up, you'll end up sitting the horse backward. Theoretically. Provided your foot could swivel a hundred and eighty degrees. Which it can't."

"This is harder than you made it sound."

"People are doing it all over the world, my young friend. Every day. It's not advanced astrophysics."

Jill seemed to be using her hands to hold the stirrup steady while she placed her foot.

"I think that's okay," the girl mumbled. "I just want to be sure my foot doesn't slip when I swing up. I'm wearing flip-flop sandals."

Norma felt her patience skid away.

"*Why* are you wearing flip-flop sandals?"

"Don't yell at me. I didn't know there was a horseback ride in my future."

"I meant why are you wearing flip-flops anywhere around here when you're camping?"

"They're comfortable. They're nice and cool. Doesn't everybody?"

"No. Smart people wear some kind of boots out here, like hiking boots. But this is not the time or place to argue about it. Hurry up and grab on to my arm."

The girl hooked her left arm through Norma's. Then she tried to swing up. But Norma had to pull hard on the arm to help.

Fred rebalanced himself as the girl settled behind the saddle, and Jill let out a frightened squeak.

"What's he doing?"

"He just shifted his weight is all."

"Ow. I pulled a muscle."

Norma ignored the complaint.

"You can hold around my waist if you're worried about slipping off. I know it's different without stirrups."

"I think I'm okay, but . . . can I just put my hand on your shoulder? Like this?"

Norma felt small, thin fingers gently grip her left shoulder near the collarbone.

"Fine," she said.

She turned the horse around on the trail and urged him forward, and the hand gripped more tightly. In fact, saying "ow" was a temptation, but Norma kept those thoughts to herself. After a few strides, the girl seemed to adjust to Fred's movements, and the grip of the hand loosened to something more comfortable.

"Thank you for doing this," Jill said. She sounded . . . maybe even humble. Definitely sincere.

"You're welcome."

They rode in silence for a time.

Norma was worried that she wouldn't recognize the use-trail they had taken. In the dark, she wasn't sure enough what that intersection looked like. The GPS would show her the direction of home, but not where to pick up the trail to easily ride there. But a moment later Fred took the turnoff on his own.

"He seems like a nice quiet horse," the girl said.

"He's a good boy."

"What's his name?"

"Fred. But the locals call him Saint Fred."

"Why do they call him that?"

"Because his name is Fred and he never does anything wrong. Well. Hardly ever."

Just as she finished that last sentence, a lone coyote stepped across the trail. The animal saw them and startled, stopping dead for a split second. It startled the horse, who stopped suddenly, his feet wide. Norma could feel the jolt of it run through his muscles.

The girl let out another one of those squeaks. Then the coyote vanished.

"What's he doing?"

"He just got startled by a coyote is all. Came out of nowhere."

"And just when you were saying he never does anything wrong."

"Spoken like a city girl who doesn't know what ninety-nine out of a hundred horses would do if something came out of nowhere like that in the dark."

"What would they do?" Her voice sounded unsure, as if she only halfway wanted to know.

"Let's just say we're lucky not to be sitting in the trail on our butts and leave it at that."

They rode in silence for another stretch, the girl's hand gradually loosening.

Norma had grown comfortable with the hand on her shoulder. Having been a mom, she found it reassuring. It reminded her of the way your child takes your hand when the dangers of crossing the street become very real.

"It's nice of you to take me back to my parents," Jill said, knocking her out of her thoughts.

"I'm doing it against my better judgment."

"Why, then?"

Norma opened her mouth to speak, but the girl just kept going— just kept spilling words.

"Oh, I didn't mean that the way it sounded. It's nice that you're doing it, whyever you're doing it, and maybe why you do what you do is none of my business anyway. It just seemed like . . . well, maybe I shouldn't say how I think you are, because I barely even know you. I only met you that one time before, and that was only a few hours ago. But based on what I know so far, you don't seem like somebody who does things that are against her better judgment."

"Normally true."

"You don't have to tell me if you don't want."

They rode quietly for a minute or two. Norma leaned forward slightly as the trail turned uphill. The girl did not follow suit.

"Shift your weight forward a little," Norma said. "Makes it easier for the horse going up a slope."

The girl brought her torso forward until her chin bumped Norma's back. Then she corrected slightly. Her other hand gripped the cantle just behind Norma's hip.

They rode in silence for a minute or two more.

"Once upon a time," Norma said, "I was married. This was a long time ago. Seventeen years with this guy. We had two kids together. Two boys. Everybody thought he was the nicest guy, my husband. And he was, a lot of the time. But he had another side to him."

She waited, feeling the familiar rocking gait of the horse beneath her. Wondering if she wanted to go further in that conversational direction.

The girl did not speak. She only waited.

"He was one of those guys who didn't handle anger well, but I was the only one who saw it. I don't know exactly why that was. Maybe his feelings were more overwhelming around me because there was love there. Maybe because I was his wife he felt entitled. I really don't understand that mindset and I really don't want to. Anyway, for most of the time it was little things, though they didn't seem little at the time. He'd grab me by my upper arms and shake me, and it would leave the nastiest bruises. One time he knocked me down and then picked me up by my hair. Not to say that's not bad enough, but for a long time it didn't progress beyond that. And then one day he tried to strangle me."

She stopped talking for a few beats. Waited. The girl said nothing. Just listened. Jill seemed to be listening so hard that Norma imagined she could hear or feel all that listening.

She hadn't told this to anybody since the day after it happened.

"I thought he was going to kill me. He choked me out until I was unconscious, and I thought I was dying. When I opened my eyes again, I was so surprised. I took the boys and tried to leave him. Well. I did leave him. But not with the boys. They wouldn't come with me. They wanted to stay with their father."

"After what he did?"

"They didn't believe what he did. They'd never seen that side of him. He'd made sure they never did. He told them it was a lie. That I was seeing another man and that's why I lied about it. They believed him. They were thirteen and fifteen. That was the last I saw of them for almost ten years. They didn't want to see me and God only knows what he was telling them about me behind my back."

For what felt like a long time, the girl said nothing.

Then she said, "I'm sorry that happened to you."

"Not nearly as sorry as I am. But anyway, thanks."

"Is that why you're doing this thing even though it's against your better judgment?"

"I can't be *that person*. You know. The one who won't take your word for how bad it was."

They crested a rise, and Norma saw her little house, on her little ranch, in the distance, bathed in moonlight.

"That's where I live," she said.

"You don't get scared, being out here all alone?"

"No. I can take care of myself."

"You don't get lonely?"

"I got this horse and two good dogs, and the fewer people I have in my life the happier I'll be. You hungry?"

"Yes, ma'am."

"I figured you must be. I'll make you some pancakes and eggs before we go."

"That would be very nice," Jill said.

—

Jill sat at her kitchen table stroking the dogs' heads, and Norma came around and gave her a cup of coffee and a tall plastic tumbler of water.

It was the first time she'd seen the girl in the light. She was almost painfully petite, with the most brilliant blue eyes. She kept those eyes slightly averted, the way people do when someone's taught them to be afraid.

"You got a driver's license?" she asked the girl.

"I *have* one. But I had to leave it behind. It was in the tent with Jake, and if I'd gone back for my wallet then he would've known I was really leaving and he never would've let me go. People don't take their wallet when they're just going out in the bushes to pee."

"Okay." Norma plunked down at the table, as if sitting would help her think. "You'd be driving without your physical license present," she said, more or less to herself. "But if we got pulled over for some reason, they would run your license, and you'd have one."

"I'm driving?" the girl asked in a brief break between gulps of water.

"I'll be honest with you. Again. My night vision's not good. And I've barely slept. I was thinking I'd drive you out of here under a blanket, so no one'll spot you. Then I figured when we're well out of the area I'd let you drive. Maybe I can even get some sleep. But you better drive carefully, because if we get pulled over for anything, your jig is up, my friend. Your whereabouts as a found person will have been established. Either that or we'll have to hunker you down here and go tomorrow night."

"I've barely slept either," Jill said. "Maybe tomorrow would be best."

"Okay, then. I guess that has to be the plan." Norma pushed to her feet with some effort. She was tired, and sore. "I know you're hungry, so I'll whip something up."

"Can I call my parents?"

"No. I'm sorry. That's one reason I was hoping to go tonight. But they're just gonna have to trust that you're coming by and by. I already called them once. That's on my phone record. If anybody ever saw that, I could pass it off as a sympathy call. But a second call has no good explanation. It just pegs me as part of this whole thing."

"I don't get it. Who would be checking your phone records?"

"Yeah, you really *don't* get it, my young friend, and it's time you started to. You've made a decision with big consequences here. You're a missing person. That's a law-enforcement case. The longer you don't show up, the more they're going to suspect your boyfriend killed you. There'll be serious investigations."

"Oh."

Then she left the girl to think on that for a time while she whipped up some pancake batter.

"You sure you still want to do it this way?" Norma asked after a few minutes. "Because there's plenty of time for me to officially find you tomorrow."

"I'm sure," the girl said. "I'm positive. Better they should investigate a fake murder than my real one. I just want to get back to my parents' house alive."

Chapter Five

The Thing

Norma woke, and blinked into the light spilling in from her bedroom window. She pulled the alarm clock off her bedroom table and squinted at it.

It was after 11:00 a.m.

Norma could think of no other time in her life when she'd slept past seven. Then again, she didn't normally go riding the trails in the dark and then make breakfast for visitors in the middle of the night.

She looked around for the dogs, but they were not in the bedroom with her.

She rose and pulled on a corduroy robe over her pajamas.

She stepped out into her small living room, which was much dimmer. She had pulled all the curtains closed out there so that, in the unlikely event anyone came to her door, the girl would not be spotted sleeping on her couch.

Norma took a minute to let her eyes adjust.

There was no one sleeping on her couch.

As she walked closer, and reached a spot where the big recliner did not block her view, she saw the girl. She was curled up on the rag rug on the floor, covered with the blankets Norma had given her. She had a hound dog on either side of her, pinning her in. She looked asleep, but as Norma walked closer, she opened her wildly blue eyes.

She blinked at Norma for a few beats, as though refreshing her memory. Then she smiled shyly.

"What're you doing down there?" Norma asked. It didn't come out the way she had intended at all.

She had meant to be her usual gruff self and spit it out like a criticism or a complaint. Instead her voice sounded soft to her own ears, and seemed to carry a note of . . . almost . . . fondness? Or partway to that, anyway.

She's not your kid, Norma told herself firmly. *She's somebody else's kid.*

The hound dogs woke up to the sound of her voice, and looked up at Norma with their tails thumping.

"Dogs are so comforting," Jill said.

"Yes they are. Want breakfast?" she asked to brush away the moment.

"Um. I'm okay for now. We did have that big breakfast in the middle of the night. If you're making coffee I'll take some, though."

"If it's morning, I'm making coffee. But first I have to feed the horse and then I have to feed the dogs. And then I can look after us."

—

"You didn't tell me your name," the girl said as Norma handed her a mug of coffee.

"No. I didn't. And I didn't tell your parents, either. I had this ever so intelligent idea that I could remain anonymous in all this. And then gradually it started dawning on me that none of that was my best thinking. All your parents would have to do is say 'Woman with volunteer search and rescue in Sloot.' Because there's exactly one of those. And I told you my giant buckskin horse was called Saint Fred and that pretty much narrows down my identity, too. I guess as long as the jig is up anyway I might as well tell you. I'm Norma."

"Thanks for the coffee, Norma."

"You're welcome. I gotta call Betty."

She pulled the receiver of the landline down off the wall and hit number two on the speed dial.

Betty picked up on the second ring.

"You were up anyway," Norma said, "right?"

"Oh yeah. What's up?"

"I think I was wrong when I said I was just tired from the riding and the lack of sleep. I think I'm coming down with a stomach bug."

"You did say your stomach was a little off."

"And now it's more than a little."

A long silence fell. Norma didn't quite know what to make of it. She had expected Betty to immediately know where she was headed with this. She waited longer, figuring Betty would get there in time.

"Are we crossing new lines here?" Betty asked after a few seconds.

"I have no idea what you're talking about."

"You're wanting us to be more like friends for real?"

"What are you on about, Betty? I'm stumped."

"You don't usually call me with newsy stuff like how you feel."

"I'm not being newsy. I'm telling you I can't come in tonight."

"Norma . . ."

"What?"

"You're off on Tuesdays."

"Oh, is this Tuesday?"

Norma heard a little huffing sound on the line. Maybe a light, scoffing laugh.

"You're not yourself, girl. Just yesterday you told me you didn't know it was Monday."

"Yeah, well. My head's kind of messy."

"I hear you. I get like that when I'm sick, too. You get something in your sinuses or your lungs or your stomach, and you expect it to leave your brain alone. Seems like the two things should be unrelated. But my head's always muddy when I'm sick. Get some rest, okay?"

"Yeah, I will. Thanks."

She hung up the phone. The exact minute she did, it hit her. She was hours late to the campground for search and rescue. And it was unlike her not to show. So unlike her that Ian would worry. He might even show up on her doorstep, which was exactly what Norma didn't need.

She dialed his cell number from memory.

He picked up on the first ring.

"Norma," he said. "Thank goodness. We were about to call up a search and rescue operation for *you*."

"Yeah, I'm sorry, Ian. I was up all night with a stomach bug and then when I finally fell asleep I slept till all hours of the morning."

"Well, just take care of yourself. We'll get by without you. Call me when you feel like yourself again."

"Will do, Ian. Thanks."

She clicked the phone off and hung it back on its base on the wall. Then she sat back down at the table with Jill. She was shaken, and she hoped it didn't show. She was trying not to let on. But that had been such a perfect example of how you convince yourself you've thought of everything, and how wrong you can turn out to be.

"What do you do here all day?" Jill asked.

She sounded bored. Or as though she could hardly bear the anticipation of boredom. It irked Norma. She wanted to say "That should be the worst problem you ever have, my young friend." She didn't say that.

"Normally I'd ride the hills looking for *you* all day. Maybe go into town for groceries. Maybe clean out Fred's paddock and give him a good groom and then take the dogs for a walk. But now I can't do any of that because I just told everybody I was sick. And now I'm kicking myself, because tonight was my night off anyway, and I never needed to call Betty and tell her anything."

"But you still would've had to call in sick to search and rescue."

"Oh. Yeah. That's true."

"You're saying we just sit here all day."

"Pretty much, yeah."

"I guess things could be worse for me."

"Glad to hear you haven't lost sight of that," Norma said.

———

All of Norma's best judgment told her to lock herself in her room and pay no attention to the interloper.

Norma never had guests in her house. If someone arrived uninvited she might occasionally seat them on her couch, offer them a glass of water, and hear why they'd had the poor taste to surprise her. Then she'd rise suddenly and mutter something about needing to get back to what she'd been doing before she'd been interrupted.

But this girl had nowhere to go until Norma took her there later that night.

She got up off the bed, sighed, and surrendered out of pure boredom.

She opened the bedroom door to see the girl lying on her back on the rug, petting the dogs' heads and staring at the ceiling. She looked over at Norma when the door hinges creaked.

"You play cards?" Norma asked.

The girl sat up suddenly.

"I can play gin rummy."

"Fine. I'll go get the deck."

———

"I haven't told my parents about how bad Jake is," the girl said. "And I'm really dreading telling them."

Norma was clutching her hand of cards, wondering if she should encourage the girl to get back to the game or suggest a pause in their playing while she got all this off her chest.

A minute later Norma sighed and set her cards on the table, facedown.

"They pretty much figured it out on their own."

"They did? What did they say?"

"I only talked to your mom. She said she figured he'd already hurt you, maybe more than once."

"Oh," Jill said.

She was still holding her cards in both hands. Too tightly, Norma noticed. It might bend them, and the bends might not come out just by putting the deck back in the box. She might need a new deck after this.

Norma didn't answer, so the girl talked on.

"I told them I tripped and fell down the stairs. And another time that I walked into a door as it was being opened. I guess they didn't believe me."

"Girl. You got any idea how old that is? That 'I walked into a door' thing? Why, I used that one in *my* day, and it wasn't even new back then. Anytime the same young woman keeps getting bruises and black eyes, people are gonna wonder. Kids, too. You take your kid to the ER too many times and someone from the state or the county's sure to come poking around to investigate. Because kids get hurt all the time, sure. Falling off their bikes and such. But they also get abused by their parents. All the time. And there's one thing the girl with her boyfriend and the kid with his parent have in common. They'll both lie to protect their abuser. But look. You said something a minute ago that doesn't make good sense. You said you're dreading telling your parents how bad Jake is. But they already know I'm sneaking you out of here in the dark of night so he won't kill you dead. Don't you think their knowing that little tidbit of information pretty much gave away the whole show? I mean, the cat's out of the bag anyway now, am I right?"

"It was worse than bruises and black eyes," Jill said. "But . . . yeah. Right."

She set down her cards in a defeated gesture. But she set them down faceup. Which meant this round was effectively over, whether anyone had intended it to be over or not.

"I just hate the idea of them looking at me and seeing what bad judgment I had."

"Everybody has bad judgment starting out as a grown-up. We're not born with good or bad judgment. It's something we have to develop. We learn it by the hard knocks of experience. People don't want to think you never made a mistake, because there is no such thing. They want to figure you learned something from it. If you lie to make people think better of you it'll always backfire. Because then they just figure anything could be true in your life and they'd never know it, because you'd never let it show. You want somebody to respect you? Tell 'em you messed up. Then the next time you say you didn't do anything wrong, they'll believe you."

The girl sighed, and picked up her cards again.

"Well, that'll never work," Norma said. "We can't just finish this round. You had those cards on the table faceup. We gotta deal again."

"Oh. Right, I wasn't even thinking about that."

"Maybe we should talk now and play cards later when you're thinking about it."

Jill sighed.

"The thing is . . . ," she began.

Norma wasn't sure when Jill planned to end the thought.

"What? Go ahead and tell me what the thing is."

"I'm not sure you want to hear all this."

"Might as well. We got the whole damn day and nothing much to do."

"Okay. That's true, I guess. The thing is, it wasn't bad judgment at first. Because at first Jake was really nice. And I really didn't know."

"No," Norma said. "Of course you didn't know. Nobody ever does."

"Really?"

"I'm telling you. There's not a person on God's green earth who ever met somebody new and had that person say 'Come be in love with me, but just know in advance I'm gonna knock you around some.' Relationships are a funny thing. There's this thing called courting behavior. You might not know the phrase, because it's probably from my generation and not yours, but I know you've seen it. It's when you only put your best foot forward. Both parties, I mean. You show the other person the very best side of you. Everybody does it whether they mean to or not. Then two people get their hooks into each other and it's pretty much a done deal that they're together, and that's when it all comes out. There's not a person on the planet as far as I'm concerned who knows what they're getting themselves into when they start a new relationship. You just throw your lot in with somebody and maybe you get lucky and maybe you get hurt. And that, in a nutshell, is why I prefer horses and dogs."

"But I stayed with him. He started hitting me when he lost his temper and he even pushed me down a flight of stairs and I didn't leave. And then . . . this is the part I didn't want to tell you when you first found me. I didn't know you. But I found out he tried to kill his last girlfriend for leaving him. Took a shot at her. I mean, an actual shot. With a gun. She wouldn't report it. But I knew her. She came out of hiding and found me, just to warn me, and it was a risky thing for her to do. And she confided in me. And I didn't leave. That was the bad judgment. That's the part I'm really ashamed of. I didn't leave. Of course by then I was afraid to leave. But that was only part of it, and anyway, I'm still ashamed that I knew and I didn't leave."

"If you didn't leave, then what're you doing here?"

"Oh. Right. I guess I meant I didn't leave soon enough."

"It takes what it takes," Norma said. "We all have a different bottom we need to hit."

"You're really not judging me?"

"I'm judging you as having a lot to learn, which makes you pretty much the same as every nineteen-year-old I ever met. We all start out in life having a lot to learn. Now stop worrying about what your parents think. They love you and they're just happy you're okay. They just want to know you're ready to go in a new direction now. Let's deal another hand of cards or two and then I'll make us that breakfast we haven't had yet today. And then I'll go take a nap, because I'm thinking we'll be up all night driving."

"I can drive some. Your night vision."

"I still got to get home when the sun comes up tomorrow."

"Oh. Right. I really appreciate your doing this."

"You said that already and I believed you."

"It's just nice. You're a nice person and I can't figure out why you don't want people to know it. You're nicer than you let on. I can't understand why you want people to think you're so tough and mean."

"Because I *am* tough and mean. I'm not a nice person and I don't even want to be. Don't take that away from me. Don't go insulting me like that again. Now come on. We've barely played cards since we started playing cards. And it's your deal."

Chapter Six

Karma

Jill skittered out to the truck in the dark, her head down, as if escaping through a line of enemy fire. She leaped through the extra cab's open door and stretched out across the back seat.

Norma stood at the truck, holding a big, dark blanket.

"I'm sorry," she said. "You're going to have to get down on *the floor* in the back."

"Why is that?"

"Because the dogs'll be on the seat."

"Oh, the dogs are coming?"

"Yeah, they have to. Otherwise there'll be nobody here to feed 'em. I can't very well ask somebody to come by and feed my dogs when I've told everybody I'm home with the stomach flu."

"Oh. Okay."

The girl shifted onto the floor, and Norma covered her with the blanket. Meanwhile a voice in the back of her head said, *If you're keeping secrets . . . if you're hiding anything . . . that's how you know you're making a big mistake.*

"Ouch," Jill said. "Now I have this transmission-hump thingy pressing on my ribs."

"Sorry. It's just till we get on the highway and get well out of town."

She heard the girl sigh, but nothing more.

She gave one short whistle through her teeth, and the dogs jumped in, leaning down to sniff and nudge their new friend through the blanket.

Norma slammed the back door and climbed into the driver's seat. She fired up the engine and pulled off her property.

Now it's a done deal, she thought. *Good idea or bad, whether I regret it or not—and I'll probably regret it—this is what we're doing.*

The girl's voice, slightly muffled, came to her from under the blanket.

"What does the horse eat while we're gone?"

"The horse is different. He doesn't overeat. Some horses would, but Fred doesn't. I can leave him enough food for the time we're gone, and he'll only eat what he's hungry for at any one time and save the rest for later. Some people can do that with their dogs. But not these dogs. They'll eat till they're sick and then starve for the second half of the thing."

"What about water? What if he runs out of water?"

"He's got an automatic waterer."

"I don't know what that means."

"It's what most horses have. It's a container of water with a float. You can leave the water turned on all the time because the float stops the water from running when it's full. When they drink it down it fills up again."

"Oh. Good."

They drove in silence for a time.

A few minutes after Norma got on the highway headed west, the girl spoke up.

"You think the police are gonna question him like he's a suspect?"

"I guarantee they will. They probably already are."

"I guess his life is gonna be hell for a while."

"If not indefinitely."

"Good. He deserves it. That's justice."

Norma did not reply.

They drove in silence for several miles.

Fortunately, out here in the middle of nowhere, there were no streetlights on the highway, and very few vehicles coming in her direction. It was the lights at night, more than anything else, that made it so hard for her to see.

"You didn't say anything," the girl said, knocking Norma out of her thoughts.

"About what?"

"About how Jake deserves for his life to be hell and it's justice."

"He probably deserves for his life to be hell. I'm not sure it's justice."

"It's Karma. Karma is justice."

"I don't know anything about Karma. I'm not even sure I believe in it. I see a lot of people doing a lot of bad stuff that doesn't seem to be catching up to them."

"The idea of Karma is that it catches up to you *in the long run*."

"Okay."

"Why do you not think it's justice?"

"I just said I don't know if it is."

"Why don't you know?"

The conversation was beginning to irk Norma. It reminded her of the time when her kids were little. How they just talked and talked and never left you a minute alone to think your thoughts in peace.

"I'm just thinking they're going to be treating him like he killed somebody. But he didn't."

"But he *would* have."

"Or so you think. But we'll never be absolutely sure you're right. Besides. Even if you're right. You can't punish somebody for what they would have done. Let's say I make a plan to rob a bank. I get a mask and a bag and a gun and I get in my truck to drive there. But my truck breaks down. You can't put me in jail for bank robbery, because I didn't rob any bank, even though I would have if I could have. Maybe if I made a complicated plan with other bank robbers, then maybe I'm legally guilty of some kind of criminal conspiracy. But otherwise, punishing me is not exactly justice."

A brief silence. A car came eastbound, shining its lights into Norma's eyes. The light had a pattern to it, like a wheel with spokes. A sort of complicated halo. Which meant Norma wouldn't be able to put off that cataract surgery indefinitely. She'd been putting it off long enough already.

"You talk like you're on his side," the girl said.

"If I was on his side I would've given you to the authorities and risked his finding you. I just have some very specific ideas on right and wrong. I like to stick to the cold hard facts, and I believe in fairness."

"It seems like . . ."

But then, for a long time, the girl under the blanket didn't say what it seemed like.

"I know I'll regret asking this, but what? It seems like what?"

"It seems rigid," the girl said.

"Funny. I would have used the word 'character.'"

"It is, I guess. It just seems like your character is rigid."

"But that's a good thing, when your character is rigid. The last thing the world needs is more people whose sense of integrity flip-flops all over the place. Besides, I'm not asking a nineteen-year-old's advice for how I should be seeing the world."

"I'm just telling you what I think."

"And it seems to me that all these thoughts from you regarding my character are a little bit like biting the hand that feeds you. Listen. Am

I going to lie awake at night and cry crocodile tears because Jake's life is hell? Of course not. But he'll be treated like a murderer, and he's not one. That's all I'm saying. Now, I'm going to pull over, and let's get you up here to drive before I kill us all."

———

Norma was three-quarters of the way to sleep when the girl spoke, bouncing her back to consciousness with a start.

"There's just one thing that still bothers me, though," Jill said. "And I can't stop thinking about it."

Norma sighed deeply and noisily, and suppressed an irritated grumble.

She looked over at the girl, who had her hands gripped tightly at ten o'clock and two o'clock on the steering wheel. Jill might have been wearing a furrowed brow, but with nothing but the glow of the dashboard lights it was hard to be sure.

"Well, I just *know* I'm going to regret asking. But go ahead and tell me. What still bothers you that you can't stop thinking about?"

"They're not actually going to put him in jail."

"I never said they were."

"No, but you said if you were all set to rob a bank, and you were on your way there with a gun, and your car broke down, they couldn't put you in jail for bank robbery. But they're not going to put Jake in jail for murdering me, because there's no body. They're just going to treat him like a suspect. If the only thing that'd stopped you from robbing a bank was car trouble, and you had to spend months or maybe even years being investigated for being a bank robber, are you honestly saying that wouldn't be fair? Because I think it would be very fair. I think it would be not only Karma but . . . I'm going to use the word even though you'll argue with me . . . justice."

Norma looked out the window for a few beats, watching flat desert roll by in the dark. Here and there the moon cast shadows of brush and boulders.

"Huh," she said, almost without meaning to.

"Huh what?"

"You make a good point there."

"I *do*?" The girl sounded downright stunned.

"Didn't *you* think it was a good point?"

"Yeah, but I never once thought I'd make a point that *you* thought was good. I just figured you thought you know everything and I know nothing and that's just how it would always be."

"I think I know more than you do out of sheer experience. But if you end up in the right on some point, I'm not going to take that away from you. Now how 'bout if you drive the truck and let me get some sleep."

———

Norma was fast asleep, her cheek pressed up against the passenger window, when the girl said her name. She might have heard it several times before responding, because she thought she was having a dream in which someone kept saying "Norma."

"What?" she asked, sputtering awake and wiping a bit of drool from the corner of her mouth.

"We need to stop for gas."

"Sooner or later that was bound to happen."

"There's a gas station up ahead. But I don't have my credit card. Do you have a credit card?"

"Yeah. But we won't be using it. Credit cards can be traced. They show exactly where you were, and at what time. I brought my emergency cash."

"My parents'll pay you back."

"Whatever. Pull over onto the shoulder here."

"What for?"

"We're gonna change seats. *I'm* driving into the gas station. I want you down on the floor in the back with the blanket over you, like before."

"I don't get—"

"Please. Jill. I'm begging you. I just woke up out of a sound sleep. Please just do as I ask."

—

Norma was blinking under the bright lights of the gas pump, holding the nozzle and waiting for the tank to fill, when she saw the back window power down halfway. The girl must have reached up from under the blanket and found the lever.

"Now that you're awake," Jill said, her voice muffled by the blanket, "nobody would know me here."

"Maybe not. But we don't really know that for a cold hard fact."

"How could they know me?"

"We've had our heads down for a couple of days now. We don't really know if the news got around."

"Why would the news of my being gone a couple of days get around?"

"Because the world is a bizarre place, my young friend. Some missing people go pretty much unnoticed and others catch the public's fancy like a wildfire."

"But there are probably dozens of people missing."

"Try thousands."

"Then why would anyone care about me?"

Norma sighed.

A young man walked by her on the way into the gas station's convenience store. He glanced back over his shoulder at Norma as if she were crazy. Norma was pretty sure he could only hear her end of the conversation.

"Yeah, that's right," she barked at the guy. "When you get to be my age you'll be talking to yourself too."

He turned away again and hurried into the bright store.

"There's a type," Norma said, her voice quieter now.

"A type of what?"

"A type of missing person who gets more attention than all the others."

"And I'm that type?"

"Oh yeah."

A brief silence.

Then the muffled voice from the back said, "I'm not sure . . ."

"Oh, come on. You live in this world just like everybody else, my young friend. You can't tell me you don't see."

"I *might* know what you mean. But help me out here. I just want to be sure we're on the same page. Otherwise I'll always wonder."

"White. Blond. Young. Petite. Blue-eyed. Pretty."

"You think I'm pretty?"

"I think you're missing the point in a big way."

"Sorry. Why do people go for that one type?"

"You tell me, my young friend. Or if you meet a psychiatrist or a psychologist, ask him. Or her. I'm the last person in the world to tell you why people think what they think or do what they do. I think the whole lot of us are crazy and prone to absolute nonsense. But my theory is that we like to reserve our empathy for the people who remind us most of ourselves."

"But lots of people aren't blond or blue-eyed."

"True enough. But the press caters to a certain majority. And we've all been trained from the moment we popped out of our mommas that some people are prettier than others. That a certain type of person matters more than others."

"I don't think I matter more than anybody else. I think everybody matters just the same."

"As far as you know, I'm sure you do. I believe that you believe what you just said. But we digest these things all our lives, and it's in there whether we really meant for it to be or not. Lots of people disappear, and when you see which ones get all the notice, then you know who our society thinks is important."

"That's an upsetting thought."

"It's true, though."

"Maybe that's why it's upsetting."

"And the other reason your news might catch on is because there was an incident of domestic abuse. Now everyone gets to decide whether they think your boyfriend killed you and dumped your body. The people who think he's innocent will argue with the people who think he's guilty, and everybody will say they *know* which is true, not just that they *figure* it was that way, and nobody will change anybody else's damn mind."

More silence fell. Norma pulled the nozzle out of the now-full tank and hung it up on the pump again. She turned back around to replace the gas cap.

"Still," the girl's muffled voice said. "It hasn't been long enough for it to really hit the news. Has it?"

"Probably not. You're probably right about that. Let's just say I'm not big on taking chances."

She opened the truck's door and climbed back into the driver's seat. Fired up the engine.

She pulled out of the station, but not back onto the highway. She stayed on a dark frontage road until she found a place to pull over.

She wanted to go far past the silent parked big rigs whose drivers were probably, but not definitely, sleeping.

"Okay," she said when she'd shifted into park and set the parking brake. "I'll give the dogs a chance to jump out and pee. Or whatever else they might need to do by now. And then you get back up here and drive again. I need to get back to sleep."

Chapter Seven

That

"Norma, wake up," a voice said. "We're here."

Norma opened her eyes. But the world still appeared dark. She could see nothing.

"Wait. Where are we?"

"We're in my parents' garage."

"You shouldn't have gotten out and opened the garage door."

"I didn't. They just left it open. And they closed it when they heard us drive in. I almost texted them from your phone and had them open it from inside the house. But then I remembered you don't want this on your phone records."

"Oh," Norma said. Her head still felt half-asleep. "Well, that was good thinking at least."

She blinked a few more times and then found herself startled by a dim face outside the truck's window. She might've let out a little sound with her breath.

"That's my mom," Jill said.

The woman opened the passenger door of the truck and stared in at Norma, who stared back. The garage light was not on, but the door was open into what looked like a laundry room. Beyond that a bright kitchen sent a glow in their direction. She reached across Norma to grip her daughter's hand tightly, but addressed Norma with her words.

"You must be our savior," the woman said.

Norma had forgotten the woman's name.

"I'm not anybody's savior."

"You might need to get used to a change in that status."

Norma stepped out into the dim garage. Jill stepped out into her mother's arms.

A man, likely Jill's father, brushed by Norma and took Jill by the elbow.

"We're going," he said to his daughter.

He steered her toward a low-slung sports car parked right next to Norma's truck in the two-car garage.

"Where are we going?" the girl asked. She sounded unbalanced, even by the grading curve of the last couple of days.

"We're taking you to Jessie's in Ukiah. Nobody will think to look for you there."

He opened the passenger door of his car and steered the girl inside, one hand on the top of her head to keep her from banging it, the way you see on those police shows.

"Wait!" Jill said. And she popped back out of the car again. "I have to say goodbye to Norma."

The girl ran in her direction and threw her arms around Norma. Held her so tightly she nearly felt smothered.

"Sorry," Jill said in her ear. "I guess I wasn't supposed to say your name."

"Doesn't really matter."

"I love you."

Those three words just echoed for half a minute or so. Norma wasn't quite sure what to do with them. She didn't love Jill—though she had developed some scant affection for the girl—so she couldn't in all good conscience say it in return. And maybe Jill didn't love her, and wouldn't have thought she did if not for the strong emotions brought up by the dire circumstances of the past couple of days. Then again, it was hard to know.

"You'll be okay," Norma said.

"Think so?"

"Yeah. Your folks'll take care of things." Norma stepped back. Brushed blond hair off the girl's face. "You have yourself a good life, you hear?"

"You do too."

"Yeah, what's left of it. I'll do my best."

Then the girl jumped into the car, and the lack of lighting seemed to make her disappear. The roar of the sports car's engine sprang to life.

Norma thought it would be the last time she would ever see that girl. In reality, it was the last time she would see her for more than five years.

"We should go in," Jill's mother said. "Before he opens the garage door."

She took Norma's elbow and pulled her into the laundry room. They stood together and listened to the automatic garage door rolling up. Then the sound of the engine faded some, and the noisy door rolled down again.

"I gotta get my dogs," Norma said.

"Oh. You have dogs with you?"

"I couldn't very well leave 'em at home. They need to get fed."

"You didn't have anybody to look in on them? Oh, I'm sorry. I shouldn't be asking all these questions. It's just that we usually don't allow dogs in the house."

"I'm supposed to be home sick. I can't very well ask somebody to come into my house when I'm supposed to be home sick but I'm actually in a different state."

"I'm so sorry. Here I am owing you so much, and I'm just not thinking. You found Jill and brought her here to us. You can bring a dinosaur into the house if you want."

"Only two hound dogs. And, just so you know, I didn't find your daughter. They did."

"Then I guess my house is their house," the woman said.

——

Norma sat at the kitchen table, the dogs sleeping on the linoleum at her feet, and watched the woman make coffee. She slipped her phone out of her pocket and glanced at the contact the girl had created on her phone. To remind herself of the woman's name. But she had changed the contact to initials only. Fortunately the initial was enough to jog her memory.

T. Teresa. Right.

She had long blond hair, like her daughter, and blue eyes that did not have the same brilliant color. They were more of a pale blue, as though they had been washed in too-hot water or left out in the sun to fade. She must have been forty, or near it, to have a daughter Jill's age. But she barely looked it.

"I need to apologize for my husband," Teresa said.

"What did he do?"

"He was quite rude to you, and I know he didn't mean to be. He didn't even introduce himself, and he didn't thank you. He does appreciate what you did. I know he does. But he's very upset right now. He feels like he wasn't protecting Jill like he was supposed to, and he just can't wait to make up for it now."

"It doesn't really matter."

"It does to me."

"Well, that's between you and your husband."

A silence fell. While it rested there between them, Teresa set cream and sugar on the table in fussy little china servers.

"You'll want to sleep before you go back," Teresa said. "I made up the guest room."

"Thanks, but I'll be on my way just as it gets light. Which ought to be pretty soon now. I slept all night in the truck while your daughter drove."

"At least I need to feed you some breakfast."

"I'll take the breakfast. Thanks."

Teresa hurried over to the refrigerator and began pulling out food. Milk, a carton of eggs. A loaf of bread. An unopened package of bacon.

"And remind me, please, before you leave. I have some cash for you. Not profit. Just gas money. Owen figured out the most he thought it could be to drive all the way here and back. Just so you're not out of pocket, you know?"

"That sounds fair enough."

"How do you like your eggs?"

"I never met an egg I didn't like," Norma said.

———

Teresa's cell phone rang as they were finishing up breakfast. She pulled it out of the pocket of her slacks and glanced at its screen.

"Oh. Owen."

She touched the screen to pick up the call.

For a minute, she only listened.

Then she said, "Yes. I will. Of course I will."

She slid the phone back into her pocket.

"He says to tell you he's sorry he ran out so fast and didn't even thank you. He said to tell you you're a hero to us, and we'll always be grateful."

Norma only grunted. Compliments made her uneasy. They always had.

"I feel like I want to ask you . . ."

But Teresa did not seem inclined to finish that thought.

"What? Go ahead."

"Like I want you to tell me what my life is going to look like now."

"How would I know that?"

"I know. That's why I almost didn't finish the sentence." She brushed long strands of her blond hair back, flipping them behind her shoulder. "For some reason I've started thinking of you as some kind of expert on everything. Like you know life so much better than I do and can tell me just about anything."

"I been around longer, is all."

"You're not any kind of oracle. I know that. But you seem to be thinking more clearly than I am about how this might play out."

"Maybe," Norma said.

"I'd like to hear your thoughts at least. I feel like . . . like everything changes from here. And it's got me off balance."

"Everything *does* change from here. My ex-husband . . . back before he was my ex, he used to say 'Buckle up, buttercup.' And oh, I hated him for it. But, really, you do need to strap in for this."

"For . . . ?"

"Well, first of all, I hope you have a plan for her to live incognito."

"Owen does. Her eyes are her most distinctive feature, so he's going to get her brown contacts. And of course she'll cut her hair and dye it. We won't really know if that's going to be enough until we see it. And of course we'll get her a new name with ID and all."

"It's going to be a very weird time for you," Norma said. "You know the way you've been living the last couple of days? On pins and needles waiting for news? Going nuts in every possible way because you don't know if your only child is alive or dead? Well, you're going to have to keep living like that's the case. For a very, very long time."

"Oh," Teresa said.

"You hadn't thought of that?"

"I guess I hadn't thought it out quite so clearly, no."

"And you'll be lying to the police every time you turn around."

Teresa was looking down at the table, her long hair falling forward. When she raised her face, Norma saw she had begun crying silently.

"You can call it off anytime you want," Norma said.

"How can I do that?"

"Just tell the police she made her way back home. But leave me out of it."

"We won't do that. We can't. What if he found her and . . . you know. Hurt her."

"Well, then you're in it now. And you're committed. You'll reach a point of no return, I expect. She might be in the news a fair bit. You'll have to play the role of grieving parent well. You'd better be damned convincing."

"It won't be an act," Teresa said, wiping her eyes in that way women do when they don't want to smear their mascara. "We'll hardly be able to see her. She's had to walk away from the family and everything we thought her life would be. It'll be real mourning. But you don't need to worry about that. You can just go home and pretend none of this ever happened."

"Oh no I can't. I have to go home and go back to riding the hills every morning, acting like I'm looking for her. How would it look if I suddenly lost interest in a missing girl?"

"I'm sorry. I didn't think about that."

"Well, fortunately I like a good excuse to ride. But people will start spouting off regarding what they think happened to her. It's gonna be a real trial keeping my mouth shut. That's not exactly my specialty in life."

"We're swimming in a sea of unintended consequences."

"You can say that again," Norma said. "Well, I wish you the best and all that. But I'd better get my show on the road now. Long drive back, and I'd rather get out of your neighborhood before it's full-on light."

Teresa pulled a few folded bills from her pants pocket and set them on the table near Norma. Norma pulled them closer and unfolded them. It was four hundreds.

"Too much," she said.

"But gas is so expensive. And it's not just gas. It's wear and tear on the vehicle. Insurance. Maintenance costs."

Norma took three of the bills and left one on the table.

"Thanks," she said.

She rose, and the dogs stirred, and thumped their tails.

"I know Jill wasn't supposed to let us overhear your name," Teresa said.

"Oh, it doesn't matter much. I told you I was a volunteer with search and rescue in Sloot. There's exactly one woman volunteer. I was never keeping my identity a very good secret anyway."

"Whatever happens, I promise we'll always leave you out of it. It'll be as though we'd never met."

"I appreciate that," Norma said.

The woman rose and walked her through the laundry room to the garage door, the dogs weaving and wagging around their legs.

"Are you a hugger?" Teresa asked.

"Not much of one, no."

"Then I'll just say thank you. Thank you, Norma."

"You take care now. And take care of that girl. She's a good girl."

Teresa's eyes softened, and a few more tears leaked out.

"She is, isn't she? She really is. She doesn't always make the wisest choices, though."

"She's nineteen. She just needs to grow up."

"Well, she'll get to now, thanks to you."

It made Norma feel a little squirmy inside, the way compliments did. She only walked around to the driver's side of her truck, waving over her shoulder without looking back.

"Drive carefully now," Teresa called as Norma was letting the dogs jump into the back seat.

"Oh, I always do."

She climbed in and fired up the engine. When she shifted into reverse, the garage door opened for her. She backed out into a silent and sleeping cul-de-sac, satisfied that it was just dark enough that no neighbors would get a good look at her, even if any were awake.

She pulled off their street and immediately saw a sign for the freeway.

Pausing at a stop sign under a streetlight, she looked at the dogs in the rearview mirror, and they looked back.

"Well, that's that," she said.

At the time she said it, she fully believed it.

But in the fullness of time, she would see that that had not been that at all. That had only been the barest beginning of that.

Chapter Eight

The New Norma

When Norma finally got home, she stumbled exhausted out of the truck. She had an eyestrain headache from forgetting her sunglasses and driving nearly eight hours without them. She could feel the buzz in her muscles as she crossed her hard, dusty lot. A ghost sensation in her body was telling her she was still bouncing and vibrating along a highway. According to her watch, she had barely three hours to eat, nap, and get to work.

The dogs wove around her legs as she walked up to her own front porch, and Saint Fred nickered at her from his paddock.

Right. Barely three hours to feed the dogs and horse, eat, nap, muck the paddock area and groom the horse, and get to work.

Her blood froze when she saw a scrap of paper taped to the glass inset of her front door.

Her heart pounding, the sound of the blood rushing in her ears, Norma pulled the note down and read it.

It said, simply, "Call me. Betty."

Betty had been here. Norma had no idea why. But she did know one thing. Betty now knew that Norma had been off somewhere in her truck, not home with a stomach bug as she had claimed.

Norma let herself and the dogs into the cool, dim interior of home and then called Betty on the kitchen phone. The landline.

"There you are," Betty said in place of hello.

"You were at my house."

"I brought you some soup yesterday evening. You know. Got to feeling bad for you and all. Then when you weren't there I got really worried that you'd gone and driven yourself to the hospital or something."

"Yeah," Norma said. "That's exactly what it was. Well, not the hospital. I got scared it was more than just a bug. Maybe food poisoning or something, so I headed to that new urgent-care place near the county line."

"Oh. Right. Is that any good? Somebody came in the pub and asked for a recommendation of where to go. Nobody I know has used that place yet, but it's the closest one. I didn't know what to tell them."

"I . . . you know what? I honestly don't know. I was half the way there when I started thinking I was being silly. It was probably nothing and so why spend all that money? I just came home."

"But I came by this morning and you still weren't there."

Norma only stood a moment, feeling the floor seem to sway. Listening to the sound of her own heartbeat.

See, this was why she never lied. This was why she had always been who she had always been. The old Norma never had to keep her stories straight, because she never set out to deceive anyone. The old Norma had only been gone for a day or two, but the old way of doing things felt, in that moment, like a grievous thing to lose.

She never did answer, because of a terror that anything she said would only dig her in deeper.

"You just never did strike me as the kind of person who keeps secrets," Betty said. "But I guess you never really know somebody."

Again Betty waited for Norma to speak. Again, Norma did not—could not. She was now utterly frozen in her fear of saying the wrong thing.

"It's nothing to be ashamed of, you know," Betty said.

Could she possibly have guessed? No. She couldn't possibly have. Maybe she had an idea what the secret was, and probably she was guessing wrong. Who could possibly guess something as crazy and improbable as this mess Norma had gotten herself into?

"What isn't?"

"Having a boyfriend."

"I don't have a boyfriend."

The words sprang out of her mouth before she could think better. That had been her "out," right there. And she had let it go by.

Only people who lie are good at lying, Norma thought.

Through the kitchen window she saw Fred pacing in his paddock, tossing his head on his long neck, because she hadn't fed him yet. She always fed him first thing when she got home in the afternoon.

Then, just like that—just as the stress began to cause the beginnings of vertigo, just as her lack of breath became something she likely could not disguise—the "out" was handed back to her.

"Well, whatever you call him," Betty said. "Fling, friends with benefits. You know I don't care. I actually think it's healthy. But . . . speaking of healthy, I'm hurt that you felt like you had to lie to me. You could've just said you wanted to go see a man."

Norma pulled in a long breath.

Settle, she told herself. *Think. Don't make any more mistakes. Get it right this time, and put this damn thing to bed before it kills you.*

"But I didn't lie to you," she said. "I didn't. I really was sick. Didn't you ever feel sorry for yourself when you're sick and feel like you want somebody taking care of you? That you don't want to be alone at a time like that?"

A ridiculous bunch of sentiments, she thought, because she would never feel that way. And more lies on top of more lies on top of more lies.

What had she gotten herself into?

"That makes me feel a little better," Betty said. "I know we're not best buds or anything, but I'd like to think you can at least tell me what's what. Good for you, anyway, for having somebody. No matter what you think he is. No matter what you call it. Anyway, listen. Take care of yourself one more night. If we get slammed and I'm dying on my own I'll call you and get your butt out of bed. Otherwise, just rest and feel better."

"I will, Betty. Thanks."

They both hung up the phone.

Norma stood another moment, the phone in her hand, staring at it as though she couldn't remember what it was. Her hands were shaking. There was a tremble deep inside her thighs. And her breath still felt ragged.

In her peripheral vision she saw Fred again, through the window. Pacing and tossing his head.

"I'm coming," she said. "I'm coming. I'll be right there."

And with that she put it all behind her as best she could and tended to her animals. Fulfilled her simple chores in a world that looked enough like the one she'd left behind.

She went to bed before it even got dark, and slept straight through till morning.

Betty never called.

———

Norma pulled into the campground at a little after eight the following morning. Late for her, by any normal standard.

She was hauling Fred in the horse trailer behind her.

She found a place to pull off into the hard dirt and let the dogs jump down from the truck, feeling more than a little bit put out.

She had lots of things she should have been doing that morning. She'd been bumped out of her normal routine for days. The laundry and the shopping needed doing, and more rest would have been helpful. But no. She had to ride around looking for a girl she knew for a fact was hundreds of miles away and not in danger. She had to waste the whole damn day on this nonsense and then work all night.

The spring weather had taken a turn toward unseasonable heat, which didn't help her mood one bit.

Ian had set up a ripstop nylon canopy to throw shade on his little impromptu command center.

She opened the back of the horse trailer, waited for Fred to come out, then used its wheel well cover as a mounting block.

She rode Fred up to where Ian sat. Or at least, as close as she could ride him without running him right into the canopy.

"Norma," he said. "You don't look so good." Before she could open her mouth to speak, he added, "I don't mean that in the insulting way. That came out wrong. I mean you look like you don't feel so good."

"I'm better," she said.

"Really?"

"Some better."

"You could've taken another day off, you know."

"If there's a girl in trouble, let's go find her."

But there wasn't. And therein lay the problem with Norma's mood.

"Make a short day of it," Ian said. "It's gonna be a scorcher."

"Yeah, when did that happen all of a sudden?"

"It just happened all of a sudden, like you said. But it might be hard on you if you're still half-sick."

"We'll see how I do," Norma said.

She reined her horse around, and pressed his sides lightly with her heels. Saint Fred didn't budge.

"What the hell?" she said to the horse. Rather loudly.

"You forgot something," Ian said.

"Like what? He goes when I say go."

Ian pulled a carrot out of his shirt pocket and broke it into three pieces. The horse leaned his head under the canopy, stretched out his long neck, and ate the pieces one at a time.

"You done now?" Norma asked him. "You happy? We can go now?"

Without being asked a second time, the horse headed for the trail.

They rode together for the better part of three hours, this time angling their trajectory down toward the hot valley. The heat built to a crescendo that shimmered off the light boulders, making the air a visible thing.

Norma never belted out any songs.

She simply was not in the mood for singing.

—

She was loading up her horse when she heard Ian call out to her.

"Norma. When you get him squared away can you come over here a minute? I need to talk to you."

And just like that, the panic was back. The shortness of breath. The cold tingling in her stomach, like her blood had been suddenly air-conditioned.

She closed the trailer door, leaving the horse untied and free inside to turn around if he chose. Though more likely he would just nibble at his hay bag.

Ian pointed to a camp chair in the blessed shade beside him, and Norma sat.

"What's this about?" she asked, hoping he couldn't hear her voice shake.

"I've been doing this a long time," he said. "More than twenty years. I know things about my volunteers just to look at them."

Norma's heart pounded harder. She had her sunglasses on this time, and she hoped it robbed him of the chance to see the fear in her eyes.

She angled her head so her hat brim blocked a bit more of her face from his view.

"Well, go ahead and tell me what you see," she said.

But he couldn't see *that*. He just couldn't.

Could he?

"See, your hands are shaking," he said. "I really think you cut your recovery too short to get back here. I appreciate the dedication to task, Norma, but I don't think you're well yet."

"Is that what you wanted to tell me?"

"No."

"What, then?"

Pound. Pound. Pound. She could feel it in her chest and hear it in her ears. And it wasn't supposed to be this way. This was never supposed to be her life. Because she never lied, and this was why she didn't.

It reminded her suddenly of that story she'd read in high school. About the murderer who thought he and his guest could hear the heartbeat of the man he'd murdered coming from under the floorboards. But it was his own guilt, if she was remembering right. His own guilt gave him away.

In a minute Ian would open his mouth and say "I know you found Jill Moss."

How he knew it, Norma had no idea. But he knew it. It was over. And, oddly, she felt it as a deep relief. She could stop lying now. She would have to face some music, but the pounding in her heart would be over.

It was over.

"If there's one thing I know about my volunteers," he said, "it's that not every case affects everyone the same. Sometimes one just stands out. Who knows why? Maybe the person reminds you of one of your own kids. Maybe their situation is like something you went through at some point in your life. Maybe someone has stumbled on two corpses in just a few months in the course of doing this work. There's a kind of

PTSD that goes with that. I've seen it. Or maybe you don't even know why. And I'm not asking, Norma. I'm not prying. It's your own business and none of mine."

"I still have no idea where you're going with this, Ian."

"This one is getting to you. I can see it. You're not taking it in stride like you normally do. It's wearing you down. I'm taking you off it. Your health and well-being are every bit as important as the missing person's. We've got a sufficient number of people out looking. I want you to go home and take care of yourself, and I'll text you next time somebody different comes up missing."

They sat a moment in silence. Norma was digesting what had just happened. Or, rather, what *hadn't* just happened.

He didn't know.

Which was . . . a relief? A disappointment? Both?

Probably both.

She glanced over at him quickly, her heart gradually settling.

He had always been honest and fair with her, and with everybody else in this town. He deserved better than to run an exhaustive operation for a girl already found.

She opened her mouth to tell him the truth, consequences be damned.

Then she closed her mouth again. Because they weren't all her consequences. It wasn't her secret to tell. Somebody else's safety was at stake, and she had promised.

She was stuck here.

"I know you want to argue with me," he said. "But I feel strongly about this."

"Normally I would argue," she said. "But I *have* been feeling pretty run down."

"Go home."

"Okay," Norma said. "Then I suppose I will." She rose. Stepped out into the blazing sun. Then she turned to look back at Ian. "Thanks."

"I'm being selfish," he said. "I need you in the long haul."

Norma climbed into her truck with the dogs and drove home.

As she drove, she realized she was in mourning. She could feel it. She would need to grieve the loss of her old life. The one that never required telling a lie. That never had her looking over her shoulder.

The one that never made her heart pound with fear because she thought somebody knew.

And now, all that was over. And it was just dawning on her—even though she'd said as much to Jill's mother—that the old way of living was never coming back.

This was her new normal.

Chapter Nine

Fuses

Norma showed up to work at eight sharp.

She stepped through the door, stopped cold, and felt her eyes go wide.

The place was packed.

Betty's eyes came up to hers. And then her coworker did something bizarrely unexpected.

"Hey folks," Betty said, her voice booming. As if she intended to address everybody in the place at the same time. "Say hi to Norma. She's on *the search and rescue team!*"

She ended the sentence with a crazy emphasis, as if saying Norma had just come back from a trip to Mars or had cured cancer right before her shift.

The crowd buzzed with mostly nonverbal noises, sounding both impressed and delighted.

Norma hung up her jacket, walked behind the bar, and grabbed Betty by the sleeve, towing her toward the kitchen.

"What the hell was that, Betty? What do you think you're doing?"

"Quadrupling your tips."

"Oh. Well, I could use that, I guess. But who are all these people?"

"Seems this Jill Moss thing made it into the news today."

"Oh" was all Norma said. It made her stomach tighten, but she reminded herself that she'd known it was coming.

As if reading the thought, Betty said, "You knew that might happen, right?"

"Well, yeah, but . . . I didn't expect people to show up *in person*."

"According to Kristen the place has been packed all afternoon."

"Who's Kristen?"

"That new day-shift person."

"Oh. Right."

Norma glanced around Betty to the patrons on the other side of the bar. They all seemed to be staring back at her.

"Well, listen," Norma said. "Don't be telling people I'm on Jill's search team anymore. Because Ian took me off it."

"What'd he go and do that for?"

"He said it was getting to me."

"Is it?"

"Yeah. Maybe. Maybe some."

"Well, I can't untell these people. Just go talk it up and collect your tips."

———

"What do you know about Jake and Jill?" a young, dark-haired woman asked while Norma was pouring beers.

The bar was surprisingly quiet considering the size of the crowd. No one had to shout to be heard. In fact, Norma had a sense that ears were tuned, waiting for her reply.

"Jake and Jill?"

"Yeah, you know. Jill Moss and Jake Willis. You must know something. You're out there looking for her every day."

"I know we haven't found her."

"You think he killed her?"

"Now how would I know that?"

Norma pushed the beers across the bar on their cork-lined tray. Then she just stood there, leaning on the bar. Braced on it with the heels of her hands, staring into this young woman's face. It felt oddly like a standoff. Like the girl was sure Norma knew much more and was challenging her to say it.

A big, booming male voice rang out.

"Well, *I* know," he said. "He killed her and hid the body and I know it."

"You were there?" Norma asked him, not entirely sure in which direction to look. "Because the police'll want to talk to you."

"No, I wasn't there."

"Then you don't know."

"I'm good at these things," the voice said.

Norma was able to locate him during that sentence. He was skin-headed and tattooed, and looked to be over forty. Maybe even getting on to fifty.

Old enough to have better things to do, Norma thought.

"Maybe you *are* good at guessing things," Norma said. "But it's a problem that you don't know the difference between guessing and knowing."

The man got up and approached the bar.

It might almost have seemed like a threatening gesture, but Norma could feel nothing. She had gone numb inside. In fact, she might have been numb for days and was only just now realizing it. It was hard to know for a fact, looking back.

He leaned his elbows on the bar and moved his head in closer to her face. His breath smelled of stale cigarettes.

"I don't *guess,*" he said. "I know human nature."

"Nobody knows human nature," Norma nearly spat. She'd had enough all of a sudden. And, just like that, there was no holding back.

No keeping it in. "What the hell is wrong with you that you think you can know things you can't possibly know? What the hell is wrong with everybody? With people in general? Have you all gone crazy? Lost your ever-loving minds all at the same time? Why, people don't even understand their own damn selves and they think they know everybody and everything else. If you don't know, then you don't know, and you're not magic, and the world would be a better place if you knew what you didn't know. Now go sit down and get out of my face, would you please?"

For a long, tense moment, nobody moved or spoke. Norma could tell that she had offended the man's pride. She could see the storm roiling behind his eyes. She just didn't know what he would be inclined to do about it. She would have to wait to learn that.

A few seconds later a more clean-cut man of about the same age came up behind him and pulled him off by the arm.

"Forget it, Mack," the new guy said. "Just let it go."

Mack walked back to his seat, and life in the pub more or less went on. With an awkward sense of discomfort, but it did.

Norma didn't know Betty was right behind her until she heard her friend's voice near her ear.

"Wow," Betty said. "Ian might've been onto something. You're on a short fuse."

"I just don't like people like that."

"You just don't like people. You want to go home?"

"Are you kidding? The place is packed."

"So what? Let 'em wait for a drink. Let 'em go patronize our competitor."

It was a small joke between them. There was only one bar in Sloot.

"I don't want to go home," Norma said. "I've been doing nothing but going home for days. I want to stay right here and tend bar like it's my job to do."

And that was what she did.

Nobody asked her any questions or tried to engage her in any way after that. And the tips weren't all that great.

—

It was about three nights later—three crowded, noisy nights—when Wanda attached herself to Norma. Or tried to, anyway.

Wanda was a tiny girl in her early twenties with a long braid down the middle of her back. The combination of the braid and the fact that she was not even five feet tall made her look like a child.

She followed Norma out into the dirt parking lot after closing time.

"Wait," she called out.

"I will not wait," Norma said over her shoulder. She did not stop walking to say it. "I'm finally off my shift and I'm going home and no one can stop me."

"But you're that lady who's on the search team."

Norma stopped. Sighed. Turned around in the dark.

"I'm taking a break from search and rescue," she said.

"But you *were* on the search team."

"I was."

"Then you know more than anybody."

"I know they're still searching. What else is there to know?"

Norma couldn't read the young woman's face, because it was too dark.

"Okay, fine. Don't tell me anything."

"There's nothing to tell. If they find her, we'll know something. Until then we know nothing."

"What do you mean, 'if' they find her?"

"You honestly don't know what that means?"

"But they'll find her, right? I mean . . . don't missing persons usually get found?"

"Usually. Not always. Now if you'll excuse me, I have a home to go to."

"Do you have to go to the highway?"

"No."

"Oh. Too bad. I was hoping you'd give me a ride to the highway."

"I'm not going that way. And I don't invite strangers into my car."

Even in the darkness of the unlit dirt parking lot, Norma could see the young woman deflate. See her shoulders droop.

Norma almost turned to go, but couldn't quite bring herself to do it.

"You don't have a car?" she asked the girl.

"No."

"How'd you get here in the first place?"

"Hitchhiked. But I don't want to hitch in the dark."

"You shouldn't even be hitchhiking in broad daylight, young lady. Don't you know what can happen to a young woman like you when you put yourself in the hands of a stranger?"

"I've been doing it since I was a teenager. Nothing's happened."

"Which doesn't mean nothing ever will. Where do you live?"

"Connecticut."

"Connecticut?" Norma's voice came out almost as a screech, but in a deeper register. "You trying to tell me you hitchhiked here all the way from Connecticut? For what?"

"I was curious about the Jake-and-Jill thing like everybody else."

Norma only stood a minute, watching a thin sliver of crescent moon, only half-visible over the mountains.

"I don't get what people find so compelling about the case."

"I sure do," the young woman said. "I'm Wanda."

"I don't want to know who you are," Norma said. "Don't take that the wrong way. It's no offense meant to you. But it's like naming a stray cat. Once you name 'em, it's a signal that you're keeping 'em. Where are you staying?"

"At that cheap motel just off the highway on the south end of Sloot."

"Get in the truck," Norma said. "I'm taking you back there before we end up with two missing girls in this town."

———

"Help me understand," Norma said as she pulled out onto the dark highway. "What is it about this case that has everybody so fascinated?"

"Well, she's *missing*," Wanda said.

"Yeah. I got that part. But you do realize thousands of people are missing, right?"

"But I don't know them."

"Oh, you knew Jill?"

"Well, no. I didn't *know her* know her. But her picture's been in the paper, and everybody on Twitter is sharing these videos she made about college life."

"Everybody on where?"

"Twitter."

"What's a Twitter?"

"You honestly never heard of Twitter?"

"I might've heard some people say it, but I don't entirely get what they're referring to. I'm guessing it's some kind of internet thing."

"Right. An internet thing."

"I stay as far away from that stuff as possible. I guess you got to feeling like you knew her somehow."

"I guess."

A long silence fell. The only sound was the hum of the engine and the rumble of the truck's tires on the pavement.

Then Wanda said, "I tried hanging out at the campground. A lot of people are hanging out there, trying to see if Jake will talk to anybody."

Norma felt her foot instinctively pump the brake for a couple of seconds.

"He's still *there?*"

"Yeah. You didn't know that? He says he's there looking for his girlfriend, and making sure the sheriff is doing everything he should be doing. But a lot of people figure that's just one of those things you say when you don't want people to know you really did it. I saw him. But I couldn't get him to talk to me."

"You do realize that he's a potentially violent person, whether he killed his girlfriend or not. Right?"

"Yeah, I heard about the domestic-violence stuff."

"Then what're you doing trying to talk to him?"

"He's not going to get violent with *me*. I'm not his girlfriend."

Norma shook her head in the dark.

"I don't understand," she said.

"Which part?"

"I don't understand any of this."

She pulled into the parking lot of the Lucky 7 motel. Its lighted sign announced "No Vacancy." She shifted into park in front of the office. Pulled on the hand brake.

The office seemed deserted, but there was a light on in front of it. Norma turned her head to look at the girl and could see her face fairly well. She looked like some kind of sprite or pixie.

"Is it possible," Norma asked her, "that because you only know a little about Jill Moss, somehow you have this projection in your head that she's a lot like you?"

"I'm not sure. I never thought about it. Why?"

"I don't know. Just, in my experience, people's empathy kicks in when somebody's in trouble who reminds them of themselves. That's when they get real interested. But you know what? Never mind. Here I am trying to understand human nature and I forgot that in a million years I never will. Anyway, you're here at your motel so you're safe for the night. But please tell me you're not planning to hitchhike all the way back to Connecticut."

"I have to get home, now don't I?"

"You could take the bus."

"I don't have money for the bus."

"And you don't have anybody who'll send you the money?"

"Nope."

"Your parents?"

"They don't give me money anymore."

"But this motel costs money."

"Not much. Even if I left in the morning it wouldn't be enough for a bus."

Norma dug the huge wad of bills from her jeans pocket. A whole night's worth of tips.

"If I gave you some money would you take a bus home in the morning?"

"No. I'd stay and spend it on more nights in this motel. I'm staying until they find her."

But they never will, Norma thought.

"What if they don't find her for months?"

"I'm hoping I'll meet a local who might let me stay."

"Don't look at *me*," Norma said. "I don't take in strays. I live alone for a reason, and it's going to stay that way. But listen. If you ever wise up and decide to go home, come find me at the pub. I'll give you money for the bus so you don't have to hitchhike."

"Thanks," Wanda said. "That'll come in handy if they find her body."

"Wait, her *body*? You're not hoping they find her alive?"

"Well, sure. I *hope*. But with every day that goes by, that's less likely. Right?"

Norma never answered. She was feeling more than a little stunned.

"Thanks for the ride," Wanda said. "See ya."

And with that she swung the truck door open and jumped down onto the tarmac. She trotted up to one of the rooms. The paint was peeling slightly on the doors of the motel.

Norma waited until the girl was safely inside.

Then she pulled back onto the highway and drove home.

She shook her head several times on the way.

At one point she said, out loud in the dark and empty truck cab, "The whole world's gone crazy."

Chapter Ten

What a Killer Would Say

It was six nights later when Jake walked into the bar. And Norma most definitely noticed, even though she had no idea who he was.

First of all, she noticed his presence immediately because he reminded her of her ex-husband. He looked absolutely nothing like her ex. Ed had been tall, dark, heavily built, swarthy. This young man was blond and, though he seemed wiry and strong, was lightly built. And yet he put Norma in mind of Ed immediately. Maybe it was the way he carried himself. Maybe it was a certain energy of challenge that followed him into the room. Whatever the reason, the feeling was undeniable.

The other reason his entrance did not go unnoticed was because every other patron in the pub noticed. The room had been full of a buzzing hum of voices. Maybe forty drinkers. And when he walked in, the place fell absolutely silent. Just like that. It was instant.

Norma had not been watching the news. She quite purposely had not been. Normally she would have watched half an hour of semi-local news out of Phoenix—Phoenix was not all that local, but then again nothing was—and half an hour of national news every day. But she had given it up until all this blew over. As the Jill Moss story was hashed and rehashed at the state level, and if and when it hit the national news,

Norma didn't want to hear about it. And she had never been a fan of getting near that social-media stuff in the first place.

As a result, his face was unfamiliar to her. Until that moment.

Clearly it was familiar to everybody else in the pub.

Norma hadn't known Betty was right behind her until she heard her coworker's voice near her ear.

"Uh-oh," it said.

"What am I missing?" Norma asked quietly. "What does everybody else know that I don't?"

"That's him."

"Him who?"

"The boyfriend. The missing girl's boyfriend."

"Oh. That's Jake Willis."

While they were discussing this sudden turn of events, Jake Willis was approaching the bar. He stood with his elbows leaning on its clean surface and looked directly at Norma. His blond hair seemed to stick straight up on top, and she couldn't imagine whether he styled it that way on purpose or if he just hadn't been taking much care of his appearance out at the campsite. His eyes were blue, like Jill's, and yet also not like Jill's. Where hers were a brilliant blue, his were a faded shade of blue that might almost have straddled the line into gray. It gave him a cool, detached appearance.

Or maybe it was not the color of his eyes giving off that impression.

"I'll have a draft beer," he said.

Norma found her midsection swelling with rage. It started in her gut and seemed to fill her up amazingly fast.

"No," she said.

"Excuse me?"

"We don't serve your kind here."

"My *kind*?" he said, his voice straining. "Exactly what *kind* would that be?"

"Let me give you a lesson about the world, young man. If a woman walks away from you, it's because she wants to be away from you. You want her to want to stay? Well, then, you have to accomplish that with how you treat her. Treat others well, they generally won't keep running away from you. You can't mistreat people and then force them to stay. I don't care if a woman is your girlfriend or your wife, you don't own her. She has full control of her own life. It might distress you a lot that she's leaving, but under no circumstances do you get to twist her arm behind her back and force her to go where you want her to go. No matter what a woman does and no matter how you feel about that woman, there is no moment when you have the right to overpower her. Never. That is *never* your right. That is *always* abuse."

Her voice sounded harder and louder to her own ears as each sentence progressed, and everybody seemed to be listening. She could somehow hear the silence of their listening, though she could not have explained how. In her peripheral vision she could see all heads turned in her direction.

He leaned closer over the bar. Norma wanted to retreat, but she didn't. She feared briefly for her safety, but she held still and let him respond.

"You think I killed her," he said quietly. "Don't you?"

"I never said that, so I'm not sure why you're thinking it."

"Because everybody thinks I killed her."

A male voice popped up from somewhere in the corner of the room. "*I* think you killed her," it said.

That was the moment when Jake Willis lost his temper and began to shout. But fortunately his rage was no longer directed at Norma.

He spun wildly around and ended up a few feet from the bar, facing the seating area.

"I did *not* kill my girlfriend!" he bellowed. "I didn't! You come say that right to my face that you think I killed her. I didn't kill her."

A silence fell. For a brief moment, Jake allowed it.

Then he said, "Nobody'll stand behind saying that? You've got nothing to say in response to that?"

Another brief silence.

Then a tall, heavy man in the corner stood. He was wearing all black except for his blue jeans—including a black leather vest. He was bearded, with a ruddy complexion.

He walked right up to Jake and towered over him. If they had been the same height, the two men would have been nose to nose. Instead the big man seemed to be looking down on the top of Jake's unkempt head.

"Yeah, I got something to say in response to that." His voice was deep and rumbly, seeming to come from a place low in his chest. "I have this to say about it: That's. Exactly. What someone. Who'd killed their girlfriend. Would say."

For maybe the count of two, the world stood still.

Then Jake Willis exploded.

He moved in swinging wildly, but the two men were already so close that there wasn't much "in" left to go. One punch passed the big man's side and seemed almost to happen behind him. The second might have landed, but it was hard to tell, because their bodies were blocking Norma's view.

The big man ended things quickly.

He simply grabbed Jake by the shirt, lifted him, and threw him like an oversize rag doll or a bale of hay. Jake flew in the direction of the nearest table. The two women sitting at that table scrambled for safety.

When Jake fell, he knocked over the table, brought it down with him, and landed on top of the edge of it. It hit him right in the center of his back.

"Ouch," Norma heard Betty say. "That can't be good. You can break a man's back that way."

Jake rolled off the table and remained sprawled there on the floor for a few seconds, not moving.

A small young woman ran to him and helped him to his feet. He was obviously in pain, and having trouble standing. But apparently his back was not broken, because he did end up on his feet, one arm slung around the woman's shoulders.

It was only when they had hobbled halfway to the door that Norma realized the young woman was Wanda.

She raised her eyes to Norma and nodded in recognition.

"Oh hey," Wanda said.

"Wanda, what the hell are you doing?"

"I'll just get him back to the campground," she said.

Norma had more to say, but no time to say it. They were out the door and gone.

Slowly the room melted, and conversation resumed. And life went on, the way it always does, no matter what's just happened.

"You know that girl?" Betty asked.

"I gave her a ride to her motel one night. She doesn't have a car."

"Then I wonder how she thinks she'll get him back to the campground."

"I don't know. In his car, I guess."

"I wonder why, though," Betty said. A little dreamily, as though thinking out loud.

"She probably just wants to talk to him. Like everybody else. You know. Pick his brain about what happened."

"I hope that's all it is."

"What do you mean you 'hope that's all it is'? What else could it be?"

"Well. You know."

"I *don't* know."

"Some women go for the bad boys. Look at the women who marry the serial killers while they're doing life in prison for all those murders."

"Yeah, that's weird. But at least they're in prison. Nice for people who say they want a relationship but they really don't. And you get to say he didn't do it, but he's locked up. You know. Just in case you're wrong. But this guy is free to twist more arms behind more backs. Nobody would be that stupid."

Norma heard no reply, so she turned to look at Betty. She was eyeing Norma with one eyebrow arched high.

"I live in *this* world," Betty said. "Where are *you* living these days?"

"Yeah, okay, I hear you."

"Do we throw that big guy out for fighting?"

"I don't know. I don't think so. He didn't start it."

"We haven't had a fight in here in years."

"I guess it's just going to be like this now. Everybody at everybody else's throat, all spouting off about this Jill Moss situation. Pretty much indefinitely. I figure this is just our new normal, and I hate that."

Another brief silence.

Then Betty said, "That's weird."

"What's weird?"

"That you would say that."

"Why is it weird?"

"Because it's only till they find her. Or find her body."

"Oh," Norma said. "Right."

And with that, the feeling came back around again. That deeply unsettling feeling that there was always something you'd forget when keeping a secret. That, hiding right around any given corner, there was always a way to make a mistake. It seemed to be waiting for you there. Waiting for you to trip over it.

Betty wasn't saying anything, so Norma added, "If they find her, sure. Yeah. Then it'll stop, I guess. Depending on what they find."

"But you said they almost always find somebody. Either find them alive or find their body."

"Some people never get found."

"Not sure why you think this'll be one of those."

"I don't know, Betty. This whole thing just has me a little off."

"Yeah, I noticed that. Ian was right about that. I'm glad he took you off the search. I think it was getting to you for some reason."

"Yeah, I guess I'm glad he took me off it, too."

They didn't talk much for the rest of the night. Every now and then, Norma would glance over her shoulder, and Betty always seemed to be watching her, and with a slightly worried look on her face.

Maybe she would need to take Betty aside sometime soon and tell her the truth about the end of her marriage. That way Betty would have an explanation in her head for why Norma was so put off balance by the whole situation.

She hated like hell to do it. It rankled her to be put in that position. It was her secret, one she'd been able to hold to herself for decades. And now here she was needing to spill it to two people in just a big handful of days.

Still, Norma had two secrets now. Better to spill that one than have Betty figure out the other one. At least that secret was hers to tell.

Chapter Eleven

What Reporters Do

It was nine days later when Wanda came to say goodbye.

Unfortunately she did so in the dark and empty pub parking lot a few minutes after closing time. And from behind. While Norma was walking along, thinking she was completely alone.

"Hey," Wanda said.

Norma startled to a degree that was unknown and surprising to her. She startled the way a person can only do when their nerves have been stretched far too thin for far too long.

She let out a small, strangled sound, and spun around with her hands out as if to defend herself.

"Oh. Wanda," she said. Her voice sounded breathy to her own ears. "You scared the living daylights out of me. Don't ever sneak up on a body like that in the dark in the middle of the night."

"Sorry," Wanda said. "I just didn't want to leave without saying goodbye."

"Oh, you're going home to Connecticut? That's probably wise. You need money for the bus?"

"No, thanks. I got a ride."

The young woman's head was turned in a direction other than Norma's face. Norma turned to look where Wanda was looking.

There was a pickup truck sitting in the dirt parking lot, its bed full of strapped-down cargo. Its engine and headlights were off. Norma could see the dark shape of someone in the driver's seat, but not much more detail than that.

"You trying to tell me you're not the only one who came all the way from Connecticut for this?"

Wanda shifted from foot to foot in the dark. She seemed edgy, but Norma couldn't imagine why.

"No. I'm not trying to tell you that. He lives in Southern California. But he offered to drive me home."

"Oh, you're seeing somebody. I get it. You met someone."

"I'm not seeing him."

"If he's currently on the Arizona-Utah border, and he lives in Southern California, but he's willing to drive you all the way back to Connecticut, I think you're seeing him."

For an uncomfortably long time, Wanda said nothing. She was shifting her weight back and forth again, signaling that something had her off balance and uneasy.

"He's still hung up on his old girlfriend," Wanda said.

"Not so hung up that he can't drive you all the way to Connecticut."

"He just likes talking to someone who doesn't think he's a monster. That's all."

For a moment they only stood. Teetering slightly in the dark. Not talking.

Norma was piecing things together in her head. Or maybe it would be more accurate to say that the things were piecing themselves. Norma seemed only to be watching them come together.

When they finally did, she marched over to the dark truck. As she walked, she slipped her phone out of her pocket and swiped her finger diagonally down its screen to bring up the flashlight button. She turned it on and shone it into the driver's face, all the time hoping she was wrong.

She was not wrong. It was Jake Willis waiting to take Wanda to a home practically on the other side of the country.

Jake winced, squeezed his eyes shut, and turned his face away from the glaring light. He threw one hand up to shield himself.

"Hey, lady," he said. "Do you mind?"

Norma lowered the phone until its flashlight lit up the dirt around her feet.

Then she marched back to Wanda.

"Are you out of your ever-loving mind, young lady?"

"I knew you'd disapprove."

"You think?"

"He didn't kill her."

"I never said he did."

"He didn't twist her arm behind her back. That got blown all out of proportion."

"Oh, he most definitely did *that*. There were multiple witnesses."

"They were wrong about what they saw. He just put his arm around her shoulder and guided her back to camp."

The flashlight of Norma's phone was still on, and she raised it and trained its light on the young woman's face. She wanted to see more about Wanda's expression. To understand better what she really thought about the nonsense she was spewing. It didn't work, though, and Norma should have known it wouldn't. Wanda turned her face away, and it was impossible for Norma to know if she looked away in shame or simply to get the light out of her eyes.

"Honey," she said, "you must know that those two things don't look anything alike."

She turned off the flashlight on her phone.

"You're wrong about him," Wanda said. Her voice was soft. Almost pleading. "He's being mischaracterized. Misunderstood. He's really a very gentle man."

"I'm not the one who's wrong about him, honey."

"But it doesn't matter anyway. I'm not his girlfriend. He's still totally in love with Jill. He doesn't think or talk about anything else. He just likes me because I'll listen when he talks about her. He's obsessed with her."

"Yeah," Norma said. "You finally hit on a true thing in that last sentence. That was the problem all along. When love comes out less like love and more like obsession, bad things follow."

"I have to go," Wanda said.

"You're making a big mistake."

"I'm doing it anyway."

"Oh, I knew you would. Nobody ever talks anybody else out of anything once they have their mind set."

"Why even say it, then?"

"Well. Here's how I look at it. If you walk away from me and something terrible happens to you, then at least I know I tried. I get to go through the rest of my life knowing I gave it a shot, anyway. Instead of going to sleep every night thinking, *At least I could have said something*. That's pretty much all there is when it comes to other people and their big mistakes. You just have to go with the fact that you tried."

"He's just driving me home. I'll be fine."

"Tell you what. I'll say a prayer tonight that what you just told me is true."

To Norma's surprise, the young woman dove in and threw her arms around Norma. She was so surprised, in fact, that it took her several seconds to return the hug.

It struck Norma that it was the second time in just a few weeks that a desperate young woman had embraced her as though she were some sort of safe parental figure. After decades of nobody getting very near her at all.

"Good luck," she said.

Wanda let go and disappeared into the dark.

Norma figured she would never see or hear from that young woman again. Never know how that story ended.

She would turn out to be wrong in that prediction as well.

—

Norma woke from a fitful sleep. At least, it was fitful in the rare moments when she was able to sleep at all. She rose, pulling on jeans and a warm sweater, and set about making coffee in the kitchen.

A strange sight caught her attention through the window over the sink.

There seemed to be a small crowd of people and vehicles just outside her gate.

The vehicles were mostly cars, but there were two vans of the type that carried transmission equipment on their roofs. And they had what Norma could only assume were TV-station call letters and logos painted on their sides. There were maybe a dozen people, two of whom balanced bulky, heavy-looking video cameras on their shoulders.

"What the . . . ," Norma said to herself and the empty room.

She stepped out into the cool morning, and the dogs followed her out the door. They ran to the gate, baying at the intruding humans, who instinctively stepped back.

Norma leaned on the gate, and a thirtysomething woman in a lavender pantsuit immediately approached her. She was carrying a microphone.

"What are you all doing out here?" Norma asked.

"You have a no-trespassing sign on your gate," the woman said.

She had blond hair, which Norma did not find especially surprising, and it looked the way a woman's hair tends to look just as she's stepping out of the beauty parlor. The wind was the normal amount of gusty and stiff that morning, but the woman's hair never moved.

Must be lacquered down pretty good, Norma thought.

"Yeah, I know I've got a no-trespassing sign, being the one who put it there and all. I didn't mean why didn't you come right in and make yourself at home. I meant what are you doing out here at all?"

Another apparent news reporter had come up behind the woman, also extending a microphone in Norma's direction. A twentysomething man with short, dark hair and a blue windbreaker over a dress shirt and tie.

The dogs sat close to her heels, one on each side, growling slightly in their throats.

"We heard you were on the Jill Moss search and rescue team," he said. "And we wanted to ask you some questions."

"I used to be on that search and rescue team, but I'm taking a break. Talk to someone who's out there every day."

"We can't find them or identify them," the woman said. "The sheriff's department won't tell us who they are."

"Then how did you find and identify me?"

"Someone at the pub told everybody there you were on the team. You're a known quantity."

"Great," Norma said. "Just great. Just what I've always wanted to be. A known quantity."

"Can you answer a few questions?" the man asked.

Norma looked up and past the two interlopers to see that the cameras were now pointed right at her face. It irked her immediately. All of this did. But the idea that those cameras might be running before she'd even agreed to an interview was just the last straw.

"No," she said, her voice hard. "I can't answer a few questions. Because I don't have any of the information you want. Now go away and leave me be. I haven't even had coffee or fed the dogs or the horse yet, and I don't need this aggravation."

"We just want to know if you think Jill Moss will still be found."

"You want to know what I *think*?" Norma shouted. "What the hell difference does it make what I *think*? What the hell difference does it make what anybody thinks? You're the news. You're reporters, and you don't even know what reporters do. They report facts. Facts! Things they can actually know. Last time I was dumb enough to watch the news, I listened to some reporter telling me what a certain congressman believes."

Norma paused a moment, and watched the two news reporters exchange a slightly confused look.

"Oh, you don't see the problem with that? And that's exactly the problem. You don't even see how wrong that is. A reporter's not supposed to say what someone believes, because they can't know that. Nobody knows what someone else believes. We only know what they say they believe. And if you don't know the difference between a fact and what someone says is a fact, then you're everything that's wrong with the world today. You with one of those twenty-four-hour cable news channels?"

"She is," the young man said.

Norma turned her face and her wrath to the woman.

"Good. I've been wanting to tell somebody this. I blame your networks for everything that's wrong with the media today, and half of what's wrong with the world as a whole. When I was growing up we had Walter Cronkite. He didn't tell us what other people were thinking. He told us what was going on, and for exactly half an hour a day. Because, guess what? That's about how long it takes to report the facts without having to stick microphones in people's faces and hear all about what they *think* happened. You need twenty-four hours of content every day so you fill it up with nonsense, and all for ratings. And yeah, before you say it, I'm sure Walter Cronkite wanted ratings, too, but he got them by being the newsman you trusted, not with nonsense meant to fill in just what people are hoping to hear. Thanks to you, nobody knows the difference anymore between what's true and what they think is true. And that's one of the worst problems we've got in this world, and you not only caused it but you're out here stoking it to this day."

The woman's microphone was no longer extended in Norma's direction. She had let it fall to her side.

As soon as Norma paused her tirade for a breath, she glanced over her shoulder at one of the cameramen.

"You can stop rolling," she said.

"I stopped rolling when she said you don't know what reporters do," he shot back.

"I'm still rolling," the other cameraman said. "But I doubt there's anything here we can use."

"You put me on TV and I'll sue you six ways to Sunday," Norma said.

"Okay," the cameraman said. "Now I've stopped rolling."

"You know how many women are missing right now?" Norma asked.

Nobody said a word.

"Why aren't you looking into any of their cases?"

For a moment, there was only silence.

Then the woman in the lavender pantsuit said, "This one has captured the public's interest for some reason."

"Yeah, well, you might want to ask yourself more questions about why that is. Now get away from my gate and leave me alone."

She turned quickly and marched back to the house, purposely not looking over her shoulder to see if they were following directions. She stomped inside, slamming the door. Then she realized she had closed the dogs out, so she opened the door briefly.

They came wagging in.

Norma walked to the kitchen window and restarted the task of making her morning coffee. Outside her gate, people were milling around, loading up their vehicles and driving away.

While the coffee dripped, she took her landline phone down off the wall and called Betty at home.

She picked up on the second ring.

"Hey," Betty said. "What's up?"

"You're not gonna believe this. But I had news crews outside my gate this morning."

"Oh, I believe it," Betty said.

"But Jill Moss has been missing for weeks. Why all of a sudden?"

"They've been here all along. You didn't know that?"

"I didn't see any."

"That's because they were out at the campground."

"Oh. The campground. I haven't been going around there."

"Yeah, they've been set up there for weeks, trying to get a glimpse of Jake, or to get him to say something. But now he's moved on and they need to stick their microphones in some new faces."

"I wouldn't call my face exactly new," Norma said. "But anyway, just my luck they found me."

"You get rid of them?"

"Oh yeah."

"I figured. Getting people to go away is pretty much your specialty in life."

———

It was Norma's day off that day, which left her with too little to do.

She needed to stay busy, and there wasn't much to keep her that way, and she just couldn't settle. Something was hanging at the corner of her mind, dragging her down with its weight, and she couldn't shake it no matter how hard she tried.

She couldn't put her finger on exactly what it was, but it seemed to have something to do with the two young women who had been forced into her life more or less against her will. They had both held her tightly and thanked her. Maybe even loved her just the tiniest bit. They had both treated her like a mother. Like someone who would take care of them.

Now they were both gone, and she couldn't take care of either of them, and she had no way to contact them and no idea if they were okay.

Around two in the afternoon she called her adult son Neal, the one who occasionally talked to her these days. He never returned the call. She tried her younger son, Rick. He didn't call back either.

Shortly before 8:00 p.m., when she knew Betty would have to start driving to make the pub for her shift, Norma called her at home.

"Hey," she said.

Then a long silence fell.

"You okay?" Betty asked. "You sound . . . I don't know what."

"I'm not that okay," Norma said. "No."

"What's going on?"

"I need to tell you something. I need to tell you this so you know why all this has got me knocked off center."

"Okay," Betty said. "I figured there was something. Since you're usually pretty dead on center. Go ahead."

Norma told her. With only a relatively small degree of sweating and shaking, she told Betty what she hardly ever told anyone. The story of the incident that ended her marriage.

She told Betty that secret because she couldn't tell her the other one. Because the other one was not her secret to tell. She had given her word, and her word still meant something to her.

It was a bond she would carefully keep for the next five years.

PART TWO

Chapter Twelve

Five Years Later

There was an elderly man missing from the campground, and Norma and Saint Fred were riding the hills in the hope they might find him.

He was an Alzheimer's patient, the missing man, and apparently near death from cancer. His now-panicky family had brought him out this way because he had always wanted to see Bryce Canyon, and had asked his grandchildren to take him there before he died.

And then he'd wandered off in the night and disappeared.

He had been out two nights. The weather was mild and springlike, with days of less than scorching heat. Still, his situation being what it was, Norma held herself braced for the fact that there was only about a fifty-fifty chance she would find him alive if she found him.

She rode the hills in silence, because the anticipation of finding a deceased person kept her from feeling like singing. Actually, she hadn't been singing much as she rode the hills. For several years she hadn't. Ever since the Jill Moss situation, singing had come less naturally to Norma.

The morning faded to midday, she and her horse grew thirsty, and she had not found the missing man at all. Not alive nor dead.

She rode back to the campground for water and lunch.

"Norma!" Ian called to her.

He waved wildly to summon her.

She rode to where he stood in the dirt outside his shaded outdoor command center.

"I'm glad you're back," he said, stroking Fred's long buckskin face. "He was found."

"Alive?"

"Yeah. Amazingly. I wish I could've told you sooner. I wanted to call you back in. Save you the trouble."

"Well, it's not your fault. If I carried a sat phone like everybody else, I'm sure you would have. How's the old guy doing?"

"Badly dehydrated and suffering some from exposure. He's in an ambulance on the way to the county hospital right now. But, all things considered, I'd say he held up pretty well out there for the better part of two days."

"Good," Norma said. "His family must be relieved."

"They were thrilled when I told them."

"It's days like this we remember why we do this. Am I right?"

Oddly, Ian did not answer. He seemed lost in his own thoughts.

Norma dismounted. She let out a sound in her throat when her boots settled in the dirt. A sort of involuntary, complaining grunt. When it hit her ears, it reminded her of the noise her grandmother had used to make every time she sat down in her chair, or levered herself up from it. It was not a sound she enjoyed hearing from herself.

She was stiff from the riding, and saddle sore. It took her legs a minute to adjust to solid land.

Maybe she was getting too old for this. The thought flickered through her mind. She was sixty-three now, and Saint Fred was twenty-two. He seemed to be in good shape for a boy his age, but Norma wasn't sure if she could make the same claim for herself.

She took the reins over the horse's head, and they walked together toward the watering trough. Ian followed along beside them.

"Speaking of days like this," he said.

But the thought didn't seem to have an ending.

"What about 'em?"

They stopped at the trough. Fred lowered his head and submerged his lips beneath the surface. He left them there for a long time, sucking in the precious liquid like a vacuum cleaner. Norma could see the muscles bulge in his upper neck each time he swallowed.

"Not sure if you keep track," Ian said. "I figure maybe nobody keeps track of this stuff but me, so I'm not sure you know what day this is."

"I give up."

"It's been five years to the day since Jill Moss disappeared."

The name hit Norma's stomach like a fastball.

Hardly a day went by that she didn't think about that situation, but she hadn't heard the name spoken out loud for a couple of years.

She had known it was approximately the five-year mark. She'd kept track of five springs coming and going. But she had not remembered the exact date.

"And you know what that means," Ian added. "Right?"

"They declare her legally dead today."

"Right."

They stood quietly for a moment, watching the horse drink. Norma was parched as well. But Saint Fred had carried her over those hills, not the other way around, and he would always be allowed to drink his fill first.

"I guess he really did kill her," Ian said.

"Well, we don't know that for a fact."

"Don't you think she would have turned up somewhere, given five years?"

"Unless she chose not to."

"But at least she would have told her parents if she was alive."

"Unless she did, but they kept it to themselves for her safety." Norma clamped down on her own molars for a moment, knowing she had said too much. "Just speculating," she added. "And this from a woman who's not much of a fan of speculation. I guess we all fall into the trap from time to time."

At first, Ian said nothing in reply.

Then, when the horse lifted his head and they walked toward the parking area together, he said, "I understand why it would be a comfort to think she might be alive."

"But legally she's not."

"Right."

He strode off toward his shaded camp chair and pulled a plastic bottle of water out of its nearby cooler full of ice. He carried it back to Norma and handed it to her. It was wet, and the coldness of it felt like a relief in her hand.

"Thanks," she said.

"I know that case had some kind of emotional significance to you."

"For some reason, yeah."

"We all have one like that. If not several. Anyway. Sorry to be the bearer of bad news."

"Not your fault," she said. "But now I'm just gonna load up my horse and go home."

She swung the back gate of the trailer open, and the horse stepped up and inside, his hooves clattering loudly on the thin rubber pads covering its metal floor.

"I'm not saying it's impossible that she's alive," Ian said. "I'm like you. I like to stick to the facts. I'm just saying it's not all that likely."

"I'll agree with you about the odds," she said.

It made her weary to have to phrase her thoughts so carefully, to be certain that what she said would be technically true. She'd been doing it for five years, and now she was just plain worn down by the effort.

"I'm going to go home and take a nap," she added.

But when she got home, sleep seemed miles beyond her grasp.

—

She didn't work that night, but Betty did.

When Betty called her from the pub it was only eight o'clock at night, but Norma had finally just drifted off to sleep. She bolted awake with her heart pounding.

It was dark, and she thought she was getting a call in the middle of the night, which was always bad news in her experience. She hadn't yet looked at the clock to see how early it was.

She sat up in bed and grabbed up the receiver of the phone.

"What?" she said, her voice breathy. "What happened?"

"Were you running for the phone?" Betty's voice asked.

"Not exactly. What's going on?"

Norma turned the clock radio so its numbers more directly faced her, and that was when she saw it was only 8:00 p.m.

"I just wondered if you knew. If you'd heard. I don't know if you watch the news much these days."

"Yeah, I heard. But . . . it was on the news? I'm surprised."

"You're surprised? How can you be surprised? How could the news not cover a thing that big?"

Norma blinked a few times in the dark. Through her bedroom window she could see the rough shape of Saint Fred in the mostly dark night. He was lying curled up like a colt in his paddock in the moonlight, his big head draped over his folded front legs.

It quickly flitted through her mind that she and Betty might not be talking about the same thing.

"It's not exactly breaking news when five years passes by," Norma said. "You pretty much always know it will."

A brief silence settled in the phone connection.

Then Betty said, "Ah. Then you don't know."

"I guess I don't. What happened?"

"Jake Willis was arrested for attempted murder."

Norma realized she was still partially asleep. Her brain felt muddy and thick, and it couldn't quite make sense of the news.

"Of Jill Moss?"

"No, not of Jill Moss. We still don't know for a fact that he killed her, and it's not like any body was ever found."

In the split second between those sentences and the ones that followed, Norma felt herself overcome with a profound sense of relief. Now *that* would have been the worst. The worst possible outcome. *Imagine that,* she thought. Imagine if they charged Jake Willis with murder in connection to Jill's disappearance, and Norma was one of only a handful of people who knew he couldn't possibly have done it. And she still wouldn't be able to tell anybody what she knew.

But while Norma was feeling grateful for having dodged that bullet, Betty was talking again.

"Wait," Norma said. "Wait. Could you say all that again? My brain was taking a trip to somewhere else and I missed it."

"I *said* . . . ," Betty began. "He was in a car on the freeway with his wife, and I guess he pulled over onto the shoulder of the road. They must've been having some kind of an argument, because he was strangling her."

Norma felt her belly go cold with the word.

"But he stopped?" she asked.

"No. He didn't stop. Some other driver saw what was happening and pulled his car over. Broke out this Jake guy's window with a tire iron and pulled him off her. Nothing to indicate that he would have stopped on his own."

A long silence fell. It tingled. Or it seemed to, anyway. Or Norma tingled, the news prickling in her skin like tiny needles.

She didn't answer. She didn't seem to have words to say.

"*Now* do you believe he killed Jill and hid the body?" she heard Betty ask.

"Well," Norma said. And then she had to do it again. As she had so many times over so many years, she had to carefully weigh and parse her words in order to say something that was true, but not true enough to spill the big secret. "The circumstantial evidence *does* seem to be stacking up."

"Boy, you never just break down and say it happened that way, do you?"

"Not if I don't know for a fact."

"Well, anyway. I just figured you'd want to know. Since that whole Jill Moss thing had such an effect on you. And because of what you told me about your own marriage, and because of the way this thing went down, I figured it was best you heard it from a friend. You know. Not just all alone in the house or something."

"I'm never all alone in the house," Norma said. "I have the dogs. And Saint Fred nearby. But anyway, I get the idea. Thanks."

She was still sitting on the edge of the bed in the dark, facing the window. Feet dangling. Her bed was high, and her feet did not quite reach the floor, and it made her feel like a child. It made her feel lost. Or something did, anyway.

"You okay?" Betty asked.

No, Norma thought.

"Yes," she said.

"Okay, I'll let you go then."

"Wait," Norma said.

"What?"

"Today is the five-year mark. It's been five years to the day since Jill was reported missing."

"You kept track?"

"Ian told me."

"Oh. What about it?"

"Don't you think that's weird?"

"I think every twist and turn of this sick story is weird, but . . . what part of it do you mean specifically?"

"The five-year mark is when they declare a person legally dead. Jill Moss is legally dead as of today."

"And . . . ?"

"You think that's a coincidence? That Jake Willis chose this exact day to try to kill his wife?"

"Might be. Or it might be that he was extra nervous about the date. How would I know? Aren't you the one who always wants to stick to only what we can know for sure?"

"Right. Sorry."

"I gotta work now. Get some sleep tonight."

But Norma got very little sleep that night. If she got any sleep at all.

Chapter Thirteen

Five Years and a Month

It was exactly one month later.

It happened just after closing time at the pub. Norma had offered to balance the cash register, and she had sent Betty home. She was behind the bar alone.

When the door swung open Norma jumped, and a little gasp involuntarily escaped her throat. She had assumed Betty had locked up behind herself. And she hadn't checked, which was unlike her. And now she had left herself vulnerable to a robbery, and it was already too late.

She instinctively reached for the pepper spray that was kept hidden under the bar. Actually, it was more than ordinary pepper spray. It was bear spray. Properly used, it could bring down just about anything.

She kept her hand on it for a second or two. But as the shape of the person who had opened the door stepped into the light, Norma could see it was a small, slight woman.

She took her hand off the bear spray again.

"We're closed," she said.

The woman continued to approach Norma. She stopped just on the other side of the bar and stared at Norma, and Norma stared back at her.

She had brown eyes and tons of blond hair, and looked like a pixie. She could not have been thirty years old.

Much to Norma's surprise, the woman made herself comfortable on a barstool and leaned her elbows on the bar, setting her chin down on one hand.

"I just told you we're closed," Norma said.

"You don't remember me," the woman said, "do you?"

But as soon as she opened her mouth and spoke—as soon as Norma heard her voice—she did remember.

"Oh," she said. "Wanda."

"Good. You do remember. I would hate to think somebody meant that much more to me than I meant to them."

"It's just been a while. You look different. Didn't you used to be a brunette?"

Wanda smiled and ran one hand through all that voluminous hair. Norma envied her all that hair. The older she'd gotten, the more her hair had thinned. And, though she didn't regret growing older in general, she did mind that aspect of the thing. That and growing a mustache.

"Yeah, I've been coloring it," she said. "And I never wear it in a braid anymore. That's kid stuff."

Wanda was wearing a black turtleneck sweater. A very thick, high turtleneck. It all but swallowed her chin. It seemed out of place on her, Norma thought—more the sort of neckline she would expect from an older woman who was self-conscious about her aging throat skin.

"What brings you back to these parts?"

Without the slightest hesitation Wanda said, "You."

"Me? What about me?"

"I know we hardly know each other. We talked maybe a handful of times. But you tried to help me. You warned me. And I wouldn't listen."

Norma only stood a moment, her hands still, letting the words sink in. Waiting for them to translate themselves and make sense. Clearly Wanda had come a long way to deliver a message, and the message was of some importance to this messenger. Norma was hoping it would soon come clear what message it was.

She looked into the young woman's eyes, her own gaze a question, and it just tumbled together all at once. The bleached blond hair. The turtleneck sweater. The long trip back to Sloot to find Norma again after all this time.

"You were the wife he almost killed," Norma said.

Wanda spread her hands wide. As if to encompass an enormous truth.

"That's me," she said. "Mrs. Wanda Willis."

"And that's why you're wearing that big turtleneck. Because you still have the bruises from that. Most people don't realize they last that long. And I guess it depends. You know. Like on exactly how much he hated you in that moment, and how serious he was about finishing the job for real. After a month they get lighter. They get more like a pale, sickly yellow and green, rather than your classic black and blue. But you can still see them a month later and quite a while beyond that."

"If most people don't know . . . ," Wanda began. "And I agree that most people don't, then how do *you* know how long the bruises last when somebody tries to strangle you?"

"I know," Norma said.

She expected the young woman to question her further, but Wanda never did. A silence fell and hung there over the bar for a few seconds.

"I'll pour you a drink," Norma said. "What are you having? It's on me."

———

"I'm such an idiot," Wanda said, rolling her orange juice around in the glass. Taking a sip.

She had turned down the offer of an alcoholic drink, though it struck Norma as an excellent time for one. So much so that she had almost been tempted to pour one for herself.

She came around to Wanda's side of the bar, and perched on the stool right next door to the young woman.

"Everybody makes mistakes," Norma said. "Especially when it comes to love."

"Yeah. Everybody makes mistakes. But not like this mistake. Not like me. I'm an idiot."

"You're not an idiot."

"I sure feel like one. You told me I was making a mistake. I wouldn't listen."

"Nobody ever listens," Norma said. "But I really don't even mean that the way it sounds."

"Not sure how there are two ways to mean that."

Norma sighed.

"Let me see if I can sort it out a little better. Nobody's more of a critic of human beings than I am. But I really didn't mean it as a criticism, exactly. It just seems to be the way we're made. The way we're wired. People can talk to us till they're blue in the face, telling us to learn from their experience. But we don't learn that way—from other people's experiences. We just don't. We learn from our own. I don't know why it's that way, but it is, and since it seems to be true of every human being on the planet, then you're not an idiot for being that way. You're just a human being like everybody else."

"Huh," Wanda said, and drained most of her orange juice in one long pull. "That's *so* not what I expected you to say. I figured you'd yell at me and say you told me so, and I was a fool not to listen."

"When a person is right in the middle of being so down on herself," Norma said, "I don't figure she needs me to pile on. You sure you don't want something stronger?"

Wanda didn't answer for the longest time. She drank the last sip of juice and stared at the bottom of the glass for a full minute or so.

Then she began to cry.

"I'm pregnant," she said.

"Oh. That sounds . . . inconvenient."

Wanda snorted out a bitter laugh.

"You think? Yeah, you could say that. My husband's in jail for trying to kill me. My parents have completely written me off. Not the world's best timing."

"You looking to keep the baby?"

"I want to. I've always wanted a baby. But I don't know. It'll be hard. I'm all alone with no one to help me."

"You must have friends."

"I guess you don't know what happens when you've been living with a control freak for years."

"I do. Actually. They cut you off from your friends. They want to be everything to you. Your whole world. No outside influences."

"Right. And now I have no idea what to do. I mean literally. No plan. From the moment I step off this barstool I have no idea what comes next."

"I guess we'll start by having you to my house for the night. And we can talk some more."

"I thought you never had people to your house."

"I never do." But as soon as she said it, an image of Jill Moss filled her mind. Sleeping in her living room, curled up with her hound dogs. "Well, almost never," she said. "Come on. Let's get out of here."

As they were walking to their cars, a thought came into Norma's head.

"Hey. Does Jake know you're pregnant?"

"Oh, yeah," Wanda said, sounding defeated. "We told our families and everything. Turns out it's better to wait and tell people after four months or so, in case something goes wrong. But we didn't know that at the time. So we told *everybody*."

"Oh," Norma said. "That's too bad."

—

Wanda sat at Norma's kitchen table while she let the dogs out one last time.

When they were safely back in, Norma asked, "When did you last eat?"

"Oh. Let me think."

"That's never a good sign if you have to think."

"Not since I left home. I was just driving and driving and I only stopped for gas."

"From Connecticut?"

"No, I haven't lived in Connecticut for years. We were living in Southern California."

"Well, I'll make us something. You can't go without eating anymore. You got somebody besides yourself to think about now. You want coffee? Tea?"

"I can't have any caffeine."

"Oh, that's right. I have some herbal tea. A mint one, and some chamomile."

"Chamomile sounds nice."

While Norma was putting the kettle on to boil, Wanda said, "You sure are being nice to me."

"I can be nice."

"I know you can. I didn't mean anything by it."

"I'm sure you didn't."

They fell silent while Norma pulled eggs and bread and milk out of the fridge. She worked in silence for so long that when Wanda spoke up again it startled her.

"This is going to sound like a strange thing to say."

"Try me," Norma said.

"Everybody is even more sure he killed her now. Jill Moss, I mean. Well, I guess you knew who I meant. After what happened with me, everybody is just more positive than ever that he killed her."

"That's not a strange thing to say."

"No, this next thing."

"Oh."

"I don't think he *did* kill her. And I swear I'm not doing that thing that women do sometimes when they love a violent man. I do love him. And he is violent. Obviously. And I'm not going to sit here and say he wouldn't have killed her, because it's pretty clear now that he's capable of it. I'm not saying he *couldn't* have or even that he *wouldn't* have. I'm saying I don't think he did. And I'll tell you why I don't think he did. The worst thing she could have done to him is leave him. And I think she did exactly that. And it drove him crazy. I could see it. For two and a half years he did searches on the internet to see if she was turning up anywhere. And it wasn't for show, because he didn't even know I knew. The first time I caught a peek over his shoulder when I walked into a room, and after that I checked his browsing history. You could see how much it was driving him crazy that she left him. Yeah, I know it's kind of weird that she never popped up anywhere. It looks bad for him. But he was behaving like a guy who really didn't know where she'd gone. And then after a while he just gave it up. Like it mattered till it didn't matter anymore. Even obsessions die eventually, if nobody's feeding them anything to keep them alive."

Norma waited for a minute to see if Wanda was done. While she was waiting she beat eggs and a little milk in a bowl with a wire whisk.

"I do think he twisted her arm behind her back and forced her back to the campsite," Wanda added. "Even though he swore that was just people getting a wrong idea."

"That's pretty much a given. There were multiple witnesses."

"Oh, that sounds so familiar. It's so weird that you first said that to me five years ago but I can just hear it all in my ears like it was yesterday. You'd think if I was listening that carefully I would have taken your advice to heart, right? But I guess we've been through all that before."

"Yeah, I believe we have," Norma said.

"You think he killed her, don't you?"

"I reserved judgment on that."

"Well, you're the only person on the planet who did."

"Yeah, I noticed that," Norma said. "I'm not very much the cross section of the American public. In general, everybody will always think he did, unless she pops up somewhere. But it's been five years. And there's a lot of circumstantial evidence at this point. Tell me, if you know. Do you think it's a coincidence that this happened five years to the day after she was reported missing? The same day she was declared legally dead? Seems like an awfully big coincidence."

"No, I don't think it was a coincidence," Wanda said. "That's just my personal opinion. It's not like he said the two were connected or anything. But he knew the date was coming up. It was wearing on him. He was worried about it, and he was on a really short fuse that day. I think he figured once she was declared legally dead it would put a lot more pressure on him as a suspect."

Norma shook her head. Several times.

She poured the beaten eggs into the preheated skillet. They sizzled.

"If you know you're more of a suspect on a certain date," she said, "trying to kill your new wife seems like a very strange way to celebrate."

"Who knows why people do the things they do?"

"Not me," Norma said. "Definitely not me."

"You know more about people than anybody else I've talked to."

"Then you need to get out more," Norma said. "Anyway, listen. If you don't mind my asking . . . what was the fight about? What did you say that set him off like that?"

"Oh, wow. This is weird. Here's the weird part, Norma: I honestly don't remember. Of course, I was without oxygen for quite a long time, and that does tend to create gaps in a person's memory. Or so the doctors tell me. But most everything else about that day I can remember. Now I wonder if it was a physical thing, an oxygen-deprivation thing, or if I don't remember what I said because it wasn't really anything. Do you know what I mean? Does that make sense, what I just said?"

"I know exactly what you mean. Even when I asked the question I realized it was wrong, what I was asking. When I said 'What did you say to set him off?' I realized that's what they do to you. That's what an abuser does, and it's what people do after the fact when they're victim-blaming and not wanting to understand. They put it off on you. They make it about what you said right before they strangled you and not about the fact that they strangled you. Not that I was trying to do that, I didn't mean it that way, but even just the question felt wrong."

"What did *you* say right before somebody tried to strangle *you*? If you don't mind my asking?"

The question hung in the air for a moment, resonating. It shocked Norma a little to be asked. But it shouldn't have, she realized. She had more or less told Wanda. She had told her enough.

"Honestly? I don't remember. And I don't think the reason I don't remember is because of oxygen deprivation. I think it's because what I said was really nothing at all."

Chapter Fourteen

Two DAs

When Norma woke in the morning, she pulled on her robe and stepped out into her kitchen. Her guest was sitting at the kitchen table crying.

"Want coffee?" Norma asked, her voice sounding husky from sleep. "Oh, that's right. I'm sorry. I'm making coffee for myself. You want juice or milk or something?"

Wanda shook her head miserably.

"Want to talk about it?"

For quite a long time the young woman offered no reply. Norma set about making a pot of coffee and left her alone to decide. She poured kibble into the dogs' dishes, still in silence. While the coffee maker was warming up and preparing to drip, she sat down across from Wanda at the table.

Wanda had changed from her turtleneck sweater to what looked like a pair of men's flannel pajamas. The bruises on her throat were a faded, sickly yellow green, and still in the instantly recognizable shape of fingers and thumbs. It made Norma's stomach flutter briefly.

"It might make you feel better," Norma said.

"I just have no idea what to do."

"If you want the baby you should have the baby. I know it's a scary thought, what with not having people around you to support you."

"That's not even the scariest part," Wanda said. "I was just sitting here thinking . . . what if I have a boy and he grows up to be just like his father?"

"He won't."

"You don't know that."

"I have some experience in the area, actually. I have two boys. They didn't grow up to be anything like their father. And they grew up with their father. Your little boy, if you have one, will grow up with you. Babies aren't born full of rage and violence. They're born innocent. The rest they learn around the house, or it's the reaction to some need they have that didn't get filled. You'll be a good mom. He'll be a good kid."

"You don't know that I'll be a good mom."

"You're sitting at my table crying about the future of a child you're not even sure you'll have yet. That's a good mom."

Norma got up, poured herself a mug of coffee, and sat back down at the table with it.

"I could help," she said. "Some, anyway."

Wanda looked up into Norma's face. Her eyes looked puffy and red, leading Norma to believe she had been sitting at the table crying for longer than she might have realized.

She didn't answer, so Norma said, "I don't have a spare bedroom. As I'm sure you noticed. But we could maybe find you someone with a room to rent. And maybe some work. And when you need to take time off work to have the baby, maybe I could help out a little financially."

"I'm really surprised you'd offer that," Wanda said. "I mean, it's very nice. But I'm just surprised is all. You never really acted like you liked me much."

"I don't like anybody much. Don't take it personally."

"And we barely know each other."

"People help other people when they barely know each other."

"How do you figure?"

"What about the guy who saved your life? That motorist. Stopped his car and broke out the window of your and Jake's car with a tire iron. Pulled him off you. Put himself at risk to defend you. I know you a whole bunch better than *he* did."

Silence for a moment. Wanda seemed to be digesting that idea.

"Why do you suppose he did that?" Norma asked. "I have my theories. But I want to hear yours."

"I guess . . . because I obviously needed somebody to?"

"Bingo."

They sat in silence for a few minutes more. Norma sipped at her coffee.

"That's nice," Wanda said after a time. "Thank you. And you might be sorry you asked, because I might take you up on it."

"I'll manage."

"Would it be okay if I used your phone? I'm not getting any reception here at all."

"Knock yourself out."

"It's long distance to Southern California."

"Anywhere in the US or Canada is all part of my monthly plan."

"Good. Thanks. I promised I would call the guy from the DA's office and tell him where he could reach me while I'm here."

She picked up the receiver of Norma's landline and punched in a number she seemed to know by heart. Norma wondered how many numbers the young woman had in her head, and how it would feel to be able to remember all that.

For several minutes she listened to Wanda's end of the conversation. How could she not hear? They were sitting right across the table from each other.

The call quickly moved from routine to earth-shattering. Not for Wanda. It was Norma's earth being shattered.

"I'm staying with a friend in Sloot. Where I told you I was going."

"I'm not sure. It's either Arizona or Utah. It's right on the state line, so you never really know. You can go out to stretch your legs and get some air and end up in the next state."

"I'm not really sure how long."

"Oh. Wait. The DA *here*? In this county? Whatever county Sloot is in?"

"Why would *he* want to talk to me?"

"Can he even do that? How can he do that?"

"Oh. Okay. Well. I'll talk to him. But I'm going to tell him what I really think. Which is that he's innocent. Of *that*, anyway."

It was somewhere right around that last sentence when Norma's stomach began to feel like it was being clamped in a vise, the thread twisting tighter.

"Let me give you the number here."

"Oh, right. Of course. It came through on your phone. I wasn't thinking."

"Okay, well, you can have him call me, I guess."

"Okay, bye."

She got up to hang the phone on its base, then sat back down with Norma, who could feel a mild shock setting in. It felt tingly and numb at the same time.

"What's up with you?" Wanda said. "You look like you just saw a ghost."

"What exactly is my local DA planning to do? Why does he want to talk to you?"

But she already knew what the answer would be.

"He's about to charge Jake with murder in the Jill Moss case."

"How can he do that? There was never any body found. How can he even prove there *was* a murder?"

Her own voice sounded strange to her. As though her ears needed popping, or the way voices grow more distant as one is slipping off to sleep.

"That's kind of what *I* said. Not in so many words. According to this guy in LA County it's unusual but not completely unheard of. You need lots of circumstantial evidence. And, let's face it. That's me. Me and my nasty neck bruises. We're the circumstantial evidence. Why do you look so upset?"

"I'll be right back," Norma said. "I have to go feed the horse."

———

She stood inside Saint Fred's stall, or shelter, or whatever one would choose to call it when it was really somewhere in between. They were both staring at the two flakes of hay she had just dropped into his feeder.

It was unlike him not to dig in to his food immediately. Norma could only conclude that he knew she was upset.

Horses know things like that, she thought. *Any animal whose fate is in the hands of humans but who speaks no human languages has an uncanny knowledge of how people are feeling.*

"The chickens have come home to roost," she said to the horse.

Oddly, he swung his head around and looked behind them. As if she might have been warning him about something he should see with his own eyes.

"And while I'm spouting old saws," she added, "no good deed goes unpunished."

Fred moved a step closer to the hay and explored it with his lips.

"Go ahead and eat," she said.

It might have been a coincidence, but he did.

"Lucky for you you're out here and not in there," she said, indicating the house with a flip of her head. "In there you've got two desperate humans who have no idea what to do next."

She watched him eat for a minute or two, the words "no idea" rattling around in her head.

"I need to talk to her," she said suddenly. "That's what I need to do next. I need to talk to Jill."

She trotted back to the house and stuck her head through the door, startling her houseguest, who was still sitting at the kitchen table crying.

"I have to go into town," she said. "Will you be okay here?"

"Sure," Wanda said.

"Need anything from town?"

"A place to live and a baby nanny?"

"I'll bring us some ice cream."

"Next best thing," Wanda said.

———

There was exactly one pay phone in the town of Sloot, and it was outside the mini-mart at the no-name gas station. That it was the only remaining one was not so much because there was anybody without a cell phone these days, but more because—depending on your service provider—your cell phone was unlikely to be of much use.

She got a pocket full of change from a grumpy teen clerk inside the store. She cashed a twenty to buy ice cream and asked for all quarters back.

She stashed the ice cream on the seat of her truck, then approached the phone as though it might be dangerous. She punched in the number that still lived in her phone contacts, just where Jill had put it.

O and T. Owen and Teresa Moss.

Teresa picked up on the second ring.

"Hello?"

"Hello," Norma said, noticing that she was surprisingly nervous. "It's a voice from your past."

"Oh?"

"Norma. From search and rescue in Sloot. You remember, right?"

A silence.

A strong wind blew through the parking lot, stirring up a swirling dust devil. It roared past Norma's ears, making it hard to hear much else.

Thankfully, there was no one around.

"Yes, of course," Teresa said.

"Good. I never thought I'd call you again. It's not something I'd do lightly. But I need to talk to your daughter."

"Look. Norma. I'm sure your intentions are good. And we all heard what happened with Jake. Hell, everybody with a pulse has heard that. But it has nothing to do with our family. It's between him and his new wife and law enforcement where they were living, and nobody on this end of things cares to relive the past. It just doesn't concern us."

"But this next part does," Norma said. "Our local district attorney is planning to charge Jake with your daughter's murder. Despite a body never having been found."

A brief silence fell. No matter how many times Norma finger-brushed her hair out of her eyes and mouth, the wind blew it right back again.

"I'm not sure I see the problem," Teresa Moss said.

"You don't see it."

"Not really, no."

"You didn't notice that the person he's about to go on trial for murdering isn't dead?"

"I guess I just think he deserves whatever they charge him with."

"Even if it's something you know he didn't do."

"But he would have, if he could have."

"But he didn't."

"But he would have."

Norma huffed out a sigh of frustration, and the wind blew it away.

"Thing number one, we think he would have, but we'll never know for a fact. Thing number two, we know for a fact he didn't. I went through the same conversation with your daughter when I drove her out to you. If I head out to rob a bank, and my car breaks down, you can't put me in jail for bank robbery. Even though the intention was there.

You put people in jail for what they do, not for what they intended to do. And how do you know I wouldn't have gotten to the door of that bank and had a change of heart? We'll never know that."

"He didn't have a change of heart when he was strangling his wife. A stranger with a tire iron had to change his mind for him."

"I admit that's no strike in his favor. And I hope they put him in jail for it for a long, long time. Hell, I hope they lose the key. But you'll notice that's a thing he did. And this other thing is a thing he didn't do. But really, I don't care if he ends up in jail even longer on a bad rap. Couldn't happen to a nicer guy."

"Then what's the problem?"

"I don't want to be the one responsible for putting him there. That's the problem. I can't have that on my conscience. Remember when I told you this thing could come back to bite us in some ways we could never even imagine? This is pretty much our worst-case scenario, don't you think?"

"You'd better not be saying you're going to break your promise to us."

"No. I'm not saying that. Not at all. I take a promise very seriously. I want to talk to Jill about whether she wants to tell that minor little secret. You know. The one about her being alive and all. And if she decides no, she doesn't want to tell, well . . . then that's not on me. She's the one with a thing like that on her conscience, not me. It's her call. But I'm in this with her. And I want to talk to her."

"I don't think that's a good idea," Teresa Moss said. Her voice had gone cool. Detached. As if the person on the other end of her phone line had suddenly become a perfect stranger. "She's started her life all over again. She gave up everything. Her identity. Every part of the life she had for nineteen years. I'm not going to upset her applecart. I'm not going to tell her you called. I'm sorry, but that's the way I feel."

Norma opened her mouth to counter that argument, but she was interrupted by the click of the call being ended.

She stood in that windy and deserted parking lot and stared at the receiver of the phone for a full minute or so.

Then she hung it up and drove home.

—

"Here's what I think you're going to do next," Norma told her houseguest when she arrived home. "It's not exactly a long-term solution for anything, but it'll give some direction to your next couple of days. I need to go out of town. Family emergency. Not really sure for how long, but I can keep you posted. I'll show you how to feed the horse and the dogs and you can be my house sitter. Take care of things while I'm gone. You can have my bed, and some privacy, and a little time to think about the future. Think you can do that for me?"

"Sure," Wanda said. "Thanks. I hope everything is okay with your family."

"That makes two of us."

She called in sick to work, wrote a few notes about the animals, packed a small bag, and that was it.

Norma was on the road.

Chapter Fifteen

The Court of Public Opinion

Norma noticed her hand trembling ever so slightly as she knocked on the door of the Moss home. She wanted that not to be true. She prided herself on being a person who was afraid of nothing and nobody. But that was just the self in her head. This was the real world, and she was headed for a real confrontation.

It was late afternoon, windy and warm, with the sun on a long slant behind the trees to the west.

Teresa Moss opened the door, and her face seemed to freeze.

They stood considering each other for a few moments, the two women. Neither was giving much away in their facial expressions.

A different emotion rose up in Norma. She felt a flare of anger.

She opened her mouth to say, "Hang up on *this*, lady."

She didn't say that.

Instead she had a flash of memory. Her mother, and the way she'd used to say "You can catch more flies with honey than you can with vinegar, sweetheart."

"Here's the thing," Norma began.

The other woman rocked back on her heels slightly in the doorway, and locked her arms across her chest. But she said nothing.

"It's very rare for me to say a thing like this—like I'm about to say. If I do something for somebody, it's because I think it's the right thing to do, not because I want anything from them. I'm not the type to go around telling people they owe me anything."

"But you're going to tell me that now," Teresa Moss said.

She didn't sound angry. Maybe just a little scared. *Maybe everybody is a little scared when they have to deal with other people,* Norma thought. *Maybe the anger is just a thin layer plastered on top of that fear.*

"Some mild version of it. Yeah. I don't want to, but I think I need to. I've been through a lot since I found your daughter and quietly turned her over to you. I've told a lot of lies when I'm not used to telling any. I've lost a lot of sleep and chewed up a lot more antacids than are normal for me. And now I want to have one conversation with her. If she turns me down, fine. I'll know I tried. But I'm not sure I can live with you making that decision for her. I'm a mom myself and I understand wanting to protect your little ones. But she's a grown woman now. She's . . . what? Twenty-four?"

"Yes. Twenty-four. And she won't turn you down. That's the problem."

They stood without speaking for a strange length of time. The wind swirled a bit more strongly than it had a minute earlier, and it felt hot.

For the moment, Norma did not ask what made her so sure that Jill would not refuse a visit from her.

Then she heard Teresa Moss sigh, and knew they had reached a shifting point in the conversation.

"You've been driving all day?" she asked Norma.

"I have."

"Have you eaten?"

"Not so's you'd notice."

"I guess you'd best come inside then," she said.

—

"My husband is still at work," Teresa Moss said.

She set a wooden board of cheese and crackers in front of Norma and sat.

"Thank you," Norma said.

They were sitting on high stools at the butcher-block island in the middle of the Moss kitchen. The sun was nearly down, and the light of dusk from outside the windows was their only illumination.

"Maybe that's for the best, that he isn't here," Norma added. Then, hearing what she had just said, she hurried to add, "I'm sorry. That came out wrong. I really didn't mean that the way it sounded."

"You got a false impression of him that one time you met."

"We didn't even meet. I just sort of watched him hurry by. But that wasn't what I meant at all. I wouldn't have judged him by that really tough moment in a person's life. Just . . . I would've thought he'd be the one more dead set on me not talking to her."

"Well, then you would be exactly wrong," Teresa said. She reached for a cracker—something with poppy seeds—and lifted it off the plate. But then she only held it between her fingers and stared at it. "I'm the momma bear in this situation. He was very upset with me because I ended your call so abruptly. He thought we owed you a lot more. And he thought Cassie should be able to make her own decisions."

"Cassie?"

"You must know she had to change her name."

"Oh. Right. Of course."

"She's more or less taken on the role of her own cousin. Explains any slight resemblance, and the fact that we might visit her from time to time. It was complicated, but I think we managed it. Owen hired a guy quietly, under the table. The kind of guy who helps mob figures disappear. He faked documents and such. Fortunately our family is very small and what few relations we have were more than happy to go along with it."

"Right. Sorry. I just wasn't thinking about the name thing."

Part of her wanted to think more about that other thing. Pretending to be her own cousin. It didn't feel quite right to Norma. It didn't seem like that safe a cover story. Wouldn't it be fairly easy to prove that there had been no cousin until after Jill disappeared?

But Teresa was talking, so Norma couldn't think it all the way through.

"And he said more. Owen, that is. He reminded me that she's always talking about Norma. Norma this, Norma that. Norma is so wise, Norma is so solid and balanced. Granted we only see her two or three times a year. But she constantly makes it clear that you're a hero to her."

Norma briefly felt a glow from that news in a low, deep part of her belly. Then she pushed it away again. She didn't want to be anybody's hero. That role came with too much responsibility.

"And also, Owen . . . he said I was robbing her of the chance to have a visit with you. He thought she would want that, no matter what you wanted to talk about. He agrees with me, though, about Jake. He figures the more crimes they put him in jail for, the better."

"Even if you know he's innocent of a particular crime."

"Yes. The world is better without him in it."

"You want him dead?"

"I've thought about it. For years I weighed taking out a hit on him. But I couldn't bring myself to do that."

"Glad to hear it."

"But it just makes me so mad that I know he's a killer, but people keep interrupting him or taking away his opportunities, and so he never gets punished like a murderer."

"Because he never committed a murder."

"But he would have."

"You don't know that," Norma said.

She took a long, deep breath. Then she stared at the plate of snacks and realized she was rapidly losing her appetite. Especially since she was about to tell—yet again—a story she never meant for even one person to know. Ever.

"I was married when I was younger," she said. "And my husband was a lot like Jake, except he was better at hiding it. He had another side to him, but I was the only one who saw it. He kept it under wraps as best he could, for a long time. But then it started to escalate. And then he just lost control of it entirely. He strangled me almost to death. I lost consciousness and was sure I was dying. But I woke up. So, obviously, somehow, he stopped. For some reason he stopped. Maybe it scared him to see how close to the line he really was. I don't know, and I'll never know. All I know is, that was not a murder. Because I'm not dead. It might not even have been attempted murder, because it might be that his intention was never to kill me. It was definitely a very bad act and it was definitely assault. And it's definitely a thing that only a horrible person would do. And yes, I agree that the world would be better without horrible people. But you keep saying you know what Jake would've done if he'd had the chance. And you don't know. You don't know whether a person is going to stop before it gets to murder or not."

A long, long silence fell. It seemed to hurt. But maybe something else was hurting Norma, and it was only an illusion that the silence was to blame.

"I'm sorry you had to go through that," Teresa said after a time.

"Thank you."

"I'm surprised."

"I'm not sure why. It's not that rare an occurrence."

"You're right. Of course you're right. I guess I had you pegged as someone who'd never been in my daughter's shoes, because you seem like a woman nobody would dare push around. But that's wrongheaded thinking. It can happen to anyone. But also . . . I guess I figured if you'd been in that position, you'd want more terrible things to happen to Jake."

"I want Jake to pay for exactly what he did. Not more and not less."

"Did your husband pay for what he did? If you don't mind my asking?"

"No."

"You never pressed charges?"

"I did. But he hired a good attorney, and I wasn't getting a lot of help from my bargain-basement guy. It became sort of a he said/she said thing. He said I was seeing another man and that's who left the marks on my neck. It didn't look like I was going to win and it was tearing my sons apart, so I let it go. I regret that. Every day I regret it. Look. Jake is going to jail. He's going to be charged with attempted murder, and there were witnesses. He'll be in jail for years. I know we like to hear about a prison sentence more like decades, but try that on for size sometime—having to leave your home and everything you know and go to jail for a handful of years. It's not nothing. Jake's a small guy. He's slight, and he's young, and he's a pretty boy. His life is going to be a living hell in there. He's about to find out firsthand how it feels to be on the receiving end of abuse. If you've been wanting him to suffer, you're about to get your wish. But this thing about a murder charge . . . well, it's not my decision, and it's not yours either. Your daughter has to decide what she wants to do."

"It's just that she's been through so much already."

"Then she's strong. It's the one way life pays us back for trouble. She's a survivor. Don't treat her like she's so fragile. Don't take away her credit for that."

—

They hovered silently over their dinner. Owen, Teresa, and Norma. Teresa had made a stir-fry with chicken and vegetables, served over noodles. For several minutes they ate without speaking. It felt awkward, to say the least.

Then Owen set his fork down suddenly. It hit his plate and made a clanging noise, and everybody jumped. Even the person who had made the sound.

"Not a day goes by that I don't regret our first meeting," he said to Norma.

"Don't get hung up on that," Norma said. "Don't waste any time on it. *I* never did. It was just a very hard day in your life."

"Not as hard as the day before it. And that's because of you. And I didn't even thank you."

He was staring down at his plate. At his uneaten food. As though there was something interesting about watching it get cold. The hair on the top of his head was thin in one big, oval spot. Norma wondered if it had been that way when she last saw him.

They were all getting older. Everybody was getting older. All of their lives were ticking by, whether they took the time to notice them going or not.

"Actually," he added, "that wasn't entirely true, what I said. It's kind of an old cliché to say 'Not a day has gone by.' There were probably days I didn't think about it. But I doubt a week went by without those old regrets coming up."

"If it helps any," Norma said, "you have my permission to let it go now."

He picked up his fork and they ate in awkward silence for a few more minutes.

Then Teresa spoke up suddenly, her fork poised halfway to her mouth.

"I think we were hoping that if Jake went to jail for a really long time she could come out of hiding."

"Well, you didn't think that through very well," Norma said. "No offense."

"I know. He'll get out eventually no matter what they charge him for."

"That's not what I meant."

"And we'll face some charges for filing a false police report. But because he honestly tried to kill somebody, I guess we're figuring they'd go easy on us. You know. If they knew we had a really good reason for doing what we did."

"That's not it, either."

"What Norma is trying to say, Teresa," Owen interjected, his voice even and firm, "is that if they put him in jail for our daughter's murder, and then she comes out of hiding, the conviction will be overturned and he'll get out again."

"Oh," Teresa said. "That's true. I guess I really *wasn't* thinking it out very well. Was I? But he'll still have to do time for strangling his wife almost to death."

She glanced nervously at Norma on the last sentence. Maybe remembering what Norma had told her about her own ancient, near-fatal marriage.

"Here's what I think you're failing to consider," Norma said. "You stay silent while a man is convicted of a murder you know damn well he didn't commit. You're willing to tell me you're okay with it, because he deserves it. Because it's just me. Just one person. But how's that gonna play in the court of public opinion, do you figure? It's a pretty brutal place, that court."

"She's not coming out of hiding, Teresa," Owen said. "We talk about this all the time. And I remind you of all the reasons that won't work. That it will never work. And then somehow you revert back to the starting line in your head."

"Even if she doesn't do it on purpose," Norma said. "It could come out. She could be discovered. The whole cousin thing seems a little weird. Like, a cousin just appeared in your family out of nowhere?"

"She hasn't been discovered in five years," Teresa said.

"Doesn't mean she never could."

"How?"

"I don't know. It's not really my field of expertise. Something with dental records maybe?"

"She's been lucky with that. She has the best teeth. She never had a cavity in an adult tooth until two years ago."

"If for some reason she had to take a DNA test, maybe? I don't know. Maybe she tells just one person because she figures it's somebody she can trust. And that person blows it wide open. Or just tells one other person who tells one more. I don't know all the ways it could happen. I can't see all the possibilities. That's the problem. Nobody ever can. That's why they say there's no such thing as the perfect crime. There's always some little thing to give you away, and the human brain just can't cover it all."

"You know . . . ," Teresa began. Then she stalled briefly. "You told me this five years ago. That we could run into unintended consequences."

"And now we have."

"I guess so."

"And I can honestly say I never saw this one coming," Norma said. "At the time it never occurred to me they might charge him with murder. I just figured they'd need a body for that. But they're doing it. And if it works, and they convict him . . . I suppose I can live with that, provided I've said my piece to your daughter. I'll just figure it was her decision, not mine. Nobody has to know I was even involved. I'm just wondering if *you* can live with that. You know. If he spends ten years or more in prison and then it comes out that Jill's not even dead and you knew it all along."

"Maybe she won't tell anybody that we knew," Teresa said. She sounded desperate now. Grasping. "Maybe she could say she was even hiding from *us*."

"You told me you go see her now and then. Like she's her own cousin. Your niece. You think a jury would believe you don't know the difference between your niece and your daughter?"

A silence fell, and hovered unbroken for a long time.

Norma shoveled food into her mouth, even though she was no longer hungry and didn't really want it.

As if hearing her thoughts, Owen said to his wife, "Did you tell her she's in Oregon?"

Norma's head shot up.

"Jill? Is in Oregon?"

"Cassie," Teresa said. "Yes."

"Well, that's gonna be a hell of a drive."

"You don't have to go talk to her in person," Owen said. "You could talk on the phone. We could even set you up with a video call."

"No," Norma said, and set down her fork. "No, I really think a talk like this should be face-to-face."

"You'll stay in our guest room," Owen said. "And drive in the morning."

—

Teresa brought in a clean folded bath towel, hand towel, and washcloth in a cheery bright yellow. *The only cheery things around,* Norma thought.

"Who's taking care of your dogs?" Teresa asked.

Norma looked up at her face in surprise.

"I'm sorry," Teresa said. "Do you not have your dogs anymore? That was five years ago, and I don't know how old they were when I met them."

"No, I have them," Norma said.

But then she wasn't sure if she should say more. Should she let on that she was giving aid and shelter to Jake's most recent victim? Maybe. Maybe it was fine. But she wasn't sure. She was tired, and not thinking clearly. Maybe there were unintended consequences to that, too.

"I have a houseguest," she said.

"Oh, I see. Well. Get a good night's rest. Let me know if you need anything."

And with that she let herself out.

—

Teresa was sitting at the breakfast table when Norma came out of her guest room in the morning. There were no lights on in the kitchen. The morning light still appeared faded and dull as it came through the window over the sink.

Teresa was cradling a cup of coffee, judging by the aroma, and staring off into apparently nothing. Norma could feel a pall in the room—some sort of sorrow that she imagined draped over everything in thick folds.

"Coffee?" she asked Norma.

It surprised Norma a little, as the woman had given no indication that she knew Norma had entered the room.

With a flip of her head Teresa indicated a spot on the counter where a clean mug sat next to the coffee maker. Next to it sat those fussy little porcelain servers for cream and sugar, but Norma paid them no mind. She poured herself a mug of coffee and sat at the table with her host. The mug was from Grand Teton National Park, and bore an image of those pointed, snow-capped mountains.

"Owen at work already?" she asked.

"Yeah. He asked me to say goodbye."

"You okay?"

"Not really. No. I don't think either Owen or I can really claim to be okay. It's not that the marriage is in trouble, exactly. We're still okay being together. Just, neither one of us is really okay. But maybe that was more than you wanted to know."

"I asked," Norma said.

She took a sip of the coffee. It was hot and strong. Just the way she liked it. Possibly even better than what she made for herself, which was saying a lot.

"I think it's just catching up with me," Teresa said. "All of it. I think it's just finally landing on me how much of a toll all this has taken."

She was wearing her long blond hair gathered up onto the back of her head, and it showed much more of her face than Norma had seen before. It seemed counterintuitive that this should be the moment she chose to reveal more of herself—to pull away that which covered her in some small way.

Then, almost as though hearing the thought, Teresa reached up and pulled out the gold barrette in one smooth movement, and her hair tumbled around her face and across her shoulders.

"You warned me five years ago," she said to Norma. "You said we'd have to keep pretending we were in that same desperate place. Pretending that our only daughter was missing, and we had no idea where she was, or if she was okay. The only thing you didn't warn me about was how it would start to feel true after a while. Especially since we only see her a couple of times a year."

Norma sipped more of the hot coffee.

"And if you had it to do over?"

"Oh, I'd do it again. To protect my daughter? My only child? In a heartbeat."

A long silence fell. Several minutes from the feel of it. Long enough that Norma expected the kitchen to grow lighter, but it never did. She looked out the window and decided it must be overcast. But in that twilight hour it was hard to tell.

"What would you have done?" Teresa asked. "If you'd been in my shoes?"

"Oh, I expect I would have done things a little differently. I wouldn't have pretended she'd never been found. I'd have put her in some kind of living situation that was safe. Really safe. Like, a setup that was to a person what Fort Knox is to a bar of gold. Security cameras. Maybe even a guard. And maybe put a tail on Jake, so I'd know the minute he left the house. Private-detective kind of thing."

Teresa's eyes had changed. They no longer looked lost and unfocused. Now they seemed to be chewing over something tricky, like a math problem.

"That sounds so much better. That makes so much more sense. Why didn't we do that?"

"Don't ask me."

"It's like she just had this idea of how she wanted it to go and we never tried to talk her out of it."

"And you ended up solving the problem the way a nineteen-year-old would."

"Exactly."

Teresa pulled a scrap of paper from her pocket and slid it across the table to Norma. It had been torn from a long, narrow, lined pad. Maybe the kind of thing a person would use to make their grocery list. On it was the name Cassie MacEnerny, and an address in an Oregon town she'd never heard of before.

"Thank you," Norma said. "Does she know I'm coming?"

"Yes and no. I didn't want to say too much in a text, so I just said she was about to get a visit from someone she considers a hero. Not sure if she'll guess right or not."

"Well," Norma said, feeling slightly embarrassed. "I'd best get on the road. It's a long drive."

"No breakfast?"

"I expect I'd best start driving."

"I put a couple of pastries in a bag, in case you felt that way."

"Well, I won't say no to *that*," Norma said.

Chapter Sixteen

Norma Knows a Lot

It was the middle of the following morning when Norma pulled onto Jill's property in Oregon, after spending an uncomfortable night sleeping in her truck at a highway rest stop.

She pulled down a long, graded dirt driveway, surprised at its rural and uninhabited feel. Somehow she had expected the address to lead to a house or apartment in a small city or good-sized town, though in retrospect she wasn't sure why.

She drove around a curve and saw an open gate, a small cabin-type house, and a paddock with two horses—a huge buckskin and a smaller, fine-boned bay. A brown-and-white-spotted hound dog immediately ran toward her truck, baying wildly.

Norma parked the truck close to the cabin and just sat a moment, wondering if it was safe to step out with the dog nearby. She took in her surroundings, nursing an odd feeling, though it took a moment to identify it. Then it dawned on her. Big rural property. Small rustic house. Big buckskin horse. Hound dog. It was a life bizarrely like her life, though she could only imagine that to be a coincidence.

A young woman stepped out of the house, but Norma didn't think it was Jill.

As she sat in her truck, watching the woman race in her direction, she still felt quite sure it wasn't Jill. The young woman was dark-haired and dark-eyed, with a shorter nose and higher cheekbones. Maybe even a different chin? It flitted through Norma's mind briefly that Jill might have transformed into this, but the idea didn't seem to fit there, so she allowed it to flit away again.

The young woman took hold of the hound dog's collar and motioned for Norma to step out of the truck.

Norma stepped down into the hard, dusty dirt of the place.

"She won't hurt you," the woman said. Norma couldn't decide if the voice sounded familiar or not. Mostly not. "She's all bark, this one."

She let go of the dog's collar, and the hound came wagging up and sniffed all around Norma's jeans and shoes.

Norma was looking down at the dog when the young woman descended on her, grabbing her up into a bear hug. It took her by surprise, to phrase it mildly.

"It *is* you," she breathed into Norma's ear. "I was *hoping* it was you. My mom said I was about to get a visit from a hero. I couldn't figure out who else besides you she would call a hero, and also I figured if it was anybody else she would've just told me who. I've been waiting all this time, just hoping it was you."

She stepped back, holding Norma at arm's length by her shoulders.

"My goodness," Norma said. "You don't look like you at all."

"That's kind of the point, wouldn't you say?"

"I guess it is. Did you have plastic surgery?"

"Yeah. Some."

"And those are brown contacts?"

"Right."

"You might be the only blond-haired, blue-eyed person on the planet who purposely went to brown hair and eyes."

"I know, right? And that's been a whole weird thing all in itself. It's just weird how much that changed everything. But I don't mean to go off on a tangent."

"Do you know why I'm here?"

For the first time since Norma's arrival, Jill frowned a little.

"I think so. Maybe so. I figure it has something to do with the fact that Jake tried to kill his wife, and the fact that the DA in your county just announced he's going to charge him with my murder."

Norma felt her eyes go wide.

"You *knew* about that?"

"They just announced it this morning."

"Announced it? Announced it where? Why would they announce a Utah murder charge in Oregon? Is your case really still that big in the media after all these years?"

"I get my news on the internet," Jill said, her frown a bit deeper.

"Oh right. The internet."

"I follow any news about him really carefully. And about . . . you know. Me."

"I suppose you would."

They stood a moment without talking. The dog tried to stick her nose into Norma's crotch, but Jill grabbed her collar and pulled her away again.

"You realize we've got a situation on our hands," Norma said. "Right?"

"I'm not sure what we're supposed to do about it, though."

"That's what I figured we could talk about."

Jill sighed deeply. As if something—a load of tension, maybe—had been straining to get out and she had finally seen fit to open the gate.

"Come on inside," she said. "I'll make us some coffee. And . . . have you had breakfast?"

"Not yet, no."

"I'll make us coffee and breakfast. I hope you're not planning to run right off again. We've got a lot of figuring to be done."

"Yes, we do."

"Wait. Where are your dogs? Who's looking after Saint Fred? Oh no. Should I not have asked that? It's been five years. Are they not still with you?"

"No, it's okay. They're all still kicking."

"Who's looking after them?"

"Now . . . that's a bit of a long story. And it's one I think is best saved for after breakfast."

They walked through the dusty yard toward the little cabin, side by side. Then Norma stopped and cast her gaze around the place again.

"Something about all this," she said.

"I know what you're going to say."

"Do you?"

"You're thinking it looks just like *your* life."

"Oh. Then you *do* know."

"Now, you can't go and accuse me of copying your life. Because it's nothing like yours at all. I have one hound dog and two horses, and you have two hound dogs and one horse. See? Totally original."

The statement brought a wry smile to the younger woman's face that Norma found contagious.

"Fair enough," Norma said.

———

"What do you do for work these days?" Norma asked over coffee.

Jill was at the stove scrambling eggs.

"I work as a technician at a vet's office."

"And it lets you afford all this?"

"Oh, no. I just caretake this place. I don't own it. It's seven hundred acres and there are cattle on the other side of that gate. I get to live here and keep my horses here in return for tending the cattle."

"Not a bad deal."

"Oh, it's wonderful. I love it here." She stirred the eggs for a few seconds, frowning. Then she said, "It wasn't entirely true when I said I wasn't copying your life. I sort of was. Does that make you mad?"

"Not sure how it hurts me any. But why?"

"I just really loved your life. I'll never forget showing up at your place in the middle of the night on that big horse's butt. My eyes were all adjusted to the light and there was a little moon, and I just looked at that cabin and the horse corral and the dogs weaving in and out. And I felt that horse moving under me, and I watched all that, and I thought, This lady's got it right. Norma knows how to live. Norma knows. Of course the fact that you'd pretty much just saved my life might've factored in. I think I was feeling overly emotional about everything. But later I guess I just figured . . . well, in a way it sucks to have to start your life over. You have to leave behind everything. But in another way . . . you get to start your life over. I figure if you have a better idea for how you want to live, it just seems like that's the time to do something about it. Break out the plan, you know?"

"We don't know for a fact that I saved your life."

"Seems like a safe bet to me. Even if Jake wouldn't have killed me for leaving him, I was completely lost and I had no water or food."

"Oh. Well, yeah. People do die of *that*. I guess we should talk about this . . . thing. This situation that's in front of us. Don't you think?"

"Do you mind if we have breakfast first? Talking about him makes me lose my appetite. Even thinking about him'll do it."

"I'm not in a hurry if you're not," Norma said.

———

"We should go for a ride after breakfast," Jill said.

Norma had been reaching for a bottle of hot sauce for her eggs, and her hand hung up in the air for a beat or two.

"I know what you're thinking," Jill said. "But a person can talk and ride a horse at the same time. I actually got the big buckskin gelding because he reminded me of Saint Fred, so I'd be curious to know what you think. He's not Fred, though. I can already tell you he's not. He's pretty darn steady, but if the mare explodes he'll occasionally jump a mile. And believe me, the mare explodes. She is one moody beast."

Norma shook hot sauce onto her eggs—a lot of it—without trying to get a word in edgewise. It struck her as Jill spoke, stringing her words together in a fast cadence, that the young woman probably really was hoping to postpone the difficult conversation.

"How old is the gelding?"

"He's seven."

"Fred wasn't Fred either when he was seven. They need time to mature, just like people. But the mare sounds like she's just reactive. Some horses are hot. It's just who they are."

Norma shoveled a few more bites into her mouth.

"I got her because I didn't think Grady would be okay out here all by himself. They always say a horse needs another horse. But Saint Fred doesn't have another horse."

"He doesn't care," Norma said. "But that definitely makes him the exception to the rule as horses go. Most horses would care. These eggs are good."

"That's because I have my own chickens and they were gathered just this morning. Anyway, about the horses—normally if I want to ride them I have to ride Grady and pony Mae along behind us or vice versa. Because I do want them to get the exercise. I could turn them out in the big pasture with the cattle. They all graze together fine. But that's the problem. They just graze. They don't run around and exercise. They just eat even more."

"Besides," Norma said, "if you want a horse to be a good riding horse you have to get on regularly."

"This is my chance to have a rider for both horses. I'm talking too much, aren't I? I'm sorry I'm talking too much. I hear myself doing it but I'm not sure how to stop. I think I really am a little nervous to talk about this thing with Jake."

"I figured," Norma said, and shoveled in another big forkful of eggs. There was also buttered rye toast and a ramekin of mixed berries, which Norma thought was a nice way to treat a guest. "You don't have to work today?" she added, her mouth still full.

"No, I have Fridays off. Which is nice, because every weekend is a long weekend. Can you stay? Can you spend the weekend? Sure would be nice to have all that time to catch up."

"Probably," Norma said, wiping her mouth on a tan cloth napkin. "I'd have to call home and make sure it's okay."

"Now tell me who's taking care of the dogs and the horse," Jill said. "You said it was a long story."

An awkward silence fell. It seemed to sit on the table for a few seconds. Norma was not the one to break it.

"I'm having trouble figuring out what could possibly be controversial about your dog sitter," Jill said.

"Might be weird for you to hear who it is."

"Can't imagine why."

"It's Jake's wife. Well, ex-wife. Well . . . estranged wife, I guess. Divorces take time."

"Wait. The one he tried to strangle?"

"Right."

"That *is* weird."

"I thought it might be."

"How do you know her? You haven't, like . . . kept in touch with Jake, have you?"

"No! Of course not. I don't even know the guy. I gave him a dressing-down once when he walked into the pub, and other than that I never even so much as gave him the time of day. But Wanda . . ."

158

She trailed off, and Jill jumped in.

"That's his wife? The one he tried to kill? Wanda?"

"Right. I actually knew her before she even met Jake."

"But *how*?" Jill asked, drawing the word out long, her voice rising to an almost howl. It was the first outward clue that she was upset, but Norma figured the upset had been there all along. Waiting to be let out. "This can't all be a big coincidence."

"No. Not really, it's not. After I took you to your parents, the whole thing with your disappearance really exploded. Which you probably know. But you might not know that Sloot was kind of the epicenter of the whole crazy thing. And then the pub ended up taking a lot of that heat because word got around that I was on the search and rescue team. We had all these people hanging around the pub and hanging around the campground. Some were reporters but a lot were just people who got obsessed with the case somehow. Who knows why people get obsessed with the things they do? Jake was still at the campground, and everybody wanted him to talk. Wanda hitchhiked all the way from Connecticut to be there."

"But *why*?" Jill asked. Her voice sounded quieter, but similarly strained by stress.

"I guess she felt like she knew you in some way. Identified with you or something. She ended up having a chance to talk to Jake, but of course I was hoping it was just to hear his story. I was hoping it wouldn't go the way it seemed to be going."

They ate in silence for a time. Several minutes. Norma was relieved, because the food was too good to let get cold.

"Isn't it odd how women do that?" Jill said after a time. Quietly.

"Go for the wrong guy, you mean?"

"Some women. I only meant some women. I didn't mean all women do that."

"I knew what you meant."

"But listen to me talking about 'some women,' like I can't for the life of me understand them, and I picked that same wrong guy myself."

"I picked wrong too," Norma said. "But we didn't know. She knew more about what she was getting into before she got into it."

"I got into it accidentally," Jill said. "But then I stayed. All I'm saying is I'm a fine one to judge. Why do you think she did it, then?"

"Hell if I know."

"I figured you would know."

"Why would you figure that?"

"Because you're Norma. I figure you know. I figure you're the one who's got life figured out. I always figured that. I think that's another reason why I was copying you. You know. With the cabin in the middle of nowhere and the horses and dogs. Modeling my life on yours. I guess I just figured if Norma picked it, then it must be the right choice."

"You should never put people on a pedestal," Norma said. "It's not good for anyone involved. I don't know everything. I've just had more life experience than you. Learned a few things the hard way. Don't do the whole 'Norma knows everything' deal, because I can't live up to that."

"How about 'Norma knows a lot'? Can you be comfortable with that?"

"Some days I might be," Norma said. "Not every day. I think either Wanda didn't believe what was being said about him, or maybe she thought the fact that he'd do it to you didn't mean he'd do it to her. Always a rookie mistake."

They didn't speak again until Jill rose and began clearing the breakfast dishes into the sink.

Then Jill said, "This is why I haven't had any boyfriends since."

"In five years you haven't had a boyfriend?"

"You don't have boyfriends. Do you?"

"No. But that's different. I was in my late forties when I left my husband. I had two kids. This is the prime of your life, my young friend. This is your youth."

Jill set a few plates in the sink, roughly. Probably more so than she had intended. She sat back down across from Norma at the table and sighed.

"I just keep thinking I'll pick wrong again, Norma. Because we don't know going in. I mean, unless we're Wanda we don't know. You said it yourself. You said when you meet somebody they never say in advance 'Just know I'm going to knock you around some.' Then how will I know?"

"Maybe you won't," Norma said. "Maybe you won't know what you're getting into and you'll make a mistake. But here's what's different: this time you won't stay."

"Huh," Jill said. "That's actually the only thing anybody's ever said to make me feel better about a thing like that."

Chapter Seventeen

My Murder Trial

"I guess we should talk about it," Jill said. She had to turn her head and raise her voice to be heard.

They were riding along a forested ridge, Jill on the mare out front, Norma following on the big buckskin gelding. If she shifted her eyes to the right as they rode past breaks in the trees, Norma could see some kind of lake or reservoir stretched out below them, looking like a stylized dragon lying flat in the glinting sun.

"Your murder trial?" Norma asked.

"Right. That."

"I suppose that's what we're here to talk about, yeah."

But they didn't get the chance to talk about it.

Just at that moment the mare exploded into panic. She reared up, then seemed to lift straight up into the air. When her hooves hit the ground she spun around and bolted right toward Norma and the gelding.

It was a narrow trail with no room for the mare to get by. It was one of those real trouble moments that a horse can drop you into without the slightest hint of warning.

"Easy," Norma said to her horse.

He danced on his feet, but trusted her and held his ground.

And Jill . . . Jill rode it out like a real pro. She cranked on one rein and brought the mare's head around in a circle, which brought the whole mare around in a circle. That eased the danger of the horses crashing into each other. But the mare was still in a panic, and she began to spin wildly on the narrow trail. Jill wrapped her legs tight to her horse's belly and rode that spin until the mare was practically in a seated position, head close to her sweaty chest, nostrils wide and blowing.

"Stop it!" she shouted at the mare. "You stop being an idiot! Right now!"

The mare decided to let the moment pass.

Jill reined her around again and headed off down the trail.

Norma breathed out her leftover fear and followed.

"What did she see?" she asked Jill's back.

"Deer."

"That can be a big deal to a horse. Especially if they're not used to it."

"They see deer every day," Jill said. "She was just looking for an excuse. She hates to lead."

"Well, why didn't you say so? I can lead."

"You shouldn't have to do that."

"Does Grady mind leading?"

"Nah. He couldn't care less."

"Well then, what's the problem?"

They rode in silence until they reached a wide spot in the trail. Jill reined the mare over to the right and Norma passed her. Even before they had pulled out front, Norma could see and hear the mare drop her head and sigh deeply.

"You've become quite the horsewoman," Norma said over her shoulder.

"I appreciate your saying that. I mean . . . you would know."

"It's true. Most riders would've come off just now. You sat that spook like a pro."

"Thanks," Jill said. "I wanted you to think I was a good rider. That's why I didn't want to ask you to lead."

"A good rider takes the horse's limitations into account. Good horsemanship doesn't look for trouble. You avoid what trouble you can and deal with what can't be avoided. It's kind of like everything else in life that way."

"I don't know what to do about the situation with Jake."

"I can understand that."

"I mean I literally have no idea. I try to think about it, and I get nowhere. I just can't figure out what's right."

"You know what's right," Norma said. "You just have to think if you're strong enough to do it."

"I don't know if that's true or not. I mean, there's right in terms of . . . you know . . . justice and what really happened. But I also need to factor in what's right for me and my life. He's already completely upended my life once."

"Just so you know, I'll accept your decision and respect you for it. Whichever way you decide to go."

For a good long section of trail, no answer came back up to her from Jill.

"You knew that," Norma said. "Right?"

"Not really."

"You didn't think I would respect your decision?"

"I figured you wanted me to be strong like you."

"Nobody's strong every time."

"But you came all this way to get me to do something."

"I came all this way to get you to make the decision. Because I couldn't live with myself for putting a guy in jail for a murder I know he didn't commit. Or even not taking an extra step or two to prevent it. But it's your decision, not mine. Whatever decision you make, that's up to you. If you can live with it, so can I."

"It's not that easy," Jill said.

"Why isn't it?"

"Because I have to make a Norma-type decision. I have to get this right."

"Sit with the idea for now," Norma said. "We've got the whole long weekend to figure things out."

———

"I understand about how you met his wife and everything," Jill said. "But I don't understand why she's at your house taking care of your dogs."

They were sitting in low camp chairs in front of the cabin, in the shade of a tree that blew in the wind, revealing the sky and then obscuring it again. Jill's hound dog was sitting at Norma's side, her big brown-and-white head heavy on Norma's knee, and she seemed to have fallen asleep that way.

Norma was drinking a glass of lemonade Jill had made by picking lemons fresh off a tree behind the cabin. The glass was adorned with two sprigs of mint that grew wild and thick under the hose bib at the side of the house.

"Okay," Norma said. "It's like this. She came to me one night and said she had a ride back to Connecticut. This was way back when Jake was just packing up and leaving the campground in Sloot. She came to the pub to say goodbye. She didn't tell me straight out she was leaving with Jake, but I saw him sitting in his truck, waiting for her. She swore she wasn't getting involved with him, but I could see which way the wind was blowing. I told her she was making a big mistake. And then when it all came down the way it did, she came back to tell me I'd been right and she should have listened to me.

And also . . . I think she needed some support and advice. She doesn't really have anybody."

Norma paused, trying to decide whether to add the last bit of information. She decided Wanda had given no indication that it was a secret.

"She's pregnant," she added. "She's trying to decide whether to have the baby or not, because she's all alone."

"She must have somebody," Jill said.

"Not really. You know how it is when you're in a relationship with someone like Jake. They cut you off from everybody."

"Her parents would take her back."

"No, *your* parents would take *you* back. Not all parents are created equal. Her parents have washed their hands of her."

"Are you going to help her?"

Jill's voice sounded reserved. Maybe a little troubled.

"If it goes that way, I likely will."

"But she can't live at your house. Right? You could never stand having anybody live at your house. Could you?"

"Oh hell no. But Betty has a spare room. And she's a sucker for babies. Goes wild over them. She had four of her own and now she's waiting for them to give her grandchildren and none of them'll do it."

They sat in silence for several minutes. Norma sipped at her lemonade, chewed on one of the sprigs of mint, and watched the dappled light change in front of her eyes.

Then Jill said, "Is it bad that I'm a little jealous of her?"

"Because I'm helping her out, you mean?"

"Yeah, because you're taking her under your wing like a parent does."

"Honey, I'm old enough to be a grandparent to you girls."

"Okay, the way a grandparent does."

"I took *you* under my wing and helped *you*."

"Yeah, but that's over now. Never mind. I'm being silly. I'm being sort of . . . ungenerous. And childish. I also feel a little jealous of her because she was married to my ex. Which is really crazy, because I don't want him back. And he nearly killed her."

"Feelings don't really respond to facts like that."

"Still. I'm being crazy."

"You're being a human person," Norma said. "It's not like you've got a bunch of other choices."

———

Norma was lying in Jill's bed in the dark, still awake. Jill was asleep on the couch, with the door open between them. Or . . . she was on the couch, anyway. Norma had no idea if she was awake or asleep until she spoke.

"My biggest fear is that I say I'm alive and the murder charge goes away, and then they put him on trial for the attempted murder of . . . what was her name again?"

"Wanda."

"Right. Wanda. And then what if a jury doesn't convict him for some reason?"

"There were witnesses. There were vicious bruises on that poor woman's neck. Seems unlikely a jury wouldn't convict. Though, look. I'm not going to try to convince you that nothing could possibly go wrong. You know me. I'm a realist. Still, the odds of him getting off are slim. The combination of the fact that you went into hiding so he wouldn't kill you and the fact that he *did* try to kill the partner he *could* still find . . . it's pretty compelling."

"But what if they only give him a year or two in prison? When he gets out, he could come after me."

"I guess if that happened you'd want your parents to help you with some real security. A tail on his movements or a bodyguard for you. And you have to know it's hard for me to advise you, because the situation comes with no guarantees. You know. Like life. And can you even imagine how bad I'll feel if something happens to you? But I'll tell you something Wanda told me. She said for about two and a half years he was still completely obsessed with you. Scoured the internet all the time to see if you'd turned up anywhere. And then after a while he stopped. Obsession is an odd duck, my young friend. It's so powerful while it lasts, but then it doesn't last forever. You think it will but it doesn't. It needs to be fed."

For a few moments, Jill didn't answer. Norma had her hands laced behind her head, staring through the window at a thin crescent moon hanging over a stand of trees. It looked almost painted on the sky, like a movie backdrop.

Norma's stomach felt prickly and ill at ease. She wondered, more directly than she had before, if she had been wrong to put Jill in this position.

"If I testify against him," Jill said, "that might be feeding it. That might wake it up again. And they'll probably make me testify. You know. About how he treated me when we were together. He might even think I came out of hiding just to testify against him. To make sure he went to jail for what he just did. It might make him mad."

"Or he might think you came out of hiding just to make sure he didn't go to jail for something he didn't do."

"Now I'm all confused."

"It's a complicated situation."

"I'm not sure where that leaves me. You know. Decision-wise."

"Well . . . ," Norma began. Thinking and talking at the same time. "Maybe this. Maybe *I* go to the DA and tell him you're not dead. If you decide to go this way, I mean. I could 'out' you as being alive, and we could let it seem like I did it against your will. And then you could resist testifying and only show up in court if they send you a subpoena. Which they probably will. But you could make it really clear that you're not testifying against him voluntarily."

"I guess," Jill said. "I guess that's better than the alternative. Better than him thinking I'm outwardly trying to hurt him. But then I worry . . . what if I make it seem like I didn't want to testify against him and he takes that as a sign I still have feelings for him?"

"Oh," Norma said. "I suppose I hadn't thought of that."

"Why is life so complicated?"

"I'll be damned if I know, girl."

They lay silent in the dark for a time. How long a time, Norma couldn't have guessed. She might even have half dozed for a minute or two.

When Jill spoke again it made her jump slightly.

"Do you have any idea how many women and girls go missing every year? How many are missing right now? Really missing. Not like me."

"Unfortunately I do."

"Most people don't."

"No, that's true. Most people don't. And once upon a time in my life I'm sure I didn't either. But then I decided to devote my free time to volunteer search and rescue. And that opens your eyes real quick."

"I've been reading up on it. A lot. For five years I've pretty much buried myself in statistics about missing people. And not just statistics but real cases. Real people. Statistics are so much easier to swallow. They're just numbers. But sometimes even the numbers are heartbreaking. Just the numbers of Native American women and girls is enough to make you cry. And you know why I bring that up, right?"

"Because nobody talks about it. Nobody even knows."

"Right. All these thousands of women and girls missing, and nobody pays any attention to them, because they're too busy paying attention to me. Do you have any idea how that makes me feel?"

Norma considered this for a few beats before answering.

"Actually, no. I don't."

"Guilty. It makes me feel guilty. And I can only imagine how it makes the parents of those other girls feel. Because it's like the media and the public are saying I'm more important. But why am I more important? Because I had blond hair and blue eyes? Because they think I fit their tiny narrow little definition of what pretty means? If you had any idea how different things are for me with brown hair and brown eyes . . ."

"You started to say something about that when I first got here. You said it was weird."

"It *is* weird. It's so different. It's not like guys never, ever treat me like I'm pretty. Just more like . . . it takes them some time to notice me. It used to be like this automatic reaction. It was instantaneous. They just looked at me and some string got pulled. I actually like it better this way. I feel safer. I just think it's weird."

"Especially since the vast majority of human women aren't blond-haired and blue-eyed."

"It's just a bad system. It's terrible for the others but it's bad for me too. Nobody wins. It's like you were saying before about not putting you on a pedestal. How it's bad for everybody involved. And then we're talking about women and girls and ignoring all the men and boys that are missing. Like the girls matter more because they're so helpless and delicate, which is total misogyny. But there's a certain truth to it, too, because women really are a lot more likely to be beaten and raped and kidnapped and murdered. But for any individual man or boy I'm not sure those statistics are very helpful."

She paused a moment, almost seeming to run out of breath. But Norma knew it wasn't really about breath. She had run out of something, but not oxygen.

"What is this world we're living in, Norma?"

"It's what we have to work with," Norma said. "It's the only world we've got."

Chapter Eighteen

The Genuine Kind

Norma wandered into the kitchen the following morning to find Jill just ducking out the back door.

"Horses first," she said. "Then I'll make us breakfast."

Norma sat at the table for a time, watching her through the window. Watching her carry flakes of hay and tip them over the fence, and measure scoops of grain into feed buckets. While she watched she could hear the contented lapping and crunching of the hound dog eating breakfast in the corner. She could hear the coffeepot hissing and dripping.

She found herself filled with an odd feeling that she only sat still with for a time, without dissecting. When she did pick it apart, she decided it felt like admiration.

Jill popped back into the kitchen.

"Sorry," she said.

"Never apologize for putting the animals first. We bred them to depend on us for everything. For their survival. That comes with big responsibilities, and anybody who doesn't take that responsibility seriously is someone I don't even want to know."

"I'll make us pancakes and eggs."

"Sounds good to me."

Norma sat quietly, watching her cook, for several minutes. Then she decided that what she was thinking was better said than unsaid. Even though not saying a thing is almost always easier.

"You've grown up to be a fine young woman," she said.

Jill's hand, which had been whisking pancake batter, stopped moving.

"Why do you say that?"

"You sound surprised. Don't *you* think so?"

Jill had her back to Norma, so it was impossible to judge her reaction by her facial expression.

"I guess I was just secretly hoping you'd tell me more about what you saw that made you think so."

"Oh. Okay. That's fair enough. Let me see. You fed the animals first."

Jill turned her head slightly, and Norma could see part of a crooked smile.

"I figured that would be your kind of thing."

"But you do it even when I'm not here, right?"

"Of course."

"These are just the little things. I'm building up to the big thing. Another little thing. The way you sat that big spook yesterday. Doesn't sound like a character-related thing, or at least I think it probably wouldn't to someone who doesn't know horses. But two people on a trail ride can always get hurt. People want to be kind with their horses, and I'm all for that. But in that moment, with no notice and no time to think, you knew your job was to keep everybody safe. And not just the people, either. Both horses were in danger if you'd handled it wrong, so if you're too soft on the behavior, are you really being kind to the horse or not? You knew it was your job to be in charge. To insist she submit to you—to your will. Not all that different from a parent who has to keep a kid from running out into the street. Sometimes the adult human just knows more. Anyway, it showed me you have good instincts when the chips are down."

"Thank you," Jill said.

Her hand began to whisk again.

"What was the big thing?" Jill asked after a time.

"The fact that you've been learning about people who are missing. The fact that it makes you mad that the world treats your disappearance like it's more important. It's a type of privilege to be the one who captures the public's fancy, and most people are all too happy to accept their own privilege. Oh, they'll tell you that's not what they're doing, because they don't think any privilege exists. They don't see it. But you see it. You see that nobody talks about the Native American women and girls. You see that men and boys go missing, too, but people feel sorrier for the women and girls. You grew up to have genuine empathy. Genuine empathy extends to everyone in a given situation. The non-genuine variety is mostly reserved for yourself and people just like you."

"Thank you," Jill said again. "It means a lot coming from you."

"Then I'm glad I spilled it."

"You know I still haven't decided what I should do."

"I do know that, yes."

"And you said you wouldn't judge me for that."

"And I'm not judging you for it," Norma said.

———

"Oh, I just thought," Norma said as Jill was clearing the dishes after breakfast, "I need to get my phone out of the truck. I left it there. I need to call Wanda and tell her when I'll be home. Unless the battery's run down. I might need to charge it first."

"You haven't called her yet?"

"No. Not yet. I pretty much left it that I'd be gone a few days. But I should give her an update."

"Well, if you left your phone turned on, and it wasn't in airplane mode, it'll be dead by now. There's hardly any reception out here, and phones tend to exhaust themselves searching for a signal."

"Sounds familiar," Norma said.

Jill was at the sink, washing and rinsing the breakfast dishes before stacking them in a draining rack on the counter. She took a quick break, wiping her hands on a dark-red dish towel printed with stars and cowboy boots. She took her landline phone off its base and handed it to Norma.

"Here, use this. Wherever you call, my bill is the same."

"Thanks," Norma said.

She took the phone and punched in her own home number.

It rang three times.

"Oh darn," Norma said, more or less to Jill. Maybe more to herself. "I hope she answers my phone. We didn't talk about whether she should answer it if it rang."

"Hello?" a tentative little voice said. Or asked. It came out more like a question.

It was hard to believe it could be Wanda. It sounded like a little girl.

"Wanda?"

"Oh, good, it's you." The voice was noticeably louder and stronger this time. "I wasn't sure if I was right to answer, but then I thought it might be you."

"And it is. You doing okay?"

"Oh, I'm better than okay, Norma. I'm great. I'm so happy. I'm so free. I had no idea how free I wasn't. I guess I'd kind of gotten used to not being free. Like I didn't even notice it anymore. Or maybe I'd never really acknowledged it, I don't know. There are so many levels in a person's brain and it's hard to figure stuff like that out. But I've been playing music I like. He didn't like the music I liked, so I just sort of put away the fact that I like it. And now I get to listen to it. Little stuff like that, but it's big to me. And I can say whatever I want, but there's no one to say it to, so I've been talking to the dogs and the horse a lot. They're fine, by the way. I'm sorry I'm talking too much."

"It's okay," Norma said. "I'm happy you're happy."

A brief silence fell on the line. Jill had gone back to washing the breakfast dishes. The running water and the light clink of porcelain plates and cups was the only sound.

"There's actually someone human you should be talking to," Norma said. "Go by the pub tonight and have a soda and talk to Betty some and get to know her. And definitely tell her you're pregnant. She loves babies. Loves them. Goes wild for them. She had four of her own way back when, and now none of them'll give her grandbabies, and it drives her crazy. And she has a spare bedroom."

"Oh," Wanda said, and she sounded a bit deflated. "Okay. I guess. Just . . . I don't really know her. I know you."

"You'll get to know her, and let me tell you, she's a lot nicer and easier to get along with than I am. Not like that's such a hard contest to win. Look. I'll be back day after tomorrow, okay? I'll leave in the middle of the day tomorrow but I'll have to sleep over one night and come back on Monday. I just have to finish up some family business. And while you're talking to Betty tell her I'll be back to work on Monday evening."

"Okay," Wanda said. "I'll see you."

"Bye."

Norma clicked off the call and set the phone on the table. Jill continued to wash dishes, her gaze trained out the window over the sink. Maybe watching her horses. Maybe taking in the distant hills. Maybe just staring off into space.

Norma was a little surprised when she spoke.

"I could only hear your end of the conversation, so I couldn't hear why she said she was happy. But don't tell me. Let me guess. She feels like this huge weight was lifted off her shoulders because there's no one controlling her every move. Except she didn't even know the weight was there—or at least she didn't know *how much* the weight was there—until it lifted."

"That's the long and short of it," Norma said. "Yeah."

"I know the feeling."

"So do I, sorry to say."

A brief silence.

Then Jill said, "I'm not jealous of her anymore. Now I just feel bad for her situation."

"And there goes another big reason why I feel like you turned into a good woman."

Jill rinsed her hands, dried them on the printed towel, and sat down across the table from Norma.

"More coffee?"

"I'm good. Thanks."

"I'm sorry you had to lie."

"When did I lie?"

"You told her you had to wrap up some family business."

"Oh. That. I'm not worried about that. That was true *enough*. You're family *enough*."

———

"I'm really confused about the best way to do this thing," Jill said.

They were sitting outside under the trees again, drinking iced tea.

Norma thought it was an interesting statement, because it made it sound as though Jill had decided she was going to do it, just not exactly how.

"I keep going around in my head about it. Over and over. About how if I pop up and say I'm not dead he might think I'm trying to save him from something and be grateful. Or he might think I'm just dying to testify against him now that he's in jail and can't hurt me. And that might make him mad. Or he might think it means I'm still in love with him, which is a whole other can of worms. If *you* pop up and say I'm not dead . . . well . . . I don't know. That's the problem. Maybe he'll think I would have just let him go down for a murder. I don't know what he'll think."

"Whatever he thinks, if I do it, there's less chance he'll associate the motives of the thing with you. If we think he's mad you weren't going to come clean we can say you'd already discussed talking to the DA with me. Or with your parents. Doesn't matter. We can just say it was already in the works."

"I guess."

They sat in silence for a time. Norma closed her eyes and could still notice the difference between sunlight and shade as the leaves blew back and forth above the women's faces.

"Won't you get in trouble?" Jill asked. "For finding me and not reporting it?"

"Maybe. But I'll take my lumps. Before I was afraid they wouldn't let me ride with the team anymore. But I'm ready to retire from that. They might give me community service or something. I doubt there'd be more to it than that."

"You would do that for me?"

"Already made it clear I would."

"I just wish I could know," Jill said. "You have to make a decision, but you really can't know how it will all play out. It's like you try to see down the road, but you can't. You just have to choose, and then find out later what you got yourself into."

"Yeah," Norma said, her eyes still closed. "There's a word for that."

"There is? Tell me. Oh, wait. Never mind. Don't tell me. I know. The word is 'life.'"

Norma opened her eyes and they stared up at the blowing leaves together.

"Now how did you know I was gonna say that?"

"Because I know you. Before I *wanted* to know you. I wanted to believe I knew you, maybe better than I really did. But now I'm starting to know you for real."

They sat for several minutes in silence.

Then Jill said, "You go tell the DA I'm not dead. That's my decision."

Norma looked over at her face, but there was nothing particularly telling in her expression.

"Good decision."

"I hope this doesn't sound silly. Or make you mad. I sort of knew what the answer was, for a little while anyway, but I thought when I announced it you might just get up and go home."

"Nah," Norma said. "I already told Wanda I'd be home Monday. And we're having a nice visit here. Why rush off?"

"That's good," Jill said. And she seemed to relax some. "You know. When you called her earlier . . . you were waiting to see if she would answer, because you hadn't specifically told her to answer the phone if it rang. And somehow in that moment I was picturing her hiding. In your house, hiding. Like I was hiding when I was at your house. Curtains drawn. Staying quiet and letting the phone ring like no one was home. And then she picked up, and I realized she doesn't have to hide. He's in jail. She doesn't have to be afraid, because he's in jail. She can feel safe now."

Norma was sensing a hesitancy in her voice, but wasn't sure if she was reading it correctly.

"Do *you* feel safe now?"

"Not really," Jill said. "I wish I did. I want to. But not so much."

———

"Are you awake?" Norma asked in a quiet voice.

She was in Jill's bed, but not asleep. Jill was a vague lump on the couch in the dark.

"Yeah," the dark lump said back. "I was just about to ask you the same question. But first I was lying here thinking that tomorrow night you won't be in there and I won't be able to ask."

"I could come visit again sometime. I could visit a lot if it's no secret you're alive."

"Oh," Jill said. "Right. I hadn't thought of that. What did you want to say when you asked me if I was asleep?"

"Just . . . I don't know. Might sound strange, but I've had my doubts about this cousin thing. Pretending to be your own cousin. Doesn't seem like the best cover story. Seems easy to crack."

"My dad came up with something about Cassie having been born in England and just moving here. And he got a pro to fake the paperwork."

"Little bit of genealogy would disprove that real quick."

"Maybe," Jill said. She sounded uneasy. "But it's held up all this time. I think the police investigation went cold before I was Cassie. Nobody really looked at the thing all that closely. They took us at our word."

"You're lucky then. And I'm a little bit surprised. I promised myself I wouldn't say anything about it, because I didn't want it to seem like I was scaring you into coming clean. You know. By suggesting people would find out anyway. But now you've made your decision, so now it doesn't matter. You've dodged a few bullets in your time, girl."

"I have," she said. "You helped me dodge some."

"Well, if you see any more headed your way, just give me a call. You know where I am."

———

"You think you'll go see him right away?" Jill asked.

They were standing by the open door of Norma's truck. Neither seemed anxious to bring the visit to a close.

"The DA, you mean?"

"Yeah. That."

"Pretty straight away," Norma said. "Depending on how tired I am."

"Okay. Still wish I knew how this was going to play out."

"Right. Don't we all?"

A long silence. It seemed regretful.

"You can go back to being Jill," Norma said. "If you want."

"I'm not sure I'd even want that."

"I'm surprised. I thought you would."

"That nice compliment you gave me. How I grew into a good woman. That was for Cassie. Not for Jill. You never said anything like that about Jill."

"Jill was just young and needed to learn some things about the world. *You* grew into a good woman, and that's not going to change, no matter what you call yourself."

Rather than answering, Jill rushed in and gave her a hug. And held on to Norma for a long time.

"Call me," she said into Norma's ear. Then, before Norma could open her mouth to answer, she added, "Oh wait. What am I thinking? You can't call me. If you could call me you would've called me all along."

"We're going public with our story," Norma said. "Everything changes."

Jill stepped back from the embrace and stood a moment, her brow furrowed.

"Wow," she said. "This is going to take some getting used to."

Then she trotted back to the cabin, glancing once over her shoulder and waving.

Norma climbed into her truck and drove.

Chapter Nineteen

Your Mad Doesn't Care

Norma was within striking distance of the Arizona state line when the overwhelming urge to call her older son got the best of her.

She tapped his number in her contact list, put the phone on speaker, and set it on the truck's bench seat.

He picked up. That surprised Norma. Neal almost never picked up.

"Hey, Mom," he said. "What's up?"

"I tried to call your brother a while ago, but he never called me back."

"Rick's backpacking through Europe."

"Huh," Norma said. "That's odd. Isn't that one of those things you do in college?"

"Well, *he* never did. And I guess he was feeling like life was flying by. What's up, Mom? Is everything okay?"

Norma glanced at the face of the phone, resting on her truck seat. As if it might have an expression, or something else her eyes could tell her. Then she looked back to the road for safety.

"Pretty much," she said. "Everything's pretty much okay. I guess I was just feeling like life is flying by."

"You're not sick, are you?"

"Oh, no. No, I'm strong as a horse. But I'm not getting any younger, hon, and sometimes you just need to keep one eye on the finish line and make sure nothing important gets left unsaid or undone. Granted, I may well be around for another thirty years or more, but you never do know. Look. I don't want to upset the applecart here. I think you boys are happy enough leaving the past in the past, but I've been carrying this for a long time and now it needs to be said."

"Okay," Neal said, drawing the word out long.

Tall cacti rushed by in Norma's peripheral vision, along with a retaining wall made of old tires. And acre after acre of dirt.

"I never cheated on your father. There was no other man."

A long silence.

"So *he* did it," Neal said.

"Does that come as a shock to your system?"

"Not entirely. I mean, you grow up. You grow up and you look back and you realize there's always a chance that not everything your father told you was true."

"I thought the reason you hardly ever called or came to visit was because you still believed him and you still hated me for it."

"I don't hate you. At all. It was just a hard thing. I had all kinds of feelings around it, but not hate. I was mad at you if Dad was telling the truth and mad at Dad if you were. And if you were, then there was the guilt. And the confusion over what to feel after all this time just makes it complicated and hard."

"He was a very persuasive man. And you were only a child. But now you're a grown man, and now . . . I just have to ask you this. Do you believe what I just told you?"

"I'm inclined to. Yeah. I have to think about it, but . . . I saw other things that made me think anger was a problem with him, but I never saw anything to make me think you'd lie and cheat. And I guess you wouldn't have called out of nowhere all these years later if it wasn't true."

"Okay. Good."

"And I'll come visit. I'll come before the year is out. Jane might have to work but I could bring the kids."

"That would be nice."

The conversation just hung there a moment. Norma wasn't sure if it was over.

"Mom?"

"Yeah, baby?"

"I'm sorry."

"Well, stop it, Neal. Stop it right now. Stop being sorry. You were a child. Nothing that happened that day was your fault."

"I'll have Rick call when he gets back."

"Good. You do that. I gotta go," she added.

Because if there was one thing Norma had always hated, it was crying in front of anybody but just herself.

———

When she arrived home, her houseguest was thrilled to see her. In fact, Wanda was thrilled in a way Norma had never seen her thrilled about anything.

"Norma!" she shouted, and jumped up from Norma's easy chair using no hands for leverage.

"Enjoy doing that while you can," Norma said, "because in six or seven months you're going to miss it."

Meanwhile the hound dogs were winding around Norma's legs, baying, and whipping their strong tails. Wanda seemed to be trying to come in to give Norma a hug, but the way would not clear.

"I'm so happy!" Wanda said, her voice raised to be heard over the ruckus of the hounds.

She was bouncing up and down on her toes as she spoke.

"So I see. Who plugged you into a wall socket?"

"I'm just happy. I talked to Betty. A lot, for a long time. Betty is *great*! She's going to let me live in her spare room until I get on my feet after the baby."

"Then you get to have the baby."

"Yes, and I'm happy!"

"Well, I'm happy you're happy," Norma said. "But now I have to go say hello to my horse."

Norma stepped out into the yard, realizing as she did how utterly bone-tired she'd become. She felt it in every limb as she walked. The inside of her head seemed to buzz with that exhaustion.

The dogs followed, sweeping in wide circles and baying their excitement. Wanda followed in more of a straight line, still talking.

"It was so nice to have dogs," she said. "Well, not have them, I know they weren't mine, but just to be around them. Have them here with me. I forgot how nice it is to have dogs. You can talk and they always listen."

As they approached Saint Fred's paddock, he lifted his head and nickered at Norma, deep in his throat. She could barely hear it over all the other sounds, but she could see the breath reshape his nostrils as he pushed out the air. She could watch the soft skin around them shudder as the sound resonated.

He dropped his head over the fence and she stroked his long face.

"Sorry, buddy," she said quietly to the horse. "I had to go take care of some important business."

"Thank you for letting me spend that time with your dogs," Wanda said. "I like them a lot and I think they liked me."

"You haven't had a dog for a while?" Norma asked, still stroking the horse's face.

"When I was a kid we had dogs. But then I was on my own and I wasn't sure I could take care of one. And then I was married. But Jake doesn't like dogs."

"That sounds about right," Norma said.

For a blessed moment, nobody said anything. Even the dogs had gone quiet. It was a relief to Norma, who hadn't had her usual amount of alone time.

"Betty doesn't like them," Norma said. "I mean, she likes them okay when they're somebody else's, but she doesn't really want to keep one around her house."

"I know. We talked about that."

"Okay, good."

"We talked about everything. But I won't be at her place forever."

"True."

Another long, sweet silence.

Then Norma said, "Don't take this the wrong way, but . . . when do you move your stuff over to Betty's?"

"It's already there. Most of it. I was just staying at your house with the dogs until you got back to take care of them."

"Thank you," Norma said.

And that beautiful, welcome silence fell again.

It was Wanda who finally broke it.

"Is everything okay with your family?"

"I hope so," Norma said. "It more or less remains to be seen. But I think the situation made a move in the right direction at least."

———

Norma showed up at the bar at eight. Betty was just coming out from the kitchen.

"Now that's what I call timing," Betty said. "We have a bunch of half kegs at the delivery door and my back is acting up."

"We have a hand truck, you know."

"Yeah, but you still have to get them on it."

"Why didn't you have the delivery guy bring them up?"

"His back is acting up, too."

"Great," Norma said, and hung up her light jacket on an empty hook. "The whole world has a bad back."

"How's yours?"

"Not great, but I'll manage."

"Welcome back, by the way."

"Thanks. Weirdly, it's actually good to be here."

"Not sure why that's weird."

"It's a bar."

"It's home."

"Which is weird."

Norma walked through the kitchen. She positioned the hand truck, and rolled and lifted the four half kegs onto it. She wheeled them up front, where she and Betty set about wrestling them under the bar together.

"Thank you," Norma said.

But she clearly wasn't thanking her for helping with the kegs, because they had barely started.

"You mean for filling in while you were gone? It wasn't really that busy. You'd think it would be this time of year, but not so much."

"Partly that, but mostly I meant for Wanda. Offering to take her in like that."

"She's a nice girl."

"As far as that goes, yeah. I suppose she is."

"She'd drive *you* crazy. She's bubbly, and she talks a lot. I don't really mind, though. It's too quiet in that big house all by myself."

"Well, that's fixed as of now."

"And there's gonna be a *baby!*"

Betty's voice came up to the level of an excited squeal on the final word.

"I figured that would be your kind of thing."

For a moment they didn't talk, because they were too busy with the physical aspects of the task at hand. Norma grunted twice but not much more.

By the time they had finished they'd ended up sitting on their butts on the thick rubber floor mats behind the bar, legs splayed for leverage. They looked at each other and sighed.

"Life just keeps getting harder," Betty said.

"I'll drink to that."

"Why do women go for guys like that Jake fellow?"

"I'll be damned if I know, Betty."

"In a fair world, guys like that would never have a girlfriend."

"You can't tell me you ever thought this was a fair world."

"No," Betty said. "I'm not stupid."

They each sighed a final time and staggered to their feet.

Betty wiped her hands on a bar towel she wore tucked in at the waist where her apron tied.

"I hope they put that jerk in jail for years," she said. "I hope he never gets out."

"Hard to know what a jury will do," Norma said.

But her stomach immediately began doing flip-flops. Because she had already called and gotten squeezed in for an appointment with the DA at his office the following day. To give him information that would likely result in Jake doing less prison time.

It made her feel like a traitor. Not to Betty, exactly. Or not only to Betty. To most of the world.

This is the problem with being an adult, Norma thought. *You're always having to make a decision that someone will like and someone else will hate. You're always having to betray someone. Decide one thing, betray one party. Turn around and decide the other thing, and get ready to be told you just burned the people on the other side. Because people's needs are always in conflict. There's no such thing as everybody happy all at once.*

Betty knocked her out of the thought.

"What's going on with you, anyway, Norma? Wanda said you told her you were off dealing with family. But you're always telling me you have no family."

"I'm trying to put things back together with the boys," Norma said, happy that it was true. Or anyway, true enough. Not the reason she was gone, but at least a true statement.

"Oh, that's nice," Betty said. "How's that going?"

"Hard to say at this point. Better than it was before I tried."

"They're not still mad at you?"

"Doesn't seem so."

"And you're not still mad at them?"

"Why would I be mad at them?"

"For picking their father over you."

"They were children."

"Yeah. Well. Sure. Your brain knows that. But your mad doesn't care."

"Hmm," Norma said.

She vaguely remembered telling Jill, "Feelings don't really respond to facts."

She let it drop from there. But, honestly, it was worth thinking about. Maybe later, when she was more rested.

Chapter Twenty

About Justice

Norma stood in the lobby of the building, waiting for the elevator. Her stomach jangled with fear, but her brain sailed in unpredictable and not very important directions.

Mostly she was marveling at the concept of a building with more than one floor, and wondering how long it had been since she'd seen one.

The elevator wasn't moving, so she glanced at the stairs and decided walking to the third floor was not unreasonable.

Halfway up to the second floor she got it in her head to call Jill. To tell her she was scared going into her meeting with the DA. Maybe it would help to tell that to someone—someone who understood what was at stake in this situation, and was allowed to know the details. And there was more or less one such person on the planet.

She pulled her cell phone out of her pocket, sure she would have no reception. She was, after all, in a stairwell.

She was shocked to see five bars.

So this is what it must be like to live in a city, she thought to herself. *Even a small one.*

Out loud she said, to no one, "I've got to get out more."

She touched the "Cassie" number in the contact list, and the line rang once.

Norma immediately hung up the phone.

She hung up because it struck her suddenly that it would be utterly unfair to tell Jill she was afraid and ask for emotional support. Nobody was more afraid than Jill at this moment. Norma should be supporting the younger woman, not leaning on her.

Norma's phone rang suddenly, and she jumped the stereotypical mile.

Not surprisingly, it was Jill calling.

She picked up.

"Hey," she said.

"You just tried to call me," Jill said. Her voice sounded tight, as if it had been twisted or stretched. "Did you see the DA?"

"Not yet. I'm literally just walking up the stairs to his office."

"Why did you call?"

"Accidental dial," Norma said.

Then she only stood still in the silence, experiencing how bad it felt to lie.

"Okay, that wasn't true," Norma said. "See, this is the problem with telling any lies at all. Even for a good reason. If you never lie, you never lie. But then if you open the door and tell one, it just makes the next one that much easier. I'm sorry. The truth is, I'm a little nervous. I was going to call you and tell you I'm a little nervous because maybe that would make me feel better. But then I hung up because I thought, I'm not nearly as nervous as you are, and it's not fair to lean on you at a time like this."

"Norma . . ."

"What?"

"We can lean on each other."

"Oh. I actually hadn't thought of that. I haven't been much of a leaner in my life."

"Do me a favor, would you?"

"What's that?"

"Don't hang up the phone. Just put it on speaker and slide it into your pocket. I promise I won't make a peep on this end. I'll put the dog where no one can hear her if she barks. I want to hear this."

"What if he keeps me waiting?"

"So? What if he does? I have an unlimited data plan."

"Oh. Yeah, me too. Okay. Here goes."

"Norma, wait. Before you put me in your pocket . . ."

"Yes?"

"I love you."

Norma opened her mouth to say they barely knew each other. That they had spent a total of only a handful of days together. Force of habit, most likely. Deflecting any kind of emotion had been a go-to move for most of her life.

Instead she closed her mouth and decided maybe love wasn't based so much on time anyway. Maybe there were other, more important factors.

She hung there in the moment without speaking for a few beats longer.

"I love you too," she said. Then a pause. Then: "I'm going in now."

—

The DA kept her waiting for a full fifty minutes. Fifty. Minutes. In her entire life Norma had never made anybody wait fifty minutes for something she had committed to do for them at a set time.

It made her extra impatient knowing that Jill was in her pocket, also waiting.

"My appointment was at nine," Norma said to the young receptionist.

"He had a couple of unexpected phone calls. He should be with you shortly."

"If they're unexpected," Norma said, "then they didn't have an appointment. I do."

"They were important phone calls," the young woman said.

"Oh, lovely," Norma said. "Just what everybody wants to hear. 'We're prioritizing everybody in order of importance and you landed on the bottom.'"

She watched the woman's expression change. It shut down, the way a store shuts down at the end of the day, locking Norma out.

It struck her that she should have been more polite for her own sake.

"Look," Norma said. "I have some extremely important information for him about a case of his. It's big. If he knew how big it was, he would prioritize me."

The young woman sighed.

Then, to Norma's surprise, she rose from her desk and stuck her head in through the door of the DA's office.

For a minute or so the young woman just hung there in the doorway, her back to Norma. If words were being spoken, Norma had no idea what they were. She couldn't hear their soft voices.

The receptionist pulled her head out of the doorway, leaving it standing open.

"You can go in," she said.

Norma rose, feeling as though her heart were trying to escape through her throat.

She stepped inside the DA's office.

He was a young man, by Norma's standards. Late thirties at most. His dark hair was thinning already. He wore a gray suit that looked like it must have cost a fortune. His head was tilted down, staring at his cell phone. He was typing furiously with his thumbs.

Norma sat in a chair in front of his desk.

"I have to leave for court in eight minutes," he said without looking up.

"Which would have been a really good reason to see me at nine. Which is when I had my appointment. Nine."

She thought he might take offense, but he didn't seem to notice or care. He still did not look up from his phone.

"What can I do for you?" he asked.

"You can give me your full attention for a split second."

That seemed to get through.

He looked up at Norma, and his eyes were an oddly dark blue. It seemed out of place for a dark-haired, dark-complected man. He set his phone on the desk.

"I have some very important information about a case. And I'm not being treated like I have anything important to say. But I do."

"If you have information about a case why not go to the police?"

"I'm going to you because you're about to prosecute this case. And so you need to know this."

Norma thought she saw him sigh. But, if so, he managed to do it silently.

"Here's the thing, Ms. . . ."

"Gallagher."

"Ms. Gallagher. I'm sorry if I seem dismissive, but people come in here all the time to give me 'really important information' and it's rarely anything actionable on my part. Usually it's more like their opinion on a thing. But go ahead and tell me what you want to tell me, provided it fits into about seven minutes, and we'll see what category it falls under."

"Okay. You're making a mistake prosecuting Jake Willis for Jill Moss's murder."

"See, this is exactly—"

Norma didn't let him finish.

"Because Jill Moss is not dead."

For a strangely long, almost stretched-feeling moment, the DA allowed silence. As if he were paying attention to her at long last. His face looked stony, but his eyebrows lifted slightly.

She waited for him to speak, but it seemed he never would.

"She ran away from their campsite that night because she wanted to leave Jake and she thought he'd kill her for it. That's why she never told anyone she was alive. For her own safety. But I've seen her in just the last couple of days. And she's doing fine."

Another long silence.

"I just figured you wouldn't want to put a guy in jail for a murder that never happened in the first place."

"You just said yourself that she had to hide so he wouldn't kill her."

"But she did. So he didn't."

"Jake Willis tried to strangle his wife to death."

"I'm well aware of that. But we're taking about justice here."

"Justice," he said. As if speaking of a lunch special that didn't sound appealing. "People talk a lot about justice. They seem quite invested in it. But we don't have a justice system in this country. We have a legal system. The two are not quite the same."

Norma was just about to say it was surely illegal to put a man on trial for the murder of someone he knew was alive. But she held the thought inside so he wouldn't shut down to Norma the way his receptionist had.

"It's hard to know what to say to that," she said.

"You don't want to see Jake Willis in prison for a good long while?"

"It wouldn't break my heart."

"Then what's the problem?"

Norma had no idea what to say, so she said nothing. She was briefly aware of Jill, listening from her pocket. She wondered what, if anything, Jill would say if she could.

"I have a problem with my hearing," the DA said.

"Really? That seems odd. You're such a young man."

"It's not really age related."

"You heard me say Jill had to hide for her own safety."

"Yeah," the DA said. "It comes and goes."

Norma had been looking at his desk, trying to make sense of all this. On that last sentence, she looked up into his weirdly dark-blue eyes. That was when she understood.

"Oh," she said. "That kind of hearing problem."

The kind just about everybody has, Norma thought. *Deciding what you will and won't hear.* Though this seemed like a particularly bald and egregious example.

Norma was surprised and yet not. All at the same time. She knew a little about the justice system from having so many connections in the sheriff's department. But it was different to see it play out in front of your own eyes.

"Walk with me," he said. "I have to get to court."

They walked through his outer office, side by side. Out to the elevator.

The DA pressed the button, and the doors opened. The elevator had been right there, on the third floor. Waiting. Though she knew it couldn't literally be true, it made Norma feel as though even the elevators in that place prioritized people and their importance.

They stepped on.

Norma opened her mouth to speak, but the DA shook his head slightly. With his gaze, he indicated a spot in the upper corner of the elevator. Looking where he looked, Norma saw a surveillance camera.

They rode to the first floor in silence.

She followed him through the lobby and out into the parking lot, nearly running to keep up. It seemed as though he were literally trying to leave her behind, or maybe as though he'd entirely forgotten she was there.

Then he stopped suddenly, and turned to face her.

"I'm in this lot over here," he said.

"Oh. I'm the other way."

"Visitor parking, I know."

Norma turned to go, but he had more to say.

"Ms. Gallagher."

Norma stopped. Waited. She knew what came next was important. She could feel the weight of it.

"If you tell anyone we had this conversation, I'll deny it. It will be your word against mine."

"Well," Norma said, "I don't think you'll have any need to do that."

"I'm glad to hear it," he said.

Then he turned sharply away and trotted to his car.

Norma watched him go for a time. The inside of her felt empty and almost tingly. A mild form of genuine shock, from the feel of it.

He had been long out of sight when she remembered she still had Jill in her pocket.

She pulled out the phone, clicked the call off the speaker mode, and held it to her ear.

"You heard all that," she said.

"I absolutely heard all that. Every word."

Jill's voice no longer sounded stretched. It sounded lighter and more relaxed.

"Is that the damnedest thing you ever heard in your life?"

"I don't know what you're feeling about it," Jill said.

"I don't know what I'm feeling about it either."

"I can tell you what *I'm* feeling."

"Yeah, go ahead."

"Relieved," Jill said. "I get to keep being Cassie. I get to keep my new life. But it's not my fault and it's not your fault, because we told him. It's his fault if he won't listen. If it ever comes out that I'm alive, we won't have to take the blame."

"Except we sort of will," Norma said. "Because he'll deny that we ever told him."

"But I taped the whole thing," Jill said.

"Oh. Interesting. Well then. I guess now I'm starting to feel a little bit relieved myself."

———

It was a quarter after two in the morning when her phone rang. Norma was driving home from her shift at the pub, with the phone resting in the cupholder in the truck's console.

She knew even before she picked it up that it was Jill.

She reached over and accepted the call, and put it on speaker.

"Hey, girl," she said.

"I know it's late. I figured you worked tonight."

"I did."

"You're not sleeping?"

"No. I'm driving home."

"I'm not sure . . . are we calling each other now? I mean . . . can we be a little less careful?"

"I guess," Norma said. "I'm having trouble figuring it all out. And the weird thing is, it's been this way from the beginning. Ever since I agreed to keep my mouth shut about you being alive and safe, I've been trying to figure out what the upshot of all this would be. Or could be. Trying to follow every possibility down the road to see where it might end up. But it feels like this is a situation that just never happens, that's just outside all the normal stuff. And my brain still can't take it all in."

"And speaking of being confused," Jill said, "I still don't know if it means we can call each other or not."

"I guess it's safer than it was before."

Norma drove through her own open gate and parked the truck beside the horse corral. She carried the phone and her young friend into the house, where the dogs wagged around her legs.

"I just can't quite get over what happened with the DA," Jill said. "I'm trying to wrap my head around it."

"I'm having trouble getting it to fit in my brain, too."

"I mean . . . you want to think the facts matter to them. That they haven't just decided in advance who they think should be in jail. How much of the time do you figure it happens like this?"

"No idea," Norma said, setting down her shoulder bag and hanging her jacket in the closet. "I've heard some stories from Ian. Prosecutors suppressing evidence. And we've all seen it play out on the news. Innocent man proves his innocence through DNA and then it comes out that there was all kinds of prosecutorial misconduct behind the scenes. And those are just the ones that come out. Still, I'm guessing most DAs are not like this one. Or it's what I want to believe anyway. I doubt it's the usual way things go. But I can't help thinking it goes like this more often than we think. More than we know. The world is full of guys like this DA, who're so sure they know who deserves what that they'll bend the world out of shape to make it so."

"It shakes your faith in the system," Jill said. "But the really weird thing is . . . another part of me is happy about it. Jake was so awful to me that I kind of like seeing someone decide he should pay a price for it no matter what."

A silence fell. Norma wasn't sure how to fill it.

"Is life always this complicated?" Jill asked.

Her voice sounded vulnerable and a little bit lost, as if she had grown ten years younger since she last spoke.

"Oh, hell yeah," Norma said. "Didn't you know that?" Then, after a brief pause, she added, "Well, life is always complicated. I'm not sure anything was ever *this* complicated."

Chapter Twenty-One

Why?

It was between five and six months later when Betty got the text.

It was evening, going onto ten, and they were working together at the pub. Betty's phone jingled with a notification, and they both seemed to know, somehow, what it was about. It was rare for Betty to get a call or text at work, but there was more to the knowing than just that. The fact that Wanda was nearly two weeks past her due date made it less than astonishing.

Betty slid her phone out of the pocket of her white apron and stared at it for a second or two.

"Her water broke."

"Oh," Norma said. "You'd best go get her then."

"You okay here by yourself?"

"What difference does it make? She needs you to do this."

"Yeah," Betty said. "I suppose if some three-quarters drunk rock climber has to wait an extra few minutes for his next drink the world won't stop turning. Regardless of what he might tell you."

She untied her apron as she spoke, pulled it off, and hung it on a hook near the kitchen.

"I'll come by after two," Norma said, "and wait with you two. Unless she's already had the baby. In which case I'll come anyway and meet the new arrival. Sure hope I don't miss that, though. I would hate to miss that."

Betty was typing on her phone as Norma spoke. Presumably telling Wanda she was on her way.

"I wouldn't worry about it," she said, looking up from her phone. "First baby? This should take a while."

"Well, I don't wish that on her. I just sure wish I could be there. You think he'd be mad if we closed?"

"For a baby? Hell yeah. For a death in the immediate family? Still hell yeah. Especially as there are two of us. He'll figure one of us can handle it."

Betty had her keys in her hand, ready to head out through the kitchen.

"See, this is the problem with working shifts with your best friend," Norma said. Even though she knew she should let Betty go. "You can never do anything together."

She was looking at the floor mats as she spoke. When she heard no reply and saw no movement from Betty in her peripheral vision, she looked up.

Betty had an odd look on her face, but Norma didn't know quite how to classify it.

"You never told me I was your best friend," she said.

"Well, who else have I got? Look around." Then she changed direction quickly. "I'm sorry. That was rude. Force of habit, to bat things like that away. Yes, you're my best friend. Now go help Wanda have that baby."

———

It was well after 1:00 a.m., and Norma was hauling pitchers of beer over to a loud table of hikers who seemed to want to talk about the town and ask directions.

By the time she got back to the bar, there was a big fortysomething man sitting there, and she worried she had kept him waiting too long.

No point turning into the DA, she thought.

"Sorry," she said. "I'm here by myself. What can I get you?"

"Just a beer. Whatever you've got on tap. What happened to the other lady?"

"She had to go. Her . . . daughter . . . just went into labor."

Norma had almost said that the woman in labor was just a friend Betty had taken in, but, in midsentence, she decided fewer details were usually better.

She poured the beer and set it in front of him, and he set a ten on the bar.

He was both tall and heavy with a wild shock of brown hair and an affable face.

"That isn't the lady who used to be married to Jake Willis, is it?"

It sent a little jolt through Norma's gut, but she didn't let on.

"Who, that lady who works here, or her daughter?"

"Right, never mind. I guess neither of them. It just seems like a weird coincidence because I know she's here in Sloot. Willis's ex. Or at least I heard she was. And she should be having her baby anytime now. I follow that whole case pretty carefully."

"So I see."

Norma turned her back to him and set about washing glasses.

"She'll have to be back in Southern California before long," the man said. "Because the trial is in just a little over two weeks. The first trial. The attempted-murder one, for the strangulation. But you probably knew that."

Norma washed glasses without indicating whether or not she had known that.

She had.

"And she's on the witness list."

"I can imagine she would be," Norma said.

A brief silence fell.

Then the man said, "I was in here five years ago, but you probably don't remember me."

She glanced over her shoulder at him, but made no connection.

"No offense," she said, "but five years ago there were an awful lot of people hanging around this place."

"Sure, I get it. I was here the night Willis came into the pub. You told him off real good. That's why I didn't forget you. You really got right in his face. And then I was the one who picked his ass up and threw him down on a table."

"Oh," Norma said. "*That* I remember."

"I hear he still has trouble with a ruptured disc from messing with me that night."

"Well, in fairness, he *was* the first to throw down."

"That he was. I'm not a violent guy, ma'am. I don't go around looking for trouble. But guys like that need to learn that some people hit back."

For a minute or two he said nothing more, and Norma let a silence fall. If one could call it silent with that rowdy group of hikers drinking, hooting, and laughing in the corner.

Then she said, "Let me ask you a question. If it's okay."

"Sure. Why not?"

"Why get so wrapped up in this case?"

"Lots of people are."

"Yeah, but they're not here to ask. And you are."

"Oh. That's true. Well . . . I don't know. I mean, she was a person."

"Who, Jill?"

"Yeah, Jill Moss. She was a human woman, and she had a life, and she didn't deserve to lose it."

"But there are so many human women who didn't deserve to lose their lives. They're all around you, every day. Why seize on this one and never let go?"

He scratched his forehead for a moment. Furrowed his brow. Took a sip of beer.

"Now that's hard to say. It just jumped out at me somehow. I just felt for her."

Norma set down the glass she was washing and turned to face him. The noisy group was just heading out the door. Other than this guy at the counter, they were her last customers. Maybe she could close up early and get to the hospital.

"But don't you ever ask yourself *why*?" she said to the lone guy. "Don't you ever look deeper down into yourself to see *why* things hit you the way they do? Don't you want to understand what's up with stuff like this?"

"Hell, I don't know. Does anybody do that?"

"I don't know anymore," Norma said. "But I sure as hell hope so."

He tipped his head back and threw down the last of his beer, and Norma decided to see if she could make a break for the hospital.

"Look," she said, "I don't know if you were planning on having another, but I sure would like to join my friends at the hospital where that baby's about to get born."

"That's fine," he said. "I need to get going anyway."

He lumbered away, and Norma followed him to the door so she could lock it behind him.

He took a few steps out into the dirt parking lot, then turned back to address her in the dark.

"Hey, do me a favor, okay? If you should happen to see Wanda Willis, give her a message for me? Tell her we're all pulling for her. We're all on her side. If there's anything I can do to help her, I will."

"Sure," Norma said. "If I should happen to see her, I'll do that."

"It's just such a small town. You know?"

"Oh, it's all of that and then some."

He turned away and moved toward his car, then stopped and turned back again. And spoke again.

"It's just that, with her about to have a baby and all . . . I feel like somebody needs to take care of her. And that baby. I mean, I know he'll be in jail and whatnot, but we don't really know for how long. And that kid deserves better than Jake Willis coming after him and trying to be a father. That woman and that kid both deserve a life without having to worry about Jake Willis."

"I'm sure when he's convicted," Norma said, "she'll file for sole custody."

In fact, she had every intention of suggesting it herself.

"I wish that put my mind at ease," he said.

And with that he turned away again and walked to his car.

Norma closed and locked the door behind him.

Then she took to hurrying around, bussing the last table and sweeping the floor. She would leave their dishes in the sink and the day person would just have to understand.

Just as she was grabbing her jacket off the hook her cell phone rang.

She slipped it out of her pocket. It was Betty calling.

"Hey," Norma said. "Everything okay?"

"'Bout as okay as a seven-pound, one-ounce bouncing baby girl can be."

"Damn it," Norma said. "I can't believe I missed it."

"You can come now and meet her."

"Yeah, I'll do that. I'm just closing up early. Hey, I thought you said this would take a while. First pregnancy and all."

Betty laughed. Norma had always thought she laughed something like a horse.

"I say a lot of things, Norma, but I'm not in charge. Wanda's not in charge, and even the doctors not so much. That little baby does what she wants and we all just revolve around her whims. But I *will* say, in regards to how completely our expectations were wrong . . . I believe she was much deeper into labor when she called than she was letting on."

"Got it," Norma said. "Give me a few minutes to do the last dishes and finish closing and then I'll come by."

———

When Norma stepped into the hospital room, Betty was sitting on the edge of Wanda's bed. She was leaning over the younger woman, holding her hand. Wanda's eyes were closed, her mouth wide open, slack. For one horrible moment Norma thought she might be dead.

"Hey," Betty said quietly when she noticed Norma.

The single word caused Wanda's eyes to flutter half-open, flooding Norma with relief.

The room was set up for four patients. But the dividing curtains were pulled back and pinned to the walls, and there was no one else there.

Well. There was one other person there.

She was in a hospital bassinet about a foot from the side of Wanda's bed. Norma moved in closer to get a better look.

She was asleep, her tiny eyelids twitching. Norma wondered if brand-new babies dreamed, and, if so, what about? It wasn't as though they had a single life experience to replay. Maybe reliving her own birth? Her eyelids were slightly translucent, showing the veins inside their ivory skin. Her little nostrils flared with her breath, like the world's tiniest horse.

It struck Norma that human bodies were astonishingly fragile. Well designed and miraculous, but not meant to accept violence or abuse. They required care.

"Isn't she pretty?" Wanda asked, her eyes drifting closed again.

The young woman's hair was hanging around her head in frizzy strands that had clearly absorbed a great deal of sweat throughout the evening.

"Pretty doesn't even say it, girl. She's beauty itself. She's a miracle is what she is."

"That's what *I* thought."

"Nice that they let her be in here. I thought she'd have to be in some kind of nursery with the other babies."

"There are no other babies tonight," Betty said. "And also the nurse wants to come in every hour or so and see if she can get them started breastfeeding. If she's awake, that is."

"Betty," Wanda said weakly. "Any chance you could go get me an orange soda from that vending machine?"

"The nurse'll bring you a drink if we ring for her."

"Sure, she'll bring me water. Or apple juice. But I really want an orange soda."

Betty pulled to her feet.

"Be right back," she said.

Norma took a load off her feet, settling down on the edge of Wanda's bed.

She looked at Wanda, who looked back. The young woman's eyes appeared bloodshot and so, so tired. But still Wanda managed to burn her gaze right into Norma's eyes.

"Now what do I do?" she asked. "Now that she's a girl?"

"What do you do about what? I thought you'd be relieved if it's a girl, seeing as you were worried if it was a boy. About history maybe repeating itself."

"But then I saw her, and she just looked so tiny and fragile and like someone I needed to protect . . . I looked at her and thought, History repeats itself with boys and girls both. A boy could grow up and abuse the person he loves and a girl might grow up and take that abuse from somebody. My dad smacked my mom around and then look at me. Following in her footsteps. It seems like it just keeps going from one generation to the next and I want to stop it, Norma. I want you to tell me how to stop it."

"Okay," Norma said. "I'll do my best. Here's what you do. You love that little girl like crazy. But you don't just love her. You tell her and show her how much you love her, both. You make sure she feels it. And you teach her to love herself and to treat herself well. People who treat themselves well expect others to treat them well, too. Self-abuse is just an open field for an abuser to walk right into. Help her value herself. Nothing is inevitable. People break those patterns all the time."

She looked up to see Betty step back into the room.

"Hey," Betty said. "Norma, can I have a word with you in the hall?"

Betty handed Wanda her cold can of soda, and Norma followed her out into the hall, her stomach feeling slightly twisted.

"Problem?"

"No, not really. Just . . . Wanda and I were thinking you might've wanted to take her to Southern California week after next for the trial. We're not clear what your thoughts were about that. But tonight we decided it might be best if I did, seeing as the baby'll have two weeks to get used to being around me and all. And I'll have to hold her and keep her happy and quiet while Wanda testifies. And we're just really, really hoping that's something you won't take personally."

Norma opened her mouth to ask why they couldn't both go.

Then she shut it again, remembering.

See, this is the problem with working shifts with your best friend. You can never do anything together.

"You okay, Norma?"

"Yeah, I'll be fine. I won't take it personally. It makes sense."

"Thanks, hon."

Betty stepped back into Wanda's room.

It did make sense. But it also made Norma feel a little left out. Like everybody formed bonds with everybody else and she was left on the outside every time. Then again, Norma hadn't wanted anyone living in her house with her, while Betty had welcomed the pregnant Wanda with open arms.

Still, that didn't do much to change the feeling.

See? she thought. *This is the problem with pushing everybody away all your life. Telling them to keep moving because you don't need or want anybody. Sooner or later people are going to take you at your word and give you what you say you want.*

She stuck her head into Wanda's hospital room once more before leaving, and Wanda met her gaze with a faint smile.

"I forgot to tell you, hon. I promised some guy in the pub tonight I'd give you a message. Well, just if I saw you. I didn't tell him I knew you or that I was going to see you or anything crazy like that. But he figured it was a small town and I guess word got around that you're back in Sloot. He said to tell you 'We're all pulling for her.' That everybody is on your side."

"Not everybody," Wanda said quietly. "There's a Team Jake."

"Sorry to hear it, but I guess that's inevitable. This world being what it is. But the vast majority of the world is on your side."

"That's something," Wanda said.

"Yeah. That's something."

"I'm naming her Elizabeth Norma Brooks," Wanda said. "I'm not giving her Jake's name. He can fight it all he wants but I'm not going to do it. She's mine and not his."

Norma made a mental note to talk to her about sole custody. Later, when she was not so tired.

"I think that's lovely," she said. "And I think you need to get some sleep now."

Chapter Twenty-Two

Anger Management

On the first day of the first trial, Norma carried her phone with her everywhere. Cell-phone service had improved at her house due to a new tower near the intersection of the interstate highways. She slid the phone out of her pocket every few minutes to make sure she hadn't missed a call. Twice she called it from her landline to make sure it was working.

She texted Betty, "Hey I thought you'd keep me posted."

After about an hour of no reply she texted, "Give me an update when you can, okay?"

She took a ride with Saint Fred, which she hadn't done in over three months, just to have something to do. As they ambled along the trail, she slipped her phone out of her pocket several times to check it.

Three-quarters of the way out Fred spooked big over a snake and nearly unseated her. She actually did come out of the saddle, but she still had one stirrup and a death grip on the horn, so she managed to haul herself back up, pulling multiple muscles, her heart drumming.

"See, maybe this is why I shouldn't ride at my age," she told the horse as they moved off down the trail together, settling. "Then again, it's what happens when you don't get a horse out enough. Even a good horse. Maybe I should be riding you more, not less."

She slipped her phone out again and texted, "Call me, okay?"

Then they rode for another hour or so, but Norma never managed to enjoy it, or take in much of the view.

"I guess I need to go one way or another," she told the horse on the way home, "riding-wise. I need to either ride you enough to keep you a good, dependable horse, or just say we're both retired."

Her phone rang, but it was only a junk call. It startled her, which startled the horse. But he only offered a muted reaction.

She declined the call and rode home.

———

It was after five when Betty finally called.

Norma had finished feeding the horse and the dogs, and had just decided to make herself breakfast for dinner.

"There you are," she said, picking up on the first ring.

"I'm sorry. I didn't know you were counting on me for news. I figured you'd be following a live blog or something."

"I don't even know what that is," Norma said.

She thought she heard Betty laugh on the other end of the line, but it might just have been a loud breath. Or a sigh.

She held the phone in the crook of her neck with her shoulder, put two slices of bread in the toaster and pushed down on the lever, and began breaking eggs. Through the kitchen window she could see Fred contentedly munching his hay. It was calming, as always.

"Today was less than exciting," Betty said into her ear. "Just jury selection."

"All day?"

"Yup. Jury selection takes forever, and they're not even quite done. The idea is supposed to be to find jurors who don't know about Jake or the case, and who don't already have a fixed opinion. But what kind of rock would that person have to have crawled out from under? Like, no such person exists in the country, right? In a case like this they have to mostly settle for people who know about it but haven't totally made up their minds. But people can say they haven't decided even if they have. It's not like they give every juror a lie-detector test or anything. And the defense attorney, well, he's all over that. He knows that's his worst enemy. So he's being super cautious."

"Speaking of the defense attorney," Norma said, beating the eggs. "Any idea what his defense would even be?"

She poured the eggs into a preheated pan, and they bubbled and sizzled.

"Funny you should mention that. We got a chance to talk to the prosecuting attorney today. He has some theories. He doesn't have any magic way of knowing, of course. There can always be surprises. But the evidence is just so slam dunk that he strangled her. There's really no way to get out from under that. He figures the defense is going to try to go for intent. Like, the intent was to assault but not murder. He figures they'll try to skate under the attempted-murder charge by saying Jake had every intention of stopping before she was dead. But even that's dicey for him, because the prosecution has medical witnesses. The ER doctor who treated Wanda is gonna testify that she was awful damn close to the line as it was. And the police took pictures of her neck that first night. The plan for fighting that defense is that even if he did mean to stop, he could have made a mistake with that. He was inches from making a fatal mistake. Anyway. We'll know more after opening arguments. I'll send you a link to one of the live blogs of the trial. Because they make us turn our phones off in court. That's why I didn't see your texts till the end of the day."

"Oh," Norma said. "Okay." She stirred the eggs in the pan and felt vaguely hurt that Betty wouldn't be personally feeding her news at regular intervals. "How's Little Betty doing with all this?"

"She *could not* be better. I only had to take her outside the court-room twice. What a good baby she is."

"You know . . . ," Norma began. She could feel the call drawing to a close, and wanted to keep it going. "When they convict him . . . I guess it's an 'if' and not a 'when,' but I just have to believe they'll convict him . . . don't you think she should file for sole custody? The fact that her baby's father is in jail for trying to murder her is a count in her favor, right?"

"We actually talked to an attorney about that already," Betty said.

"You did? You never told me that."

"I figured we'd wait and see how that panned out before making you the third person in our group to never get any sleep at night. He wasn't really all that encouraging."

Norma felt an odd tingling in her lower belly, and under her jaw.

"Wait. He doesn't think a judge would grant her custody?"

"Oh, he didn't say *that*, exactly. She can go to court for custody and probably win."

"Then what's the problem?"

"We just worry that after Jake gets out he can sue for shared custody and probably have a pretty good case. Especially if the attempted-murder charge doesn't stick and he goes down for simple assault. I think when a convicted person has done their time, the court is supposed to see them as rehabilitated. Unless they do something to prove otherwise. I think it's just how our justice system is set up."

"We don't have a justice system in this country," Norma said. She turned off the fire under her eggs so they wouldn't dry out. "We have a legal system."

"I'm not sure what that means," Betty said.

"It's something our local DA told me. I can't say for sure exactly what he was thinking when he said it, but I took it to mean it's more about following the letter of the rules laid down by the law and less about delivering common-sense fairness."

"Yeah," Betty said. "That's the part that has me losing sleep."

"You said you talked to an attorney. What did he say?"

"Oh, all kinds of things. I could barely keep up. I have notes some-where. The one thing he said that really scared me is that you can never really predict with one hundred percent certainty what a judge will do. But one thing that would help, speaking of our local DA, is if he could win that murder trial against Jake. If he'd been convicted of both attempted murder and murder, I don't figure he'll be able to get near that kid. Over my dead body, actually. I still have my late husband's shotgun, and I know how to use it. I'm good with it. I'll drop that son of a bitch on my front porch if he comes around."

"Betty . . ."

"What?"

"You can drop him with a shotgun if he breaks in and tries to hurt somebody. But you can't kill him for showing up on time for his court-ordered visit."

A long silence fell on the line.

"Well, anyway," Betty said. "We'll hope for good legal outcomes. Especially with that murder trial."

It stuck a little going down, like barely chewed food. Because Norma had been more and more tempted to stop that trial before it happened. Only with Jill's blessing, of course. But at any point they could speak the truth publicly instead of quietly and privately to the DA.

But now there was Little Betty to think about.

It felt something like being handcuffed. Like the innocent people involved in this mess were the ones wearing the handcuffs, not the attacker.

———

Jill called on Norma's cell at a little after 2:00 a.m.

Norma was just changing into pajamas, exhausted from tending bar on a busy night without her usual help.

"Hey," Norma said, and set the phone down on her pillow.

She clicked the call over to speaker, set her head next to it, and closed her eyes.

"Opening arguments tomorrow," Jill said.

"So I hear."

"I've been following it on a live blog."

"Then I guess it's official. Everybody on the planet knows what that is except me. I was hoping they'd put it on TV. It's big enough news."

"I guess the judge decided it was enough of a media circus even without the cameras."

"Yeah, that's what I heard too," Norma said.

For a moment, no one spoke. Norma almost slipped off to sleep. She was that tired.

"I've been thinking of just going public," Jill said.

"I've thought about it too. Not without your permission, of course."

"It would be hard on my parents is the thing. That's what's mostly holding me back. Might get them in trouble. Might get you in trouble."

"I'll fend for myself," Norma said.

"But another part of me . . . I don't know. I really want him in jail, Norma. Is that bad? Does that make me a bad person?"

"No, you're not a bad person. Anybody would feel that way. Instead of feeling all guilty about wanting that, maybe mostly want it for the baby's sake. Because Wanda is a lot more likely to get sole custody—and hang on to it—if he gets convicted of murder."

"You don't think he'd hurt the baby, do you?"

"No, I doubt that. Different emotional dynamic. I think he'd hurt Wanda by hanging on to some place in their lives. Control her by controlling custody of their daughter."

"Oh yeah," Jill said. "*That* he would definitely do."

Another long silence fell. How long, Norma didn't know. Because she briefly fell asleep.

"Norma?" she heard.

It popped her up into consciousness again.

"What? I'm here. I'm sorry. Must have drifted off for a second."

"I know it's late. I'll let you go. I just want to ask you one question and then I'll let you sleep. How come guys like Jake never go to anger management?"

"Oh, they go. Usually when a judge says they have to. It's the judges keeping those programs full."

"Right. Exactly. They get court-ordered to go. But they never just go. They never just decide to go because they're hurting someone. And I know it's just so easy to say they don't care. That they only care about themselves. But Jake loved me. It sounds weird to say now, after all this, but he did. I know it."

"I expect he did," Norma said.

"Why don't they go, then?"

"Because they want their anger. They don't want to let it go. It makes them feel powerful. It makes them feel safe."

For a moment, no reply.

Then Jill spoke, and it was clear from her voice that she was crying.

"I knew you'd know," she said.

"I don't know everything," Norma said.

"But you know a lot."

———

Over her morning coffee, Norma tried to find this thing called a live blog.

Betty had apparently forgotten her promise to send a link to one, which struck Norma as equal parts aggravating and understandable.

She spent the better part of half an hour and got exactly nowhere.

She was able to google the trial, but all that seemed to turn up were news articles that gave the background of the case in great detail, but not what was literally going on in the courtroom that very day.

In time she grew frustrated and decided to give Saint Fred's paddock and shelter a deep clean instead.

He hadn't finished his breakfast hay, so she tossed it over the fence and turned him out onto the larger property. Then she loaded up the wheelbarrow with a shovel, manure fork, and push broom, and wheeled it into his paddock. She parked it just outside his shelter and began to clean up the straw and shavings that sat on the rubber stall mats, forming the base of his sleeping area.

The horse did not go far, as he was interested in finishing the hay she had dumped just outside the fence.

Norma spoke to him as she worked, and he raised his head to look at her in between bites, as though he found it important to understand her message.

"It kills me not to know what's going on," she said.

The horse's jaw worked visibly with his chewing. Then he dipped his head again.

"The thing I love about you is that you're always in the moment. You're never all twisted up about something that's going on somewhere else, and you never seem worried about some problem that might or might not come up down the road. The dogs are like that too. You just live. Right now. People are always happy to give you an earful about how we're so superior to the animals, and why we are, and I think when I was young I used to buy it. I think most people just buy it automatically and never give it another thought. But we turn ourselves inside out trying to meditate for thirty seconds, and our mind just flies away. You've been meditating all your life. And if that doesn't make you better, then why are people always trying to do it?"

He looked into her face, still chewing, then sighed and dropped his head again.

She pulled her phone out of her pocket, but there were no messages or calls. Which made sense, since Betty had already told her they had to turn off their phones in court.

It would be all day.

She turned off the phone completely and stashed it back in her pocket.

"Remember when I told you I was grateful to you for being a horse and not a person?" she asked Saint Fred, and he offered her his attention in return. "Well, you should be grateful too. You should be grateful you're a horse. Because being a human is not all it's cracked up to be."

It would only take her another hour or so to scrub his stall mats, let them dry, and lay down fresh bedding. And an hour didn't feel like much to kill.

Then again, when she was done out here there was always the house.

———

Betty called around six.

Of course by then Norma had made sure her phone was back on. She had been in the process of picking up the food dishes to feed the dogs, and when she sat down to take the call they were disappointed, to say the least.

She picked up on the first ring.

"How'd it go?"

"I thought you were going to follow a live blog today," Betty said.

"I thought you were going to send me a link to one."

"Oh. Oops. Sorry about that. The baby was fussy and Wanda was freaking out and I forgot all about it."

"Did she testify?"

"She did."

"How did it go?"

"Oh, I don't know. It went how you'd expect it to go, I guess. She just got up there and told every detail of what happened. When the defense cross-examined her, you could kind of tell that the prosecuting attorney was right with what he told me. He just kept asking her how she could be so sure he would have killed her, and how anybody could possibly know such a thing. But she held up okay. Cried a lot, but there's no law against that."

Both hound dogs had their heads on Norma's lap as she listened, their tails thrashing the air.

"Wait," Norma told them.

"Okay," Betty said.

"No, not you. I was talking to the dogs. He takes the stand tomorrow?"

"No. That's what's weird about the whole thing, Norma. The defense rested today. And he never took the stand."

"Wait."

"Who, me or the dogs?"

"You this time. Both the prosecution and defense rested."

"Right."

"Just that fast."

"Well, I think it's possible," Betty said, "that in the great scheme of things . . . you know, as trials go . . . one day of arguments might be on the short side. But when you're sitting there in court for seven hours listening to all the details of the thing being hashed out, it seems long enough. Especially with a cut-and-dried case like this one."

"And he never took the stand in his own defense. That seems odd. Does he have a lousy lawyer or something? Is this one of those court-appointed attorneys who shows up drunk or falls asleep in the middle of arguments or stuff like that?"

"Hardly. His mommy and daddy bought him this legal team, and from what I'm hearing, they're not the type that come cheap."

"Hmm," Norma said. "That can only mean one thing, right?"

"I figure it means his lawyers knew he'd hurt himself more than he'd help the case."

"That's what I'm thinking too, yeah. So when's jury deliberation?"

"Closing arguments first."

"Oh. Right. I forgot that. Send me the link to that blog thing this time, okay?"

"I will. I promise. I gotta go. The baby's crying and Wanda is losing what's left of her sanity."

"Okay, thanks for calling. Bye."

Norma ended the call and just sat a moment, feeling the breeze from the dogs' swishing tails. After waiting all day, that was all the news she was going to get. It left her feeling strangely hollow inside.

She sighed, set down the phone, got up, and fed her hounds.

Chapter Twenty-Three

Farley Says Hi

In the morning, there was a link to a live blog in a text Betty had sent to her phone.

It was too early to read anything about that day's closing arguments. Court had not even been gaveled into session for the morning. Norma read up on the events of the previous day instead.

It was slow, and detailed, and less than fascinating, just as Betty had suggested. And that was just the summary.

The only thing that really jumped out to Norma was the extent to which Wanda had fallen apart on the stand. Betty had told her Wanda cried quite a bit, but this was a much more vivid and detailed description.

According to the author of the live blog, who was some kind of legal expert, Wanda sobbed until she choked. Her words were barely intelligible. But when she could be understood, she told the jury she had fallen more deeply in love with her baby daughter than she even knew was possible, and that the worst part of knowing Jake could come back to finish the job was the idea of her daughter being hurt in the process, and/or growing up an orphan. She'd made it clear that her concern was for the baby far more than for herself.

It also seemed, from the blog summary, that the defense attorney stepped over the line quite a bit when cross-examining her. There were many objections, mostly along the lines of badgering the witness.

They were all sustained by the judge.

This is the problem with buying your son a pit bull lawyer, Norma thought. *Sometimes a little bullying can get you somewhere, even though it shouldn't. But too much bullying will come back around on you and bite you on the ass.*

At least, she certainly hoped it would.

———

The trial was partway through the second closing argument—the defense's closing argument—when Norma's cell phone rang.

She half expected it to be Betty. She shouldn't have, because Betty was in court, and had to keep her phone turned off. Still that was her first thought.

The little pop-up window said it was an unknown caller, but from her own area code.

She picked up anyway, figuring there was maybe a fifty-fifty chance it was a junk call disguised to look local.

"What?" she said, mostly wanting to get back to the trial blog.

"Hey, Norma," a mousy voice said. "It's Veronica."

Norma didn't think she knew anyone named Veronica, so she offered no response.

"The new day person at the pub," the shy voice said.

"Oh right. Veronica. What's up?"

"My two-year-old daughter is spiking a fever. Almost a hundred and four. I usually leave her with my grandmother when I work, but she doesn't drive anymore."

"You're hoping I'll take your shift."

"Would you? It's only four hours. Four o'clock to eight. It would have you working twelve hours straight today, though."

Norma sighed.

"You take care of your daughter," she said. "I expect I'll survive. I could use the money anyway."

While Veronica gushed her thanks, Norma realized—but did not say—that it really wasn't about the money. Or hardly about it, anyway. She needed something to do with her time. With her brain. Constantly refreshing the live blog, even though it refreshed automatically when there was an update, had been putting a strain on her nerves. She felt as though she was trying to push the news, the outcome, with the sheer force of her mind.

It was exhausting. It was driving her into a very dark state.

—

A crowd was waiting at the pub at four. Just hanging around in the parking lot, looking dirt smudged and tired, and as if they wished someone would come unlock the door.

It wasn't entirely surprising.

In the land of hikers and rock climbers, the end of the day had to beat the sun by a comfortable margin, and no one seemed inclined to glance at their watch before seeking out a cold beer or three.

Norma parked her truck near the back door and checked the live blog on her phone.

The jury had begun deliberations several minutes earlier.

She was suddenly overwhelmingly relieved that she had agreed to work. They might be in deliberations for an hour or a week—more likely days—and the distraction would keep her sane.

Norma let herself in through the kitchen and then opened the front door from inside.

The crew came spilling in. Maybe twenty of them, all told.

She began setting up behind the bar, and a young woman came and sat in front of her, waiting.

"You all one group?" Norma asked.

"Yeah. We're a team. We were climbing a route at Escalante."

She was maybe in her late twenties, with a thick, dark ponytail of hair thrown forward over her shoulder. She wore a sleeveless strappy tank top that exposed long, sinewy arms smeared with dirt. She smelled like pungent sweat. But then, most of the customers did.

"What can I get for you?"

"I guess we'll start with four pitchers. But expect that to go fast."

"I can bring them to your table."

"Nah, that's okay. You're here by yourself. And we're a handful." She allowed a quick silence to fall while Norma poured the first half of the first pitcher. "You following the trial?"

"Closer than is probably good for me."

"I figured. Since it all kind of started here in Sloot."

"Jury's in deliberations."

"I was just about to tell you the same thing."

"It's late in the afternoon. Maybe an hour earlier in SoCal. I can never remember. Are they on daylight savings there right now?"

"Don't know," the young woman said. "We're from Colorado."

"You're from Colorado and you come here to climb?"

"Gotta mix it up now and then. Besides, we don't have red rock in our little part of the state."

"Well, anyway," Norma said, "my point is . . . we probably won't know today." She finished pouring the pitchers in silence and placed them on a tray. "You sure you can handle these?"

"If I can handle the route we climbed today, I can handle anything."

She held out a credit card, but Norma waved it away.

"I'll run you a tab till you're ready to pack up and move on."

The young woman picked up the tray. It seemed to take her a minute to get the hang of the balance, but once she'd steadied herself, Norma was willing to believe she was up to the task.

"Speaking of not knowing today," the woman said, "what really kills me is how they do the sentencing phase later. Like, sometimes weeks later. Provided the jury sees the guy is guilty, and I don't see how they can miss it, that's really what you want to know, am I right? It's all about how much time they give him. That's what everybody's hanging on, waiting to find out."

"Yeah," Norma said. "That part kills me too."

—

It was roughly an hour later when the woman shouted it out. Norma didn't know how much time had gone by, because she was quite purposely refusing to look at her phone.

It was the same young woman who had carried all five rounds of four pitchers each from the bar to their tables. She was looking at her phone, and suddenly blurted out a pronouncement at a volume that not only overshadowed the din of voices in the room, but stopped it cold.

"Guilty on both counts!" she crowed.

"You're kidding," Norma called over. "So soon?"

"An hour and five minutes of deliberation," she called back. "I guess when you know, you just know."

"Do we know when the sentencing hearing is scheduled for?"

"Not yet. But I'll keep refreshing."

Norma wanted to tell her that those live blogs refresh themselves. She didn't, because she understood the urge all too well.

—

Betty called on Norma's cell phone six minutes later.

"Guilty on both counts," she said in place of hello.

"That's what I'm hearing."

"Where are you? Who are all those people in the background? Are you at work?"

"Yeah, I took over a shift for Veronica."

"Who?"

"The new afternoon person. Her kid is sick."

"Oh, her. Right. You're going to be fried come two a.m., my friend."

"I'll live. Do we know when the sentencing hearing is?"

"Two weeks from tomorrow."

"But you two aren't going all the way back to Southern California for that, are you?"

"No, we've got an in. We met a lady here. Teresa is her name. The dead girl's mother. She's coming to the sentencing. She lives near here. She promised to text us the minute there's news."

Norma opened her mouth to say "Yes, of course. Teresa Moss. I know Teresa Moss." Then she realized that, in the eyes of the world, she did not know Teresa Moss. She closed her mouth and said nothing.

"He could get as much as nine years," Betty said.

"Which still makes Little Betty a minor child when he gets out."

"I know. Believe me, I know. It's all Wanda and I have been talking about. But at least we get to find out before the second trial. The murder trial. The conventional wisdom seems to be that if the judge goes light on the sentence in this case, there'll be a chance to make up for it after the murder trial. At least, that's what I've picked up hanging around the courthouse for a few days."

"But that's only if they get a conviction. It's not so easy to get a conviction without a body."

"Norma, please," Betty said. "We have to hope for *something*."

"Sorry."

The knowledge washed over Norma, yet again, that her recurring urge to come clean about Jill was likely not an option. Her hands were tied. Or, at very least, it was an option with a high price tag. Which might have been okay if she'd been the one who would have to pay it.

"Oh, I almost forgot," Betty said. "I met someone here who knows you. He said to say hi. Farley something is his name."

"I don't know anybody named Farley."

"Well, he knows you. He said he was in Sloot not two weeks ago, sitting talking to you at the bar."

"Oh, right. I think I know who that is. Big guy?"

"That's the one."

"He's the guy who picked up Jake Willis in the bar that night and nearly snapped him like a twig throwing him down on a table."

"I remember that happening," Betty said. "I don't remember anything about the guy who did the throwing. He doesn't seem like the type. He seems more like the gentle-giant sort."

"He swore to me he's not a violent man, but I guess anyone can be if the circumstances line up just right. We figure he went all the way down there for the trial? He must be really obsessed with this case."

"Everybody is," Betty said. "But I have no idea why."

"Well, I hope you're not looking to me to sort it out. Because I've got nothing."

Chapter Twenty-Four

All That Pretending

The night before the sentencing hearing, Norma didn't sleep at all. Literally. Not one minute, as far as she could tell.

She stayed in bed as though she were sleeping, eyes closed. Willing herself to sleep. Knowing she had to work the next day, which increased the stress of the insomnia, which created more insomnia.

At about eight in the morning she gave up, got out of bed, and fed the dogs and the horse. Her stomach felt rocky from exhaustion and her eyes felt as though she had rubbed sand into them.

She made herself scrambled eggs and toast, but no coffee.

When she was done eating she pulled the curtains closed in her bedroom, went back to bed, and tried to transition straight into a nap.

At first it didn't go any better than the night had.

Then her phone rang, and it blasted her up out of sleep—a sleep she hadn't felt herself fall into in the first place.

She glanced at the bedside clock as she picked up her phone. It was nearly eleven thirty.

It was Teresa Moss calling. Because she still had Teresa in her contacts, the initials O and T read out clearly on Norma's phone.

She touched a button on the screen to accept the call.

"Hey," she said.

"Did I wake you?" Teresa asked.

"I didn't sleep last night, so I was trying to nap. But it's okay. What's happening?"

"They gave him sixty-four months."

Norma's brain, which was still partly asleep, twisted uncomfortably as she attempted math in her head.

"Five years and four months?"

"That's right."

For a moment, neither of them spoke.

Norma lay on her back in the dim room, watching the way the world appeared vaguely light only at the edges of her curtains. Watching the way the hound dogs slept on the floor, their heads on each other's backs like one of those yin-yang symbols. Trying to absorb what five years and four months meant in the real world. And how she felt about it.

"Is it okay that I called you?" Teresa asked in time. "Cassie said it would probably be okay now."

"Yeah, I'm sure it's fine. What do you think? About the five years and four months, I mean."

"I'm not sure what to think. It could have been better. I also suppose it could have been worse. I just keep thinking about that sweet little baby girl. She'll be five when he gets out and comes after her mother again. Unless they manage to win that murder trial, which is dicey with no body."

"You worry about the baby more than your own daughter?"

"The baby is easier to find."

Another silence fell.

Again, Teresa was the one to break it.

"I promised Betty I'd text her as soon as I knew. She's your friend, right? I'm going to do that now. But I just had to call you first. Because I know you. But of course I didn't tell her I knew you."

"Thanks for that."

"You'll probably hear it from *her* in a minute, and you'll have to pretend you're hearing it for the first time."

"I do a lot of pretending these last few years," Norma said. Then, against her better judgment, she added, "It's how you know you took a wrong turn somewhere."

Norma thought she heard a sigh on the other end of the line.

"I know you feel that way," Teresa said, "but I still want to thank you for not going to the DA and telling him she's alive."

"But I did go to the DA. And I did tell him she's alive. Didn't your daughter tell you that?"

"She . . . did not."

A pause, which Norma allowed. She figured the other woman had thinking to do.

"Then why is there about to be a murder trial?" Teresa asked.

"Because he didn't want to listen."

"He hates Jake as much as I do?"

"I don't know. I'm not inside his head. But it seems to be something like that, yeah."

"Then I guess I should thank you for not going straight to a newspaper or the TV news or something."

"I've thought about it. She's thought about it. I think at this point it's mostly that baby girl holding us back."

For what felt like an awkward moment, even by the standards already set in the conversation, nothing more was said.

"I'm going to text your friend now. Thanks for everything."

"You talk like we'll never see each other again."

"Will we?"

"Don't you have to come testify in his trial?"

"Oh, you'll be there?"

"I wouldn't miss it. It's only about thirty-five minutes from my house. Of course, we'll have to pretend we're only just meeting."

"But then from that point on we can admit that we know each other. Because we met at the murder trial."

"That's true," Norma said.

"Then you're right. This is not goodbye. More like . . . almost a beginning. I just hit send on that text. Hang up the phone now. Your friend is about to call you."

Norma hung up the phone.

She climbed out of bed. Stretched. Slid her feet into slippers. Clumsily, the way a person does after not nearly enough sleep. She pulled on her robe and dropped the phone into one of its big pockets.

She stumbled into the kitchen to make a pot of coffee.

Norma was counting in her head. Counting the seconds until the phone rang again. She was surprised when she got to fifty. Then again, Betty had to tell Wanda the news first. It was nobody's business more than it was Wanda's. Nobody was ahead of her in line.

Or, at least, nobody *should have* been.

On the number seventy-two, the phone rang.

"Hey, Betty," she said, clicking into the call.

"Sixty-four months," Betty said.

"Okay. That's . . ."

"Not enough. Okay, well . . . it's five years and four months. Which is not enough."

"But there's this next trial."

"And it better go just the way we want it to go. Because five years, Norma. This innocent little baby'll just be going into kindergarten. And that's if they don't parole him early or give him time off for good behavior or whatever other crap they might have up their sleeves."

Norma had already filled the coffee maker with water and grounds while she counted. She plugged it in and hit "brew."

"Not much we can do but wait," she said into the phone.

Wait . . . and keep her mouth shut about the minor detail that Jill Moss was not dead. How much of a traitor would she be if she came

232

clean now? How would she feel if something happened to Wanda, or that child? And of course if anything happened to Wanda it happened to the child as well.

Handcuffs. For the innocent parties.

"I'm scared," Betty said.

"I hear you."

"Wanda is just beside herself."

"I can imagine."

"You're going to that trial, right?"

"Try to keep me away," Norma said.

Chapter Twenty-Five

But Jake Willis Is

"This is the first time I've ever seen you nervous," Betty said.

It was two weeks later—the two weeks they had all been so anxious to see pass—and they were sitting on a hard wooden bench in the courtroom, waiting. And waiting. And waiting. Wanda was sitting on the other side of Norma, swinging the baby back and forth to keep her from fussing.

"It's not the first time," Norma said. "I get nervous plenty, just like everybody else."

"Well, it's the first time I could ever see it on you."

"Okay, I'll buy *that*."

"I know why the trial's not starting," Betty said. "It's because the defendant isn't here. But *why* isn't he here? They're bringing him over from a jail. It's not like he's home and might've slept through his alarm or something. You think it's normal for things to run late like this?"

"I have no idea," Norma said. She turned her head to the right to address Wanda. "You have any idea if this is normal?"

"I'm not an expert on trials," Wanda said. "Fortunately."

"I'm going to go ask the DA," Betty said.

The DA had wandered in on time, about twenty-five minutes earlier. He had come down the aisle, locked eyes with Norma, then looked away again. It had seemed to Norma that they both took great pains to keep their eyes blank.

Now he stood at his table in front of the court, his back to them, jacket off and draped on the back of the chair. At the moment he was shuffling through some paperwork.

Betty trotted up to the front of the room—at least as far as she could go and still be in the area that was not off-limits to observers—and tapped him on the shoulder.

They leaned together and spoke for a few seconds.

Then Betty came back.

It flitted through Norma's mind—along with a jolt down through her midsection—that Jake Willis could have escaped somehow. Maybe taken advantage of the transport from prison to court. She put the thought away again, not because it was completely impossible for it to be true but because she didn't want it to be.

Betty slid back in on her left and sat.

"He says with this judge you can set your watch by the start of proceedings."

"Then everybody's watch is going to be running slow today."

They sat without talking for several minutes. Norma was trying not to jiggle her leg in that obsessive way people do. Normally she didn't, without having to try to control anything, but today was hardly normal.

Owen and Teresa Moss were there in court, sitting on the other side of the aisle and a few rows in front of them. They had met eyes with each other once, and it had been much the same experience as with the DA.

Smile blandly, the way one does with a stranger. Show no reaction.

Betty seemed to notice where Norma kept looking.

"That's Teresa Moss," she said.

"Right."

"Oh, you knew that?"

"I saw them on TV," she said.

"Oh, yeah. Sure. I guess everybody in the world knows what she looks like by now. She's the one who took my number and texted me after the sentencing hearing. And that's her husband. I forget his name."

"Owen," Norma said. Then, before her friend could question the knowledge, she said, again, "I saw them on TV."

"Right, right."

"I'm going to go over and introduce myself."

Norma rose, and waited a few seconds for Betty to move and give her access to the aisle. Then she walked up to where the couple sat.

When they saw Norma standing over them, they both rose.

"I hope you don't mind," Norma said. "I just wanted to introduce myself to you. Norma Gallagher."

She reached out her hand to each of them in turn, and they both shook it.

"I live near here in Sloot. I'm on the volunteer search and rescue team for the area. Or at least I used to be. I used to ride my horse with the team all the time, but we're both getting older now. I think we're semiretired. If they ever really needed another hand I might step in, but mostly they get by without me. But I was riding search those first days when we were looking for your daughter. I'm awful damn sorry I didn't find her."

There were people everywhere. Behind them. In front of them. Not many people were talking, so it was a safe bet that every word they said to each other was being overheard by many.

"I hope you're not blaming yourself," Teresa said.

"Not really. Just wishing I could have returned better news."

"Yeah," Owen said. "That makes three of us. But it was nice of you to come over and introduce yourself."

"You seem like a nice woman," Teresa said. "I realize we just met and all. But can I have your phone number? Would that be okay?

Maybe I could give you a call sometime. We could talk. Maybe we could even be friends."

"I'd like that," Norma said.

She took Teresa's phone when it was offered to her. It was still turned on, with Norma's contact pulled up on the screen. Maybe Teresa had been waiting for the proceedings to finally, finally begin before turning it off. Or maybe she tended to flout the rules.

Norma added her home landline to the contact, because her cell phone was already there. She changed the name of her contact from the cryptic "Lady" to "Norma Gallagher."

"It was nice meeting you," she said.

"You too," Teresa and Owen said at almost exactly the same time.

"Now we know each other," Norma said.

"Yes," Teresa said. "Now we do."

Norma walked back to sit by her friends. Betty slid in to give Norma the seat on the aisle.

"They seem nice," Norma said.

"You gave her your phone number," Betty said.

"I did."

"That's nice. You thinking of keeping in touch?"

"Maybe so. Yeah."

Norma had planned to say more. Instead she noticed that a bailiff was leaning in and having a quiet conversation with the DA. When their heads came apart again, the DA grabbed his jacket and put it back on. He began hurriedly gathering up his papers.

The bailiff took a position in the front of the courtroom, not far from the judge's bench, and addressed the crowd.

"Excuse me. Can I get everyone's attention, please?"

The room fell deadly silent.

"You all need to go home," he said. "There's not going to be any trial today."

Owen Moss leaped to his feet.

"What? *Why?*"

"I'm sorry," the bailiff said. "I don't have any other information I can share with you at this time."

Norma saw the DA hurrying down the aisle, and she took off after him. She chased him out into the hallway.

"Hey!" she shouted. "Hey!"

"Walk and talk," he said over his shoulder.

Norma ran to keep up with him, barely succeeding, until he pushed through an outer door. They stepped out into the bright, warm sun of the parking lot.

That was when Norma lost it.

"Wait!" she shouted. Really shouted.

He stopped.

"Will you please stop running away from me when I'm trying to talk to you?"

"I'm a busy man."

"Except this morning I figure you're not, because you thought you were in trial all day. And now, suddenly, not so much. Your day just freed up and I think you have a minute to tell me what's going on."

"I'm not sure I'm at liberty to say."

"Seems to me we've already told each other all kinds of things we might not be at liberty to say. There's a precedent there."

The man sighed deeply but held still. He did not seem inclined to speak.

Norma's gut had filled with a deep dread, thinking he was about to tell her Jake Willis really was on the loose.

And he seemed to be in no hurry to explain.

"Why is there no trial today?"

"Because the defendant has been shot."

"Shot?"

"Yes ma'am. Shot."

"Who shot him?" She heard herself ask the question even as it seemed too unreal to address.

"That I don't know. Someone in the crowd when they were bringing him from the van into the courthouse. I believe the police have someone in custody as the shooter. But I don't know much more than that."

"Is he okay?"

"I have no idea. He's on his way to the hospital. That's most of what I know."

Norma thought that was an interesting way to phrase the thing. "Most of what I know." As though he felt compelled to admit that he was withholding information. But she couldn't think about it long. Her mind felt as though it was running in circles, and she had so many questions spinning around in there. She honestly didn't know which one would pop out first.

"Don't they usually bring the person in through a back way in a big case like this one? Just for that reason?"

"Often they do, yes. I guess in this case they didn't."

"Did they at least put a bulletproof vest on him?"

"I have no idea, ma'am."

"Well, it's not that hard to figure out, is it? If he's in critical condition, they probably didn't. If the bullet pretty much bounced right off him again, they probably did."

For a few beats, they both just stood there in the sun. The man seemed to be staring into her face now, but she had no idea what he was hoping to find there.

"Jake Willis was shot between the eyes," he said.

It took Norma a few seconds to digest that visual before speaking.

"Well then, that pretty much answers the question of whether he's okay, doesn't it? It's not too likely that he's okay."

"I would say the chances that he's okay are quite slim."

"We never heard a shot."

"The entrance is pretty far from the courtroom."

"But here's what's even more important," Norma said, realizing it and speaking it at the same time. "We would have heard a siren. And there was no siren."

"I assure you this happened," the DA said. "I would have no reason to make a thing like this up."

"I'm not suggesting it didn't happen. I'm saying when a person is injured and bleeding out, but there's still some chance he could survive, you call an ambulance, and it shows up with sirens blaring. And then after they load him up, they would drive off with sirens blaring. Because they're in a hurry. Because the guy might still make it."

"Yeah," the DA said. "I guess I see your point about that. Look. I should get back to my office. And you should go home and turn on the news. I'm sure the details you want to hear will hit the airwaves soon enough."

He turned and walked away.

Norma turned back to the courthouse and walked inside to find her friends, so she could tell them. She did it as though sleepwalking, her mind muddy and her body tingly and partly numb. But she did it.

When she swung the door open into the dim corridor, they were all there. Everybody in the building who was known to her. Betty. Wanda with the baby. The Mosses.

"Did you catch him?" Betty asked. "What did he tell you? Anything?"

"Somebody shot him."

"Somebody shot the DA?"

"No, not *that* him. Jake. They were bringing Jake in for the trial. And somewhere between the van and the entrance, somebody in the crowd shot him between the eyes."

They all stood a moment without speaking.

"Is he alive?" Wanda asked.

"That's not confirmed yet," Norma said. "But you'll notice the ambulance didn't run their siren taking him away. I don't know if that absolutely, positively proves he's not alive. But I'm thinking nobody likes his chances at this point."

"Oh thank God," Teresa said.

It came out all at once, on a rush of air. As though she'd been holding it in under pressure and then lost control of it.

Norma's eyes had begun to adjust to the dim light, and she saw shame on Teresa's face.

"I'm sorry," Teresa said. "I guess I shouldn't have said that. We should never be happy when somebody dies. But . . . the thing is . . . I'm not saying I'm not. Happy, I mean. I really do feel that way. I just know I shouldn't."

"After all this," Norma said, "I think you get to feel any way you damn well please."

Chapter Twenty-Six

What to Feel If You're Not a Baby

Norma sat in her truck in the courthouse parking lot, not starting the engine. Not moving. The sun beat down on the windshield and the roof of the cab, and after a minute or two she turned the key to "accessory" and powered the windows down.

Then she picked up her phone off the truck's seat and called Jill.

"Norma," Jill said, her voice sounding agitated and desperate. "He's dead. Did you know?"

"I was just calling to see if *you* knew," Norma said.

"I'm following it online."

"I was sitting in the courtroom. But we never heard any shots. And there was no siren, so that was a clue that he was dead, but we didn't know for a fact that he was. They wouldn't tell us much. But I cornered the district attorney and he told me Jake took the bullet between the eyes. That says a lot."

"I read that he was killed instantly. And that's not an internet rumor. That's the Associated Press."

"I guess that's what happened, then."

"I don't know what to feel about it, Norma."

"I can't tell you what to feel."

"You can tell me what *you* feel."

"Can I? I'm not even sure I know."

A group of nine or ten people passed behind the truck chattering excitedly, and, because her windows were down, Norma waited before saying more.

When they had moved sufficiently away, she said, "I'd be lying if I said I wasn't relieved. But that's not the whole story. It's still not right. Nobody should've taken the situation into their own hands like that. It shouldn't have ended that way. What he did was bad, but it wasn't death-penalty bad."

"Could have been," Jill said. "If nobody had stopped and broken out that car window and pulled him off her, she'd probably be dead. And he might have gotten the death penalty for it. But I know what you'll say. You'll say 'But someone *did* stop and break out the window, and he *didn't* kill her.' I know you by now."

Norma pulled in a long, deep breath. Possibly the biggest she'd taken since all this began more than five years earlier. She released it as a noisy sigh.

"Maybe I need to lighten up," she said. "Maybe he got the death penalty in a much higher justice system, and maybe I should just leave all the judgments alone."

"Wow. Norma changing?"

"I'm not such an old dog that I can't learn a new trick. So, listen. I need to get going. Everybody is headed over to my house. Betty and Wanda and the baby and even your parents. I don't exactly remember why, but that's the plan we landed on."

"Wait. My parents?"

"Yeah, we officially all know each other now, because we introduced ourselves in court. Now that's out in the open."

"Oh. Right. Of course."

"When they go again, I'll give you another call. Later today or maybe tomorrow if the day gets away from me. We'll both know better what we're feeling by then. But in the meantime, don't be too hard on yourself over what to feel. If it makes you happy, then feel happy. There's no law against feelings."

At first, Norma heard only silence on the line.

Then Jill said, "I used to love him."

"Well, there's no law against feeling that either."

"I'm happy for Wanda. And that baby."

"Yeah, me too."

"This may sound strange . . ."

"Today? After everything that's happened? I doubt it. Why not just go ahead and spit it out?"

"I'd like to meet them."

"Wanda and Little Betty?"

"Right."

"We'd have to let them in on the big secret."

"It's not as big a secret as it used to be."

"I don't mind asking her how she feels about it."

"Maybe it was just as well that we didn't blow this whole thing wide open to save him from a murder trial. Since he was never going to make it to that trial."

"Unless that's why someone shot him. Because they figured he was guilty of a murder he might never pay for."

That just sat on the line in silence for an awkward length of time.

"I'm sorry, never mind," Norma said. "I shouldn't even have brought that up. I was just thinking out loud. Don't take it on. We'll never know why people do what they do. Probably this shooter did lots of bad things that had nothing to do with you, so I think we're making a mistake to fall into guilt over it. Besides, if that was the case, then a person would've waited to see if Jake was going to pay a price for that murder in court."

Still, after they'd said their goodbyes and ended the call, Norma couldn't help thinking, *See? I told you there would be unintended consequences that we'd never in a million years see coming.*

—

When Norma arrived home, her guests were already inside the house.

The Mosses were sitting on her love seat, and Betty and Wanda sat on the couch with the baby propped in between them. The hound dogs were sniffing the baby's face, which made her laugh.

For just a split second, Norma envied Little Betty, and wished she were a baby. Nobody had to tell Little Betty what to feel.

Dog noses are funny. Simple.

"I hope this is okay," Wanda said. "I still knew where the spare key was."

"It's fine. Whatever." It was and it wasn't, but it just was not important enough to take on in that moment. "Help me get some cold drinks for all these people."

Betty pulled the baby closer to her side, and Wanda followed Norma into the kitchen.

"How're you feeling?" she asked over her shoulder.

"Free."

"That's understandable."

"It's like I forgot how it feels not to be afraid. For five years I was afraid and I didn't even know it. Well. I knew I was afraid when something set him off. But I didn't know I was afraid all the time. It's like . . . when you feel something every minute of every day for long enough, you don't even know you're feeling it after a while. It's just what *is*. And so now I'm not afraid and I totally forgot how that even feels."

"Yup," Norma said. "That's how it goes, all right."

"But also . . ."

Norma waited, but Wanda didn't go on.

Norma opened the refrigerator and pulled out two kinds of juice, and bottled water. She opened a cupboard and brought down a glass pitcher that she filled with ice from the freezer door.

Wanda still had not finished the thought, so Norma took a shot at finishing it for her.

"But also you loved him, whether he ultimately deserved it or not, and he was the father of your baby."

"Right. I think I *shouldn't* feel that, but I do. But also the other thing, about how nice it is not being afraid."

"Yeah, life has a way of hitting you with two things at once like that."

They gathered up the water and juice and ice and carried them out to the coffee table between the guests. Betty and Owen seemed to be having a spirited conversation, but Norma didn't really click into the content of it, because she turned right around and stepped back into the kitchen for glasses.

When she got back, she heard Owen say, "I just don't see what the problem is. I mean, good riddance. Right?"

And Betty said, "You can't be advocating for shooting a person between the eyes."

"*I* wouldn't do it," Owen said. "I've thought about it, I won't lie. But mostly I wasn't willing to be ripped away from my wife to do all that time in jail. That felt like just another harm for him to do to my family. But if some guy in the crowd wants to do it, I don't see the problem. If anybody deserved it, it was Jake."

"*I* see the problem," Norma said, plunking into her big recliner. "The problem is, some random guy with a gun is getting to decide who deserves to die. Let's just say, for the sake of conversation, that this guy was right. Assuming it was a guy. How long is it going to be before a guy with a gun decides some other person deserves to die, but he's wrong? How can you put that kind of power in people's hands? Hell, I'm not even a fan of the state doing that."

"You don't believe in the death penalty?" Teresa asked.

"I'm not a big fan of it, no. I'd be happier with life in prison, no possibility of parole."

"Even for a guy like Jake," Owen said. He didn't make it sound like a question. He'd decided. "A man who would have killed this beautiful young woman and the daughter growing inside her if some passing motorist hadn't intervened just exactly when he did and not a minute later. Even for a really bad guy like that."

"Jake was a really bad guy," Norma said. "We agree on that. But that's the thing. That's my problem with the whole thing. Aren't we supposed to be better? I'm just thinking *he's* supposed to be the bad guy and *we're* supposed to be better."

Owen seemed more agitated now. He pulled his body forward until he was perched at the very edge of the love seat and leaned in to the conversation.

"But we *are* better," he said, his voice hard and strong. "We are. Because he was going to kill somebody innocent. Somebody who'd done nothing to deserve it. We're talking about killing a potential killer."

"Okay," Norma said. "Except . . . I think we're supposed to be *much* better. And I'm sorry if that offends you, but it's the way I feel. Having said that, I never want to celebrate that somebody's dead, but I can't honestly say I think the world is poorer without him."

"I'll drink to that," Owen said.

And with that, attention turned to the refreshments. Ice clinked into glasses, and juice and water were poured.

Betty was looking at her phone. Scrolling. She was the one to break the silence.

"It *was* a guy," she said.

"The shooter?" Norma asked.

"Right. It says here they have a forty-two-year-old man in custody. And . . . oh, crap."

For a strange length of time she said no more.

"What?" Norma asked. "What does it say?"

"It has the suspect's name. Farley McMaster."

For an oddly stretched moment, no one spoke. No one else but Norma knew why the name would matter. Norma knew why it mattered, but, for a few seconds, she did not know what to say.

"I assume," Norma said, "what with Farley being an unusual name and all, that McMaster was the 'something.' You know. When you told me his name was Farley something."

"Yeah," Betty said. "Now that I hear it . . . that was definitely the 'something.'"

———

Norma stepped outside to stretch her legs and get some air. Or so she said. It was maybe half an hour later, and she was already wishing her house weren't so full of people. She was already needing to listen to some silence for a change.

She took her phone with her, because she intended to call Jill.

Instead she bumped into Wanda by the horse corral.

She had known Wanda was out of the house. Wanda had announced several minutes earlier that she was going for a walk. Norma just hadn't known that the walk would be out to see Saint Fred and no farther.

She slipped her phone back into her pocket and joined the younger woman at the fence, leaning her elbows on the top rail.

Wanda was stroking the horse's long face, and didn't stop when she realized Norma was there.

"Do you know that guy?" she asked. "It sounded like you know him."

"Not *know* exactly. He was in the pub a couple of times. That I know of. He's the guy who picked Jake up and threw him down on a table. And a couple weeks before the first trial he was sitting at the bar talking to me about the case. He's also the guy who sent you that message about how everybody's on your side."

"Why do people get so wrapped up in this case?"

"Honey, that is a question for the ages."

They stood in silence for a minute or two. Saint Fred moved his face over and bumped Norma's elbow with his soft nose, and she petted it. Then he turned his attention back to Wanda.

"He knows we're upset," Wanda said.

"Yeah, horses are good at that."

"He misses the search and rescue thing. I know it sounds weird to say that. It's not like he told me so in regular English words or anything. But I could just tell. I could feel it."

"We're both getting older," Norma said. "But maybe we'll do a day's ride next time somebody goes missing. For old times' sake."

"Why did he do it?"

"Whoa. Jumping topics."

"Yeah. Sorry."

"Why did who do what? That Farley guy?"

"Right. He brought a gun to the trial and just . . . took Jake down. He must have planned it. Now he'll be in jail for years. There's no way he didn't see that coming. Right? He just gave up a bunch of his life to change the way this whole thing went down. But why, Norma? Why would somebody do that?"

"All I can do is tell you what he told me. He said your kid deserves better than Jake Willis coming after you guys and trying to be a father. He said both you and the baby deserve a life without having to worry about Jake. But I can't tell you if that's the real story behind what he did, or if it's the whole story. If you want, we could ask him."

"How could we do that?"

"He'll be in a jail somewhere. Likely not so hard to find. But right now I should get back in and be with the company."

At the moment she said it, Norma thought she'd still slip away and call Jill. Instead she was hit with an overwhelming wave of exhaustion. She could do it later, before bed. Or maybe in the morning when she'd gotten some rest.

When she got back inside the house, the Mosses were just getting up to leave.

"Oh, good. Norma," Teresa said. "We hated to take off without saying goodbye. But it's such a long drive, and it'll already be the middle of the night when we get home."

"Walk us out," Owen said. "Please."

They stepped out into the bright sunlight together, and Norma walked with them to their massive SUV.

"I meant what I said in court," Teresa said. "I wasn't just playacting for the crowd. We got off to a rocky start but I really do think we could be friends."

"I'm game if you are," Norma said.

Teresa rushed in and gave Norma a quick hug, then climbed into the passenger seat and slammed the door behind her.

Owen only stood. He looked at Norma and Norma looked at him, blinking in the sun's glare.

"I'm sorry if I offended you with what I was spouting off about in there," he said.

"You didn't offend me. I respect your viewpoint. It's not mine, but I respect it. You're a father, and he abused your little girl. Well, she wasn't a little girl at the time, but I'm a parent, and I know you always think of them that way. So you hated the guy with the heat of a million white-hot suns. That's just a normal human reaction, I think. But look. If you're willing to hold still for a little unsolicited advice . . . your hate likely didn't set him back much when he was alive. I guarantee you it's not going to hurt his feelings now that he's dead. But it'll do plenty of damage to *you*."

Norma couldn't see much of his expression due to having to squint into the sun. But she heard him bark a rueful laugh.

"You want to show me where the off switch is on that?"

"Wish I could, friend. I'm not suggesting you can turn it off. But don't hold on to it too tightly either. If there's ever a time in the future when you feel like it's moving farther away . . . just let it move. Don't get too attached to it. Don't make it a nice little bed in the corner and put down a bowl of water. The less we feed something, the more likely it is to move along."

He said nothing in reply.

Then, much to Norma's surprise, he moved in and embraced her. It was not a quick, half-embarrassed hug like Teresa's. He held on to her as though he were a drowning man and she was the only buoyant object in his world.

A minute later he seemed to shake himself into a different mode.

He stepped back, smiled sadly, climbed into the driver's seat, and drove away.

———

Norma went to bed for a nap the minute the company left. When she woke, it took her a minute to realize that everything had changed. That it was a different world after the events of the day, and that there had been a great lifting. She woke as if it were any other day in the past five-plus years. And then the news came sliding in.

It came as a voice in her head.

It's over.

She took her phone off the bedside table and called Jill, who picked up on the first ring.

"Hey, Norma."

"Hey. You okay?"

"Pretty much. Still processing. You?"

"I was taking a nap and I woke up just now and it hit me right between the eyes. Oops. Scratch that. Very bad choice of phrasing. I may never use those words again. Anyway, it dawned on me: It's over. In a good way, I mean. All that stress and tension. Over. Gone."

"I had the exact same feeling. Except it came to me as 'We're free.'"

"Works either way," Norma said. "Look . . . I haven't talked to her about it yet. Wanda, I mean. I haven't told her about you being . . . you know. Not dead and all. And wanting to meet her and the baby. But I will. There was just so much going on. I want to really feel her out about keeping a secret."

"You can wait till things settle down if you want."

"We'll see. I did tell her I'd go with her to see Farley what's-his-name in prison. She wants to know why he did what he did. I figure there's no law saying we can't ask."

"Except it might turn out we killed Jake with our secret."

"Or it might turn out we're off the hook for that. Now that I know who it is . . . I had a conversation with this guy at the pub some months back. He seemed mostly upset about the baby. Thinking Jake might make life bad for that little girl. So I'm ready to know. But I won't tell you if you don't want."

"No, tell me," Jill said. "If you find out, I definitely want to know."

Chapter Twenty-Seven

And Pay for It

"I'll take the baby," Betty said. "You go inside without us."

They stood in the hot parking lot outside the county jail, baking in the sun. Norma was waiting to see if this new idea of Betty's would stand. It was the first Betty had indicated that she didn't plan to go in.

"You sure?" Wanda asked. "You don't want to talk to this guy? Hear his side of the story?"

"I don't think the baby should be exposed to that world," Betty said.

"She's a baby," Wanda said. "She doesn't understand."

"Oh, she understands plenty."

Wanda and Betty both looked at Norma for a moment. As if she were the ultimate referee and would break the tie.

"She's not my baby," Norma said. "It's not my decision."

"I think we should wait outside," Betty said again. More firmly this time.

Wanda and Norma exchanged glances. Asked a question or two with their eyes. Then they shrugged and walked inside.

They had already applied and paid a small background-check fee online, but they still had to fill out a form and show identification. Meanwhile Wanda kept looking over her shoulder and out into the parking lot, even though it was clear that Betty and the baby had walked off and could not be seen. She still was not used to leaving Little Betty with anyone.

An older woman guard buzzed them through a door and led them down a long corridor and into a room.

It was not the type of room Norma had been expecting. There was no long desk with a Plexiglas wall separating prisoners from visitors. There was no collection of tables for everyone to sit together. It looked more like an interrogation room. It had one bare wood table in the middle with chairs on both sides, and that was pretty much all it had. Otherwise it was just dim and bare. Vaguely discouraging. The only window was a small one set into the door, but it was milky and shot through with metal grating. The door had been left standing open.

They sat nervously on one side of the table.

For several minutes, nothing happened. The room was filled with only the sound of their breathing, somehow amplified by the silence.

Then Farley McMaster was led into the room.

He was wearing prison-issue jeans and a short-sleeved blue work shirt, and his hands were cuffed together. He was being led by a young male guard who took him to the other side of the table, unlocked the cuff from his left wrist only, and secured it to something on the other side of the table. Something Norma couldn't see. Then he backed into the far corner and stood leaning against the wall.

Norma looked at Farley and he at her.

He looked scruffier and more unkempt than when she'd seen him last. His hair was wild. Uncut and uncombed. He wore a graying beard that seemed not to have been trimmed anytime too recently. But his eyes were very clear. They looked calm and knowing.

"I know you," he said.

"Yeah you do."

"I know you, too," he said, turning his attention to Wanda. "I haven't met you in person, but I know who you are."

Wanda only smiled nervously.

Norma expected him to ask why they had come, but he didn't seem interested in that detail.

"It was awful nice of you ladies to come see me. I was going to try to get in touch with you. *You*," he clarified, drilling his clear gaze into Wanda's eyes. "I was going to try to call but I didn't want to freak you out, and, most important, I didn't know how to get your number. But I've got a sentencing hearing coming up. You know I pled guilty, right?"

Wanda seemed frozen, so Norma answered.

"We've been following the thing, yes."

"Yeah, well. There was a big crowd of people watching the shooting, so there wasn't much getting out from under it, not that I was planning to try. But anyway, about the sentencing. I guess I was hoping you and the baby might come to the hearing."

Again, he made it clear with his gaze that he was addressing Wanda.

For a distressingly long time, nothing was said. It seemed to be Wanda's turn to speak. She seemed utterly incapable of taking her turn.

Finally she shifted in her seat and spoke.

"Are you hoping I'll say something at your hearing?"

"If you wanted to," he said. He sounded almost shy, like a young boy who thinks he might or might not have the right to speak.

"I hope you don't think I'm going to say anything in support of what you did. Because I couldn't ever support that."

"I don't have any special expectations," Farley said. "I mean . . . in a perfect world maybe you would say it's a relief to be safe for a change. But I really don't need you to say anything if you don't want. Mostly I just thought it would be nice if the baby was there. Because I'm going to tell the judge I did it for her. And if she's there, all tiny with her sweet little face, I think he'll understand."

"You did it for the baby," Norma said.

It was obvious on the face of the thing, and he had just said it fairly clearly. But it was so key to the purpose of their visit that Norma felt the need to clarify.

"And for Wanda. But yeah. I needed to change the world. It was wrong, so I needed to change it. And before you say it . . . sure, I know I only changed it a little. I know there's still plenty of bad in the world, plenty of people getting beat up, but I changed what I could. Like that old story about the man throwing starfish back into the ocean even though there are about a hundred thousand of them washed up on the beach. Some guy comes up and tells him he's not making a difference, and he throws one more starfish back in the water and says it made a difference to that one. I changed the world for that woman and her little girl. That's how you do it, right? You just change what you can."

"Then this was not because of what happened to Jill Moss."

"It was terrible what happened to Jill Moss," he said. "But there's nothing I can do to help her now. It's too late. But it's not too late for these two. I knew I could still fix it so he couldn't come around later and try to hurt them. So he couldn't kill that little girl's mother right in front of her. Or even if he didn't kill her. Even if he hurt her in a way that heals. People think black eyes and broken bones are the worst a person can do to you, but they heal. But when a kid watches their mom getting beat up, that doesn't heal. Not ever."

It was beginning to dawn on Norma that he might not be talking exclusively about Wanda and Little Betty anymore. But she didn't say so. She didn't say anything. She just waited to see if there was more he cared to say.

"This way she can't go back to him," Farley added.

It was a more vehement statement than he had made before, and spoken in a harder tone.

"I wasn't going to go back to him," Wanda said.

"Well, you say that. But you might've changed your mind. My mother said that. Every time. And then every time she changed her mind and went back to him. And he just kept beating her. Just like she knew he would."

"Your father?" Norma asked quietly.

"My stepfather. And he never strangled her. Oh, no. He never wanted it to be over. Then he'd have no power anymore. No, he wasn't into ending anybody's misery. He wanted her alive and helpless and thrashing. He was into battery. You know. Inflicting as much pain and damage as he could until he felt better. But I guess he never felt better, because he never stopped. He finally died of a heart attack when I was fifteen. Happiest day of my life."

The room fell into a long silence.

Norma was the one to break it.

"I'm sorry you had to go through that."

"It's too late for me," he said. "Just like it's too late for Jill Moss. But these two still have a chance. My mom had this thing she used to say. She must've said it a hundred times when I was growing up. She'd say 'Farley, in this life you can choose whatever you want. But take a look at the price tag first, because you're going to have to pay for it.' I thought of that when I was driving out to the courthouse that day. I had my gun in the glove compartment, but I hadn't decided whether I was going to use it or not. But I thought of what she used to say. How I could choose what I wanted, so long as I was willing to pay for it. I figured the price would be around fifteen years, but I decided I could pay that. So that's what I chose."

Norma couldn't help but jump in.

"But what if you choose something and you're hurting somebody else and not just yourself? What if somebody else has to pay the price with you? I'm thinking right now Jake's parents are paying the price, too, and they didn't choose it."

He didn't answer right away. He seemed to be ordering his words carefully in his head before speaking them.

"That thing my mom said? She used to say it about going back to him. That's how she used it. That's what it meant to her. That she could choose him if she was willing to pay the price. I figured the world was full of guys who were a much better bargain for the money, but she hung on to her right to choose him, so long as she paid for it. But she dragged me back to live with him too. And I had to watch him use her as a punching bag. Break her teeth and her nose and black her eyes. From the time I was five to the time I was fifteen and he dropped dead. So, yeah. Other people have to pay the price right along with you. And it's not fair. But I was an innocent kid. Jake's parents are not innocent kids. They're a big part of how he got to be the way he was, and I don't see myself losing any sleep over them."

As he spoke, his tone morphed into something different. The man morphed into something different. He started out in the voice of a reasonable man. But by the time he got to the last couple of sentences, Norma was afraid of him. In front of her eyes he had turned into a man who would take up a gun and execute another man with a single premeditated bullet to the head.

It froze the moment, and several minutes passed in silence.

Oddly, it was Wanda who spoke again.

"At least you get to do your time in here," she said. "You could do worse than the county jail. Not so dangerous as those terrible state prisons."

Farley barked out a bitter laugh. Norma thought she saw a smirk on the face of the guard in the corner.

"Oh, you think that, do you? I'm only in County because I'm awaiting sentencing. As soon as they sentence me they'll shuttle me off to just that place you were talking about."

"Oh," Wanda said. "Sorry."

"Will you come to the hearing?"

"I'll have to think about that," Wanda said.

Then, without any notice or announcement, without any hint of goodbye, she rose and hurried out of the room.

Norma followed her out into the hallway.

As she did, she heard Farley call out after them.

He said, "Thanks for coming, ladies!"

The older woman guard was still there, as if waiting for them. Without speaking or asking any questions, she escorted them back toward the front entrance of the building.

"Now I feel guilty," Wanda said quietly.

"What've *you* got to feel guilty about?"

"He did what he did for me and the baby."

"You drop that guilt right now, then, Wanda. You didn't tell him to do that."

"I guess that's true."

"Seriously. I mean it, Wanda. Drop it. It's not yours. Never pick up some guilt that's not yours. Bad enough we've got to deal with our own our whole lives."

—

Betty was waiting for them just outside the door, swinging the baby back and forth and smiling for her.

When Little Betty saw her mom, she began to fuss, and Wanda took her and held her.

"That clarify anything?" Betty asked.

She seemed to be asking Norma, but maybe it only seemed that way because Wanda was occupied with her child.

"Oh yeah," Norma said. "It painted a very clear picture. Painfully clear, in fact."

"I'm not going to the sentencing hearing," Wanda said. "I don't want any part of what he did. I don't want anyone thinking I'm on his side, or trying to help him get off easy."

"No one can decide that but you," Norma said. "And I think I'd feel the same way if I were in your shoes."

They walked together in the direction of Betty's car.

"That really messed him up," Wanda said. "What happened to him as a kid."

"Yeah it did," Norma said.

"I'm glad Little Betty doesn't have to grow up in that."

"That makes all of us," Norma said. "Look. Wanda. Drive home in my truck with me, okay?"

"But the baby's car seat is in Betty's car."

"Then send the baby home with Betty and we'll be right behind her. I'll take you right back to Betty's house. I just want to talk to you about some of that stuff in there."

Betty rolled her eyes and lifted the baby out of Wanda's arms.

"Fine," she said. "Leave me out of the thing. See if I care. I guess it's what I get for not going in there with you ladies."

Norma unlocked the passenger door of her truck for Wanda, then walked around to the driver's side. She got in and started up the engine, and they drove away while Betty was still strapping the baby into her car seat.

She glanced over at Wanda, whose face looked stony.

"You okay?"

"I just hope you're not going to tell me I should go to that guy's hearing."

"I already told you it's your decision and I'd probably feel the same. I'm not sure why you think I'm about to tell you a thing like that."

"I just can't think what else there is to talk about. You know. About what happened in there."

"Actually," Norma said, "I told a little white lie. What I wanted to talk to you about has nothing to do with Farley McMaster."

"Oh," Wanda said.

Then she said nothing more for a moment. Neither one of them did. It wasn't a long pause. Maybe just three or four beats. But it felt long. During the silence, Norma was strangely aware of the distant red-rock mountains sliding by in her peripheral vision.

"You keep a good secret?" Norma asked.

"Yeah, I can keep a secret. Why?"

"This one is pretty important. I wouldn't want you telling it to anyone. Not even one other person."

"Not even Betty? Because she's sort of like my mom or my grand-mother now. Or both."

"Here's the thing, though," Norma said. "Here's the whole thing about secrets. Nobody just blasts them all over the place. Well, maybe somebody does. But most people don't. Most people just tell one person. Somebody close to them. And then that person tells one person. And a thing can get around pretty fast even at that rate."

"This is making me nervous, Norma."

"Sorry. But I need to know this'll stay between us."

"Okay, fine. I won't even tell Betty."

"Good. There's somebody who wants to meet you. You and Little Betty."

"Somebody who has something to do with this whole Jake disaster?"

"Yeah."

"And I've never met this person?"

"No."

"Okay. Lay it on me. Who wants to meet me?"

"Jill Moss."

They drove in silence for two or three miles. Norma glanced over at her passenger's face now and then. It was impossible to read what she saw there. But it was also impossible to discount the possibility that Wanda might be angry that this news had been kept from her for so long.

As if she'd been reading Norma's thoughts, Wanda asked, "How long have you known where she is?"

"All along. I found her when I was riding search and rescue. Not too long after she disappeared. She begged me not to tell anybody she was alive because she was so afraid of Jake. Because she was leaving him. I wasn't in touch with her the whole time, and I didn't know exactly where she was living or under what name. But I knew she was alive."

Another mile or so of silence.

Then Wanda asked, "But her parents know she's alive, right?"

"I'd rather leave her parents out of this."

"You were both just going to let him go on trial for the murder of a person you knew wasn't even dead?"

"No. We were not. I discussed it with her and we decided she was willing to put herself at some risk to keep that from happening. So I went into the DA's office and came clean."

"Then why was there ever a trial?"

"He refused to hear me. Said he had some kind of selective hearing loss."

"That son of a bitch."

"Yeah," Norma said. "He kind of is."

"You still could have gone to the local paper or the evening news."

"And don't think we didn't consider it. The main reason we didn't do it was Little Betty. Especially after they only gave him just over five years for nearly killing you. Even without early parole or anything, he'd have dropped back into your lives right around the time she was in kindergarten. And it was really hard to think about making a move that could put her in danger. Or you. Or both of you. I mean, how would we have felt if something went really, horribly wrong?"

A few more miles of distant red-rock mountains flashed by in silence.

Norma had no idea what Wanda would say when she was finally ready to speak, but she expected there would be some anger involved.

"That must've been a really hard decision for the two of you to make," Wanda said.

"It was."

"I'm sorry you had to do that."

"I thought you'd be mad."

"Well. I tried to be. I figured I should be. But ever since I almost died, everything looks different to me. It's weird, and I'm not quite sure how to explain it. But now I just look at everybody and figure they're probably doing the best they can. Maybe not Jake and maybe not Farley, but most everybody. Well, maybe even Jake and Farley. Maybe people are doing the best they can at that moment even if their best is really terrible. I don't know about that one. It's too complicated for me. But, sure. I want to meet Jill. I'm sure we have a lot to talk about. A lot in common. Too much in common, and not any of it good, but it might feel like putting some kind of final chapter on all this garbage."

"I'll figure out how to make it happen," Norma said.

———

As soon as she'd dropped Wanda off, Norma called Jill, set the phone on speaker, and left it on the seat before driving away.

"Norma," that wonderfully familiar voice said.

Jill's voice had become a sort of balm to Norma's spirit. The way most people feel when hearing from their own children and grandchildren.

"You at work?" Norma asked.

"Yeah, but it's not busy. I got a minute. Did you go see that guy?"

"We did."

"You actually went into a prison and sat down and had a talk with a stone-cold killer?"

"You know there are guards around and everything, right? And he was handcuffed to the table."

"Yeah, but still. On an emotional level. Creepy. What did you find out? Anything?"

"It didn't have anything to do with our keeping your secret. You can let go of that. He's got all this trauma left over from watching his stepfather beat his mother, and he wasn't going to let that happen to Wanda's baby."

"Man, it just keeps going, doesn't it? You think it's over when a person stops hitting, but the damage just keeps going. What else did he say?"

"A few interesting things," Norma said. "I'll tell you all about it when we come up for a visit."

"We? Are there hound dogs in that 'we'?"

"No, I'll figure out somebody to take care of them for me. Probably Betty. The 'we' I had in mind was me, Wanda, and the baby."

"You know," Jill said, and her voice sounded lighter. Freer. "I worried it was too much to ask for, but I was kind of hoping that was the 'we' you had in mind."

Chapter Twenty-Eight

Hurt People

Norma glanced over at Wanda as she drove. They were going through a long stretch of nothing in Nevada, and Wanda was sleeping with her cheek pressed up against the passenger window of Norma's truck. She had dyed her hair back to its original dark-brown color so it wouldn't look strange while it was growing out.

The baby was in her car seat in the back, also blessedly asleep. Or maybe it wasn't a blessing. Maybe it just meant she would be up all night.

She glanced over again, and Wanda opened her eyes and looked back at Norma.

"What?"

"Nothing," Norma said.

"I know I'm sleeping a lot, but I figure this way I can drive through the night."

"That would be good, actually."

"That's what I thought. Why were you looking at me?"

"I don't get the question. I shouldn't look at you?"

"I'm sorry. I guess I'm being weird."

For a long time Wanda just stared out the window, as though there were something important to see out there. But really it was just a long, straight stretch of highway with not much in the way of scenery.

"I guess I'm nervous about meeting Jill," she said after a few miles.

"Not sure why you would be."

"Maybe I'm feeling like she'll judge me."

"For what?"

"Being an idiot."

"Oh. You mean for picking out the same guy she did?"

"Okay," Wanda said. "I guess I see your point about that."

The baby began to fuss lightly, and Wanda briefly took off her seat belt, leaned over her seat into the back, and retrieved Little Betty's pacifier. When she handed it back to the baby the truck fell silent again, except for the soft suckling sounds.

"Just as well," Wanda said. "We don't want her sleeping all day and then being up all night."

"I was thinking about that, too," Norma said. "If you really want to know why I was looking over at you, I was thinking I like you better with your natural brunette hair."

"Oh, that. Right. I like me better this way too. It's strange how I didn't think to change it back sooner. Like the minute he landed in jail. It was never my idea to go blond. It was always about Jake. But I sure got a lot of attention as a blond. I mean, automatic male attention. After a while, though, I wasn't really sure that was such a good thing." She paused for a time, staring out the window. "You know what's weird about relationships?"

"Everything?"

Wanda let out a short bark of a laugh.

"Okay. Yeah, maybe. For me it was how I put away all these parts of myself that didn't fit with him. Stupid stuff, like what kind of music I liked, or what I thought about a political situation. I guess I told you something about this a while back. I didn't lie about what I liked or what I thought. I just let it sink down to some spot where it wouldn't get in the way. Not because I thought his way should win, even though now—looking back—it seems like it always did. But more because . . . it was like the difference between my day going smoothly or everything turning into a total mess."

"I get it," Norma said. "I think we all do that in all relationships. But when we're with someone who's easily upset, we tend to do it to an abnormal degree."

"I'm thinking you've been there," Wanda said. "You've said some things that make me think you've been there."

"I've been there. Yeah."

"But there's an upside to it, though. It's that time when you get to stop. And you discover all these parts of yourself you nearly forgot all about. It's like a Wanda renaissance all up in here. You want me to drive now?"

"Yeah," Norma said. "Pretty soon I'll take you up on that."

———

Norma woke in the passenger seat, unsure as to how much time had passed. It was still dark, and the truck was not moving. She glanced over at Wanda in the driver's seat. Wanda was awake, staring off into nothing. Maybe lost in thought. The baby seemed to be asleep in her car seat in the back. Or, at least, quiet and still.

As her eyes adjusted to the darkness, Norma saw they were parked in front of a gate. The more her eyes took in, the more convinced she became that it was Jill's gate.

"How'd you find your way here?" Norma asked.

Wanda startled.

"Oh. Norma," she said, her voice breathy. "I had no idea you were awake. You had your phone open to it on the maps app."

"Got it. What time is it?"

"Not even five in the morning. Didn't seem like a good time to wake her up and tell her we're here."

"I figured we'd get here in the late morning," Norma said, "but that's because I didn't know you'd be willing to drive all night."

She had barely finished her second sentence when they heard the baying of a hound dog. It was off in the distance, but growing closer.

"I think her dog is on to us," Norma said.

A minute or so later, Norma was able to make out the shape of Jill in the dark, holding her dog's collar and approaching the gate. She used no flashlight or other form of illumination. Another way in which she was just like Norma, who simply let her eyes adjust and then navigated in the dark.

The night was far too artificially lit up already, Norma felt. In general. Everybody seemed to want to chase the darkness away, like it was some sort of disease and not just half of a normal day.

Jill came through the gate and walked up to the driver's side of the truck.

Wanda fumbled to put the window down, seemed to realize it wouldn't work with the engine off, groped in her pocket for her keys, then gave up and opened the door.

Jill peered past her at Norma.

"You're here," she said, sounding as though that was a very good thing.

"Sorry about the early hour."

"Oh, I'm always up at four." Jill then turned her attention to Wanda. "You must be Wanda," she said.

"Pardon my manners," Norma said. "Or lack of same. This is Wanda Willis. Wanda, this is Cassie MacEnerny. And, remember, if anybody asks you who we visited, that's exactly what you tell them. We went to see Cassie MacEnerny. She's Jill Moss's cousin, and we wanted to talk to her to get a sense of closure. As much as is possible without being able to talk to Jill herself."

"Got it," Wanda said.

She climbed out of the truck, opened the narrow little door to the back seat, and unclipped the baby from her car seat.

"Oh, look. She wasn't even asleep. She was just being really quiet and good."

She pulled the baby into her arms in the glow of the dome light.

Norma slammed the truck door, throwing them back into darkness. The three women stood together without speaking for a time, the baby fussing in Wanda's arms, the dog sitting close to Jill in the dirt by her heel.

There was a small sliver of moon nearly ready to set over the western hills, but it didn't throw off much light.

"I understand if you say no," Jill said. "But may I hold her?"

"Sure," Wanda said. "Of course."

She handed over the baby, and Jill rocked her slightly and made cooing noises directly into her face in the dark.

"Oh, she's beautiful. What I can see of her anyway. But when we get inside I just know it'll turn out I'm right. Oh, I want one. So much! I want this baby, Norma. Well, not *this* baby. I know this one is yours, Wanda. I want one of my own. I've always wanted one."

"Well," Norma said, "first of all, you're not even halfway through your twenties, so don't talk like that ship has sailed. You've got tons of time. Second, even though I realize a lot of women choose to do it on their own, and I'm not discounting that or speaking against it, it seems like a good next step would be to actually have a date. You know. With a male person? I mean, this is assuming you want a relationship again anyway. If I'm wrong, just say so."

They turned and walked through the open gate together, and Norma closed the gate behind them at Jill's request.

That left the two younger women walking side by side up ahead, with Norma never quite catching up. But she was close enough to hear their conversation.

"You haven't been dating?" Wanda asked.

"Not really, no."

"Ever since you left Jake?"

"Right."

"That's a long time, girl."

"I know, but . . ."

"Yeah. I get it. I mean, I sort of get it. I totally plan to date. Soon. But then, I'm completely crazy."

"You're not crazy," Norma said, raising her voice to be heard. "Don't let me hear you talking that way about yourself again."

"Yes, ma'am," Wanda said.

She sounded half-kidding in her delivery. But it seemed to Norma that the other half of her was not kidding at all.

———

They sat in Jill's living room, in just a dim spill of light from the kitchen, drinking coffee. Except Wanda, who was drinking herbal tea because she was still breastfeeding. The two younger women sat on the floor, their backs against the couch. The baby had fallen asleep on Jill's lap.

Norma sat on the love seat, two soft throw pillows behind her back, nearly falling asleep herself in spite of the coffee.

"The thing is," Jill said, "we're not crazy. I really believe that now. We might've made some unfortunate choices. But being with Jake wasn't as bad a reflection on us as everybody thought. I mean, maybe after we saw what he was like when he lost it. But he was a normal guy to hook up with. Or he seemed like it anyway. And I keep hearing and reading people talking like it was our fault for being with a guy like that."

"People like to do that to the victim," Norma said, "because it makes them feel safe. If they can wrap it up neatly as you doing something they would know better than to do, then they never have to feel like the world is a dangerous place where bad things can happen to them too."

"That works better for you two guys, though," Wanda said. "You knew less about what you were getting into."

"Still, you didn't think it was all true, or that he'd do it to *you*," Norma said. "Right or wrong, for whatever reason. It might be wildly, unreasonably optimistic on your part, but it wasn't a death wish or an invitation for him to hurt you."

"If Jake had been some kind of monster . . . ," Jill began. "And I mean, I know in a way he was, but if he'd been *nothing but* a monster through and through, we wouldn't have been with him. But we both saw something in him. Something worth loving. Though I have to say it's really hard to wrap my head around that now."

"I just figured I was crazy to see anything good there," Wanda said. "You listen to people talk about him, and he was just a total monster according to them. According to the whole world except us. I figured I was wrong to ever think otherwise."

"What do *you* say, Norma?" Jill asked.

Norma jolted a little at the sound of her name, being half-asleep again.

"Nobody's just a monster," Norma said. "The worst person has something good about them. The best person has something bad. People just won't frame it that way in their own minds because they like their reality in nice clean blacks and whites."

"But it never is," Jill said.

"No. It never is. But people will turn their damn selves inside out trying to see it that way. And anything that doesn't fit with that way of looking at the world doesn't get into their heads. It just gets rejected or falls away unnoticed."

"Ooh," Wanda said. "That explains so much. You know what I remember about him that wasn't monstrous? The way he used to love to watch cartoons."

"Yeah, I remember that," Jill said. "The old-fashioned ones. Bugs Bunny and Daffy Duck. I remember he was watching the one with Elmer Fudd and the whole 'Wabbit season, duck season, wabbit season' thing. And the duck had to reach down and pick up his beak and stick it back on again. And Jake just laughed and laughed and laughed. It was the funniest thing—not even the cartoon so much but the effect it had on him. But what I really remember most from the not-monster department was the way he used to say his prayers before bed."

"Down on his knees beside the bed with his hands in a steeple in front of his face."

"Like your parents teach you to do when you're five. That always used to make him seem so young and vulnerable to me. You know his mom hit him, right?"

"Oh, hell," Wanda said. "She did worse than hit him. Once she made him take a bath in scalding water because he sassed her, and he ended up in the emergency room."

"I didn't know that one," Jill said. "I knew a couple of bad ones, like the tying his hands with an electrical cord and locking him in the closet. But I didn't know the scalding-water one. That makes me feel sorry for him. Norma. You're not saying anything."

Norm had been half-asleep again. She had heard everything the younger women had said, but in a detached way, as if from a distance.

"What is there to say?"

"Am I crazy to feel sorry for him?"

"That's a complicated question," Norma said. "Even for me, and I'm not all that afraid of complicated questions. Empathy for an abuser tends to push people's brains and hearts farther than they want to go. On the one hand. On the other hand, most abusers were abused. When he was a little boy our hearts would go out to him because his mom locked him in a closet and scalded him. What person in their right mind wouldn't feel sorry for that kid? But then that violence shapes the kid in a bad way. Then he's an adult, and he's in exactly the shape it pressed him into, and we hate him for being in that shape. Some people get help, but I don't know why some do and some don't. I mean, yeah, when he turns it outward and hurts somebody else he's crossed a line. I don't know. I had an old friend when I was married who used to say 'Hurt people hurt people.' That doesn't offer much in the way of a solution, but I think it's true."

No one spoke for a time.

The baby woke up and fussed quietly, and Jill handed her back to her mom, who began breastfeeding her.

"This may sound weird," Jill said, "but it almost makes me want to have some kind of memorial for the part of him that wasn't a monster. But I'm not going to. Because right at the moment I need to feel sorrier for us."

Chapter Twenty-Nine

What Not to Carry

Norma was napping in Jill's bedroom—the only bedroom—when Wanda came in and woke her for dinner.

"Hey," Wanda said.

Norma blinked into the light pouring through the thin curtain and then said, "Hey," in return.

"Jill made spaghetti. I hope that's okay. She doesn't eat any meat. But you probably knew that."

"Fine with me. I like spaghetti."

Wanda plunked down hard on the edge of the bed, as if she had something weighty to say.

"What if I wanted to stay here a little longer?"

"How much longer?"

"A few days. Maybe a week. I'm not saying *you* have to stay. Jill said she'd chip in some money so I could take the train home with the baby. Only thing is, that means you'd have to drive all the way back to Sloot on your own."

"I can make the drive on my own. I've done it before. I'll just have to stop over one night to sleep is all."

"Then it's okay? That would really be wonderful if it was okay. Jill and I are kind of hitting it off. We have a lot in common. She's an only child and I'm an only child and now it almost feels like this is how it would be to have a sister. And it's nice."

"Well, I'm glad you found that in each other," Norma said. "Now move out of the way so I can go eat. Never stand between me and my food if you know what's good for you."

———

The baby sat in her car seat at the table, wide awake but happy enough. She looked around at the faces and the faces all looked back at her and smiled, which she seemed to find amusing.

Norma tore off a chunk of garlic bread and set it on the plate beside her spaghetti.

That was when Wanda spoke up.

"Here's a game we can play. What do you both feel guilty about?"

The words sat on the table surrounded by silence for a minute or so.

Jill said, "About this Jake situation? Or in general?"

"I pretty much meant . . . yeah . . . you know. Recently. I'll go first if you want. I feel guilty that I didn't leave Jake sooner. After the first couple incidents. I figured it was my own choice and nobody was getting hurt but me. But I stayed until it was almost a murder, and now he's dead because of that."

"I wouldn't put that on yourself," Norma said.

"I know maybe I *shouldn't*. I know I didn't kill him. But you go back and you think how things could have turned out differently if you'd made a different decision at a certain time. What about you, Norma? You want to go next?"

"What've *I* got to feel guilty about?"

"Oh, come on," Wanda said. "You're Norma. You take everything so seriously. You play everything by the book. There must be something you regret."

Norma had been lifting a big forkful of twisted spaghetti to her mouth, but she set it back down on the plate and sighed.

"I do feel bad about lying to my search and rescue team. Not outright lying, but omitting the truth, which is more or less the same thing. Ian had to have guys out there searching for weeks. All those resources. All that effort. And Jill was safely on her way to the plastic surgeon. But it was the decision I made. I do have some regrets about that, though."

"I'll tell you what *I* feel guilty about," Jill said. "All those search and rescue hours. All the times Norma had to lie for me when she hates lying. All the women whose disappearances weren't getting any attention while everyone was busy being obsessed with mine. And almost getting Wanda killed."

Norma had gone back to eating, and she nearly choked on a hunk of bread.

"Wait," she said, her mouth still full. "How did you do that?"

"Well, I just ran away from the situation. I didn't come right out and make it public how much of an abuser he was. I let people believe what they wanted. So in a way I guess I just sort of . . . sent him on to the next relationship. Without going on record that the woman involved in that next relationship had better really watch her back. What about you, Norma? Did you go on record about your husband when you left? Really put it out there for the next person to consider?"

Norma set her fork down again. Not only because she would need to speak, but because she was feeling distinctly less hungry.

"Not really," she said. "I started to. I filed charges. But he denied them. Vigorously, and with very good legal representation. I had a pro bono lawyer and he had an expensive shark, and I wasn't going to win. It was getting really hard on the kids, so I just dropped it and went on with my life."

They all sat without speaking for a time. Just sat. No one went back to eating. The baby began to fuss, picking up on the change in mood.

"Here's an idea," Norma said. "How about we drop all this and leave it behind? I know we can't turn it off like flipping a switch. But every time it comes up, maybe we can tell it how it's not welcome here. Not a one of us woke up on any morning of our life meaning anyone harm. The only people who should feel guilty are Jake and Farley and my ex, but it never seems like they do. And I'll be damned if I'm going to carry all that crap for them. From now on, I'm just letting it go."

More silence.

Then Jill said, more or less in Wanda's direction, "See? Norma knows everything."

"I don't know everything."

"But you know a lot," Jill said.

Then, amazingly, they all went back to eating. That seemed like a good sign in Norma's mind. If you can drop things and leave them behind, they don't spoil your appetite or keep you awake at night. They leave you alone for a change.

———

Wanda walked Norma out to her truck in the morning, when it was time for her to get on the road. She didn't have the baby with her, so Norma figured Little Betty must have been in the house with Jill.

"It's really nice of you to let me do this," Wanda said.

Norma stopped short, standing still with her boots in the loose dirt. Granted, she was almost at the door of her truck anyway. But it was the younger woman's words that had stopped her.

"I'm not *letting* you do anything," Norma said. "You're a grown woman and you get to do as you please."

"Oh. Right. I guess that was a throwback to my time with Jake. My Wanda renaissance needs a little more work."

"Takes time," Norma said.

"Still. Part of what I meant was that it's nice of you to drive home all by yourself instead of telling me we had a deal to go up here and back as a team."

"I'll manage fine."

"You're a good person," Wanda said, her voice changing. Her face changing. Suddenly everything was deadly serious to her. "You're nice. You don't seem to want people to know it. But you are. Not sure if I already said that to you or not."

They stood in silence for a moment. Norma wasn't clear on how to respond to a statement like that.

Then Wanda added, "Jill wants to say goodbye to you, too, but I have to go in and take care of the baby so she can."

She rushed in and gave Norma a quick but enthusiastic hug. Then she turned and ran all the way back to the house.

A few seconds later Jill popped through the door and ambled in Norma's direction, hands pushed deeply into her jeans' pockets. Smiling. A little shyly, Norma thought.

When she arrived at the spot where Norma waited by her truck, they both just stood considering each other for a moment. It felt almost as though actual words were optional for them now.

"I'm going to remember that thing you told me," Jill said. Before Norma could open her mouth to ask which thing, Jill said, "The thing about guilt. Five years tearing myself to pieces with guilt because the world was fixated on me and ignoring everybody else who's missing. But I'm not one of the ones who think I'm more important. People were doing it in my direction . . . I mean, I was the subject of it, but I wasn't doing it. I'm not really sure why I was carrying so much guilt for so long."

"Pretty easy to carry guilt that should belong to someone else. Sometimes I think we don't even know we're doing it."

They fell silent. Deeply silent, as though Jill had something important to say but wasn't ready to say it.

Then, suddenly, she opened her mouth and let it fly.

"It's really over now."

"Yeah," Norma said. "It's definitely over. But you don't say that like you're relieved. You say it almost like you're disappointed."

"Oh, I'm relieved. It's just . . . I hope *we're* not over. I mean, we bonded over this weird situation. And now it's over."

"Sure," Norma said. "We bonded over the thing with Jake. And we probably never would have without it. But now we're bonded. And that doesn't just disappear."

She watched Jill's face soften.

"That's what I wanted to hear you say."

Jill moved in for a hug. They embraced for an extended time. Like a promise. Like putting something in writing about the future. Then Jill let go and stepped away.

She turned and moved a couple of steps toward the house. Norma had hold of the truck's door handle when Jill stopped, turned back, and spoke again.

"You ever get lonely out there? Just curious. Living by yourself out in the middle of nowhere instead of with a family?"

"Not really, no. The horse and the dogs keep me from getting lonely. They *are* my family. But, that being said, a little extended family doesn't hurt. What about you? Same question."

"Same answer," Jill said. She smiled shyly again. "Drive safely."

"Oh, I always do," Norma said.

And she did.

———

Norma stopped over one night at a cheap motel, and drove onto her own property midday the following day.

There was a strange car parked near the horse corral. One she had never seen before. There was a man sitting on the steps of her front porch.

He was maybe in his thirties, with a neatly trimmed dark beard. He wore a hat that shaded and obstructed the top half of his face. He had his sleeves rolled back two turns, and he was looking at his phone. He looked up when he heard Norma drive in, but that didn't reveal much more of his face, because he was wearing big, dark sunglasses under the hat brim.

Her hound dogs sat in the dirt at his feet.

She parked her truck and approached him, leaving her overnight bag in the truck for the time being. The dogs rose and whipped their whole bodies back and forth in their joy over her return.

"Can I help you with something?"

He pulled off his hat with one hand and his sunglasses with the other.

"Mom," he said. "It's me."

"Neal." She almost didn't have the breath to say it. "How long've you been sitting here on my front porch?"

"Oh, not too long. I actually got in late yesterday. Kind of wanted to surprise you. I'm not sure why I had it in my head this way, but I honestly didn't think you did a lot of traveling."

"Normally I don't."

"Well, anyway, I went to the pub, and your friend Betty told me you were off visiting that dead girl's cousin, and that she was feeding your animals. She put me up for the night. She was real nice. When you called her and said when you'd be home . . . that's when I headed over."

"She didn't say anything about you on the phone."

"No, I told her I wanted it to be a surprise."

"It sure *is*."

"But a good surprise, right?"

"Of course. You're my son. Of course it's a good surprise. Come on inside. I'll make some coffee. You want coffee?"

"I could drink some coffee."

He rose to his feet. He was much taller than Norma remembered. Taller than she would ever have expected. He slid his phone into his shirt pocket. Dusted off the seat of his jeans.

For a moment Norma thought he might move in for a hug. Or she might. But they both seemed to get lost in their awkwardness instead.

Norma unlocked the door and they stepped inside.

"Sit down," she said, indicating her kitchen table.

He sat. He hung his hat on one post of the high-backed wooden chair. His hairline was receding early. Just like his father's.

"I figured we were overdue for a long talk," he said.

"Only by a couple of decades."

He smiled, but the smile looked sad.

"The kids had school, so I had to leave them home with Jane. Next time."

"Yeah," Norma said, filling the coffee maker with water. "Next time."

"Rick couldn't make it."

"Next time," Norma said.

She sat down at the table with him as the coffee maker bubbled and heated, then dripped. She wanted to say something, anything, but they got lost in that awkwardness again. For a minute or more, there was only silence.

"I need to ask you a question," she said. "It might sound strange."

"Okay. Shoot."

"Your dad's second wife. Your stepmom. What was her name again?"

"Patty."

"Right. Patty. I'm not trying to disrespect her by forgetting her name. Just, it was a long time ago and I wasn't in your life much after that."

Norma could hear that the coffee had finished dripping, so she got up and poured them each a big mug.

"You take anything in your coffee?"

"Nope. Just black."

"Just like your mom." Then, because she was still faced away from him, she asked, "Did he hit Patty too, do you think?"

A long silence came back to her.

She walked to the table and set the coffees down. Sat again.

"She said he did. That's why she left."

"Oh. See, I didn't even know they'd split up."

"Oh, yeah. Years ago. He denied it, and we never saw it with our own eyes. I guess we chose not to believe that either. I can't speak for Rick, but that made it a little harder to dismiss. But I never really looked that straight in the eye. It was like . . . if I had, I might have had to admit I was wrong about you, and then I'd feel so bad. I have a lot of guilt about that."

"Let it go," Norma said.

She sipped her coffee, but it was much too hot.

"Then why ask about Patty? I believe you now, if that's what you're getting at. I don't need any more proof."

"No," Norma said. "That wasn't really why I asked. I've been feeling funny about the fact that I dropped the charges against your dad and just quietly moved away and said no more about it. Now I'm wondering if that was just setting up the next woman in his life, because she wouldn't know. Just kind of passing the whole mess on to her. I was talking to some friends about stuff like that, and now I have it on my mind."

"She wouldn't have believed it anyway," Neal said. "She heard about what happened and she chose to believe him. If you'd done more, she

282

just would have been madder that you carried the lie further. What she called a lie, anyway. You can't tell anybody anything. Everybody has to figure out everything on their own. It's just the way the world is. That's just people."

"Wow," Norma said.

"What?"

"You sound just like me."

Neal smiled a crooked smile. Once again, Norma thought it looked a little sad.

They blew on their coffee and sipped it in silence for several minutes. Norma worried that they had already run out of things to say.

It was Neal who broke the silence and spoke up.

"It wasn't entirely true what I said to you about Rick before. I said he couldn't make it. He *could have* made it. But he didn't. We talked about it, but he's just not ready."

"It's okay," Norma said.

"Is it?"

"Yeah. I mean . . . it's fifty percent more okay than it was before you showed up."

"He'll get there, though. I really think he will. I know him. And he'll come around. But just . . . he'll get there the way he gets everywhere. You know. On his own damn schedule. He just needs more time."

"Honey," Norma said, "I've got nothing but time."

———

Betty knocked on her door the following morning around seven. Norma answered the door still in her robe and slippers.

"Oh, hey," she said, surprisingly happy to see Betty's face. Which was a whole new experience with drop-in visitors.

"Did he leave already?"

"Who? Neal? No, he's asleep in my bedroom."

"Was I right to put him up and tell him when you'd be home? You wanted to see him, right?"

"Of course I wanted to see him. He's my son. Let's talk outside where we won't wake him up. I have to feed the horse anyway."

They walked side by side to Saint Fred's paddock. Norma fetched two big flakes of hay out of the feed room and tipped them over the fence into his feeder. And that absolute darling of a horse came over and puffed his warm breath into her face instead of digging right in. He even took time to say a polite hello to Betty.

"Did it go okay?" Betty asked when the horse left them for his morning hay.

"So far so good," Norma said.

"What about your younger boy?"

"Oh, he told you about that?"

"He said he just thinks Rick needs more time. What do you think?"

"I think the same. He always was that way, from the time he was a baby. Always slow to jump. But I really think it's gonna be okay, Betty."

"I hope you're right. I don't know, though. Grown kids and their parents are so hard. But you must know something that makes you say that."

"Not really," Norma said. "Just a gut feeling."

They stood a moment in the crisp morning chill, watching the horse chew happily on his breakfast. Now and then Saint Fred looked over at them and sighed contentedly.

Then Norma's cell phone rang in her robe pocket.

She pulled out the phone and checked the caller ID. It was Rick calling.

She quickly turned the phone in Betty's direction so she could see who it was. And besides, she needed a quick extra breath before answering it.

"See?" Betty said. "Told you it was gonna be okay."

Norma opened her mouth to argue, but then noticed the twisted smile on Betty's face. It was the one she tended to wear when she'd just said something she thought was funny, whether anyone else did or not.

"Oh you did, did you?"

"Well. That's how we're gonna rewrite history anyway."

Then Norma picked up the call.

BOOK CLUB QUESTIONS

1. At the beginning of the novel when Jill is hiding from Jake, she texts her parents and tells them she's leaving Jake and could be in grave danger. As a parent, what would you do if your child said these things to you? To what lengths would you go to protect them?

2. When Jill first goes missing, the press gives her case a lot of attention. What do you think it was about this story that was so newsworthy, when so many others have gone missing and barely been mentioned?

3. In the novel, Norma tells Jill that most of us have had some kind of experience loving somebody we shouldn't. Ultimately, Jill comes to regret her past with Jake. Do you think that's a common reaction? How do you think she might respond differently in a future relationship after the lessons she has learned by the end of the book?

4. Because they don't believe it will be effective, Jill's parents don't even attempt to get a restraining order before sending Jill into hiding. In this quote from Norma, she says, "You can call the police to come enforce it, but some women die before the police get there. Some die before they can pick up the phone to call." Do you agree with Norma's assessment and the decision Jill's parents made?

5. Throughout the novel, Norma is very concerned not just about her own lying but about the consequences for everyone involved. She stresses how easy it is to make a mistake and that telling just one lie makes the next one so much easier. Regarding Jill Moss's situation, do you think that the lies told were justified? Or do you think there was a better way to handle the situation?

6. The main characters in the book face extremely difficult decisions after Jake is arrested for attempting to murder Wanda. Clearly, Jake has anger-management issues, but does that make him someone to lock up, so nobody gets hurt in the future? Do you agree with the choices the characters made, faced with this kind of dilemma?

7. Norma and Jill believe that maybe a higher justice system was in play for what happened to Jake. Previously, Jill had stated, "The idea of Karma is that it catches up to you *in the long run*." How does the concept of Karma ultimately work within the book?

8. What do you think Norma meant by the statement "Hurt people hurt people"? Do you think that can be used as an excuse for violence committed against others? How do you think generational trauma plays into this statement?

9. After Jake's death, when Jill is finally safe, her father still holds on to a lot of anger because his little girl was abused and her life threatened. Norma reaches out to him and says, "If you're willing to hold still for a little unsolicited advice . . . your hate likely didn't set him back much when he was alive. I guarantee you it's not going to hurt his feelings now that he's dead. But it'll do plenty of damage to *you*." Do you believe that her advice will help Jill's father to heal?

10. Near the conclusion of the book, Jill tells Norma that she loves her. Up until now, Norma has been a very private person and pushed love away. How does her reaction show the transformation of her character?

ABOUT THE AUTHOR

Catherine Ryan Hyde is the *New York Times*, *Wall Street Journal*, and #1 Amazon Charts bestselling author of more than forty-five books and counting. An avid traveler, equestrian, and amateur photographer, she shares her astrophotography with readers on her website.

Her novel *Pay It Forward* was adapted into a major motion picture, chosen by the American Library Association (ALA) for its Best Books for Young Adults list, and translated into more than twenty-three languages for distribution in over thirty countries. Both *Becoming Chloe* and *Jumpstart the World* were included on the ALA's Rainbow Book List, and *Jumpstart the World* was a finalist for two Lambda Literary Awards. *Where We Belong* won two Rainbow Awards in 2013, and *The Language of Hoofbeats* won a Rainbow Award in 2015.

More than fifty of her short stories have been published in the *Antioch Review*, *Michigan Quarterly Review*, *Virginia Quarterly Review*, *Ploughshares*, *Glimmer Train*, and many other journals; in the anthologies *Santa Barbara Stories* and *California Shorts*; and in the bestselling anthology *Dog Is My Co-Pilot*. Her stories have been honored by the Raymond Carver Short Story Contest and the Tobias Wolff Award and have been nominated for *The Best American Short Stories*, the O. Henry

Award, and the Pushcart Prize. Three have been cited in the annual *Best American Short Stories* anthology.

As a professional public speaker, she has addressed the National Conference on Education, twice spoken at Cornell University, met with AmeriCorps members at the White House, and shared a dais with Bill Clinton.

For more information, please visit the author at www.catherineryanhyde.com.